# DOUBLY CROST

## A NOVEL

By

**MITZEL**

Published by Calamus Books
92B South Street
Boston, MA 02111


Book design: Patricia Rasch, www.bookandcoverdesign.com

**ISBN: 0914852191**

This book is dedicated to:

Billy Wilder

and

Michael Bronski

It was towards the end of a three day party. That much I recall for certain, I think. And, in the cycle of things, on the down beat. I last remember being in a room filled with people and smoke. Two TV sets were going. One beamed a football game, out of focus, colors jumping about. The other featured a videotape of *Gentlemen Prefer Blondes*. Someone kept making it go back and forth. The sound was off on both sets. My hosts worked two turntables. One moment Billie Holiday, the next Malcolm McLaren. A bong circulated. The phone rang endlessly. A cat flew through the throng. People gabbed while chopping up white powder for their noses. Two parrots eyeballed the crowd, then screeched. Poor critters. *Who was having any fun?*

It was after a bong hit that I did for purely social reasons that I carefully rose from the beanbag chair I had occupied and climbed to the top floor of the townhouse where my hosts had installed a steam room. The top floor was empty. I pulled off my clothes and dropped them to the tiles. I found a clean towel outside the steam room and wrapped it around my waist. After I entered the chamber, I pulled the metal door tight behind me and turned the steam on full blast. I reclined on a marble ledge with my legs propped up against the wall. Every muscle, every joint, ached. My cheeks felt like they were lead.

The steam quickly filled the cubicle, the tiny light in the ceiling receding behind a cloud of water droplets. I breathed deeply. Coughed. I wiped my hand against the damp tiles. I was enveloped. By steam. By a post-drug fatigue. By a willingness to just let myself fade into the wet warmth that aggressively assaulted my body. I closed my eyes and drifted away.

*This was heaven.*

I had no idea how much time had passed. The room was still filled with steam, but it was cold and clammy, not warm and sensuous. I blinked awake. I reached over to adjust the steam handle. It wasn't there. The light seemed muted. My hand groped along the cold tiles looking for the device. My hand stopped. On flesh. I had brushed up against a limb. Someone must have slipped into the steam room while I was dozing. I pulled my hand away but squinted through the dank moistness. I could see no one.

"I was looking to turn up the steam," I said politely.

"The steam is always on." It was a deep and authoritative voice.

"It just feels cold suddenly."

I felt a warm hand take one of mine. Suddenly the lingering moisture dissipated and I saw a handsome white middle-aged man sitting next to me. I suspected he was ten to fifteen years older than I. He had bright brown eyes, salt and pepper eyebrows and a thick crop of wavy grey hair. His skin glowed. His body was in good shape.

I stared at him for a minute. "I don't recall seeing you at the party. Were you a late arrival?"

"Which party was that?" he asked sweetly.

I pulled my hand from his and quickly brushed both my hands over my face and scalp. "I don't know. There've been so many. They blur together in time. I sometimes forget whether it's West Hollywood,

Fire Island, the Russian River or Beacon Hill."

He chuckled. "I'm pleased to hear it. We expect that."

I felt water-logged. It was many hours since my last hit of acid. I needed to find something familiar. "I expect we should get back to the party."

"We could. But for now, the party, such as it exists, will *always* exist, and it can wait. We have more pressing matters. I think you should come with me."

The stranger rose, standing before me, naked but for the white towel wrapped around his waist. There appeared to be no moisture on him at all, whereas my body was dripping and my towel was saturated. He held out his hand to me. I rose and took his hand.

Suddenly, *everything changed.* We weren't in the steam room. We weren't in the townhouse. Nowhere familiar. But we had to be somewhere. *Where were my clothes?*

It was a dressing room, carpeted, bright lights, full-length mirrors, and racks and racks of apparel. My companion went to one rack and said, "Let's wear bright orange nylon jumpsuits." He modestly turned his back to me, whisked off his towel and tossed it into the air. *It disappeared!* He slid into an orange jumpsuit, selected another, handed it to me and pulled my towel from my waist. My skin was dry by now, how I did not understand, and I slipped into my new attire. It was oddly slinky and pleasant.

"We think you'll like it here," he said. In a second, the dressing room was gone. I got frightened, but actually enjoyed the sensation of a bit of fear. I hoped I was in good hands. This might be a new adventure.

We were in a blank white room. Four walls, one floor, one ceiling, everything painted very bright white, a harsh white light glaring everywhere, the source of which I couldn't detect.

"In fact, we think you'll fit in nicely."

I'm not one to cling, but I did take the stranger's arm and leaned close on him. "*We?*"

He smiled on me. "Yes. *We*. All of us."

I was coy. "You haven't introduced yourself."

"You noticed. Well, in fact, I am usually given names by others. Have been for years. So I'm not too picky. What would you like to call me?"

"Mr. X?"

"Too generic. My career demands specificity."

I looked at him out the corners of my eyes. "You're the type that runs this place?"

He chuckled. "Close. Actually, I impersonate types."

"Who is this 'we' you keep referring to?"

This time he laughed loudly. "I'm glad I picked you right. I was sure you'd be more interested in the authority imprint than the actual geography of your brand new life."

I let go his arm. "I must ask. *Am I dead?* Is this the after-life?"

Mr. X pursed his lips. "Your questions indicate novel concepts. And, to be candid, I'm not one to answer hard questions. But, no, my dear, you are not dead. And, no, this is not heaven, whatever kind of impossible place that might be. This is a very real place where I have invited you, as my guest, to stay."

I was clearly getting nowhere. I walked away from my companion and explored the room. It went on and on and then somehow curved back on itself, so that no matter how far I walked away from Mr. X I wound up right back standing beside him. I gave up and parked myself next to him.

"Different rules around here, huh?"

"I like having you near me." He leaned over and kissed my forehead. "It's such a shock to cross over. Especially for someone like you in the condition you were. You were so tired. Would you like a drink?

Some sex? A good night's sleep?"

I stared at him. "I think you're mad."

"Millions would agree."

"You say I've crossed over. But what is this place?"

"It's all the here we need. Or can imagine. That's why I brought you over. I thought it'd suit you. And vice versa."

"Brought me over *where*?" I was getting impatient.

"Here. There. Everywhere at once. It's hard to describe until you experience it."

"Try me."

Mr. X reached out one index finger and gently toyed with my nose. "Here is here. You'll come to understand. We appreciate your being inquisitive; so many aren't. We like that. But you'll quickly adapt. It'll be such fun."

I figured two could toy together. "Alice Toklas said about Oakland, 'There is no there there.'"

"And wasn't she right? You'll love Alice. She runs a swank beauty salon for the vanity set." He smiled. "At first, it's a little hard. But relax and take your time. Which you have lots of now, by the way."

I remained skeptical. "You swear I'm not dead?"

Mr. X gave me a tolerant smile. "I keep forgetting. You Americans and your need-to-know empiricism. Look, I swear it. On an old stack of *Life* magazines, *Playbills*, *Opera News*, whatever is your bible. Here!"

Suddenly, we were in a hospital emergency room. Bright, antiseptic lights. Bland voice over intercoms. White uniformed nurses and doctors buzzing to and fro, as worried loved ones hovered near disabled family members.

I was in a chair. Mr. X was pumping a tourniquet around my arm. He slowly let the air out.

"Your blood pressure is fine, with an indication of some stress, which is quite understandable, given your immediate situation." He opened the top of my jumpsuit and put his cold stethoscope to my chest. He listened. "Your heart is a humdinger. Satisfied. Want a certificate of aliveness?"

"OK. You win. I believe you."

"Always my problem. People believing in me. But, in this case, you're what the doctor ordered."

The hospital scene melted away and we found ourselves in a plush office. Bright sunlight dappled through grey Levelors. The beige carpet ran wall to wall beneath blond, solid office furniture. Mr. X sat on the corner of a large white-wood desk. It had a clear plastic lay-in top that caught the sunlight. I stood next to a leather-strap chair.

"I've decided what I will call you," I announced.

"Oh, good! What?"

"Sage."

"How nice. Because you see me as a great wise man?"

"No. Because you remind me of a gentle-but-deranged hippy. So I thought I'd give you a little flowery-spicy name."

Sage sighed.

"So, now that I've named you, you must give me a direct answer."

"Just direct? Or must it be truthful as well?"

"Won't my friends at the party I left miss me?"

Sage cracked his knuckles. "Profundity comes, usually, on the second day. You're rushing things. Why should your friends miss you? You're still there or wherever you went along to after you left the party. But you must pay that no mind. Your life is here now."

"Back to here, again. I suppose my name has changed as well?"

"Anything you'd like." Sage crossed his arms and leered at me. "Are you uncomfortable?"

"Frankly, yes."

"It's a normal response. If it continues, I can always take you back to that steam room and cross you back over." He shivered at the thought. "No one remains where there is no consent, though this consent problem is hydra-headed. Beings come and go as they wish. We are like neither the state nor religions. We are like...*nothing!*" Sage smiled limply.

I sat in the leather-strapped chair. "Shouldn't I be frightened?"

"I would say: never again, unless, of course, it somehow pleases you to choose fear."

"When the libido goes, I can always rely on cheaper impulses."

Sage smiled, walked behind me and began massaging my shoulders and neck. His hands were cold, a complete contrast to the hot hands in the steam room. What gives? In front of the two of us, where the desk had been, a large screen appeared from nowhere. The screen was filled with a wide-angled image of a busy downtown street at lunchtime. Little blurry images of people darted across the screen. Traffic wended its way through the crowd. The people seemed to be wearing clothes from lots of different decades.

"This may as well be our training film," Sage said, "though in fact this scene is actually going on somewhere that you know well." The image zoomed in and closed on an old hag lighting a cigarette, switched to a news vendor making change, and then lingered on a young man, whom I recognized from some community meeting years back as he blatantly cruised two schoolboys who were rolling their bums for him.

I was bored. "What's the point?"

"Have you ever dreamed of a world where people get exactly what they think it is they want?"

"Bad screenwriters are paid a lot of money to develop that kind of product."

"But the kind of world where it's not just the rewards but all the details as well. You asked after the point of it all. On the appearance of it," Sage said, gesturing at the full screen of busy people, "so inchoate. Yet intricately structured. People do sort themselves out. You, for example, don't bowl."

"I once did."

"Nor do you attend church. Nor own a car. Nor have you ever married. Nor cared much for popular opinions or tastes. Nor have you ever visited California. That one I find rather odd."

"You keep rap sheets? You paint me as an undesirable demographic."

"Don't be vulgar. If I want A list, I get A list." We watched the screens as two young brown men were busy with the contents of a shopping bag. "It all works out one way or another. With some direction of course. People, if they work it right, get where they plan on going. Or staying. Which, I may as well tell you, is *why* you are here."

I leaned my head far back into Sage's gut and looked at his handsome face upside-down. "You're telling me *I* planned to get here?"

"You were everything but your own reception committee. So that's why I'm here. I drew the Welcome Wagon slot."

"Sorry about that. I would never want to be an imposition. But I'm confused. *I just sort of blew in?*"

"We're not really sure how it works, and it doesn't always work consistently. Just like life, full of surprises. Some we wanted very much never made it, and some with very modest claims came roaring over, well, this impulse to make judgments."

"How long have you been here, Sage?"

"It's hard to determine. We don't really keep calendars around here. It seems like no time at all, which probably means that I'm all too comfortable. What is certain is that so many have filled the ranks, coming over from lots of places, so, I guess, a lot of time has passed. I don't pay it much attention."

I stood up and looked Sage directly in his eyes. "First, make that go away," I said, indicating the large, noisy screen. Sage shrugged and it disappeared. His desk reappeared in its place. "Secondly, I hate imprecision."

"I know."

"And since you grabbed me from the steam room, you have been unable to tell me who you are, where we are, why I am here, how long you have been here, how long I must be here, or, essentially, what is happening to me."

"Right on all counts. I am guilty as charged. Don't hate me. I want you to stay. May I kiss you?"

No one had asked this of me in over twenty-eight years—I had counted! "Go ahead." I offered a cheek for a chaste buss. Sage grabbed me and landed a wet one on my lips. Then he kissed me again. *Was he an old lech?* I didn't feel much of anything, and necking isn't my scene—I tend more to the hard core. But I was polite.

We fell apart.

"Do all the boys get this treatment?" I was curious.

"So many folks arrive on a regular basis. Most stink. Babies and old people. Ugh. There is a preferred demographic. You make the cut."

"When do I get to meet the others?"

"Right now, if you'd like."

"Right now is ideal."

"OK." Sage winked at me and the office was suddenly gone.

We stood in the pulpit of some great baroque cathedral. In front of us, in the choir and in the sanctuary, was a flock of individuals, all smartly turned out in choir-boy outfits, though clearly many were oldsters. Their voices rose in a loop from some 17th or early 18th century mass. It was a spectacle.

"They always do either the 'Kyrie' or some 'Gloria' but never a 'Te Deum.' It is not allowed. Down that path, you know, lies the errors of the ages." Some of the congregation waved at me. "It's the kind of thing we do on welcoming day. Usually for groups. But you're the only one to be brought over lately. Yes, slim pickings. Like trying to find a good book editor, it just keeps getting harder and harder." Sage paused. "But if I decide I don't like them for some reason, I change the program and we do the Brecht *Mass*. It can say so much."

I cased the premises. It was a gorgeous period structure of the high baroque. Huge vaulted spaces with little over-decorated recesses. Odd windows in narrow spaces. Everything a sequence of contrasts, giantness with gaudiness, massiveness with fragility, openness with privacy. The voices were carried throughout the space with perfect acoustics. Someone around this joint had taste *and* money.

"It's delightful," I whispered to Sage, "but a little bit of this goes a long way. I'm the simple country type."

"My sentiments exactly."

In a bright flash, the church setting was gone. We stood, still clad in our orange slinky jumpsuits at the entrance to the small foyer of a third-class *pensione*.

"Like all our American visitors, you will adore Florence. You will never want to leave." Sage played combination host/bellman. "I will take you to your room," he said, giving me a little bow.

"I suppose I should be tired by now."

"Suppose anything you like. Just be sure to play it well."

We climbed the stairs. Sage opened the door to a small guest room. It had a sloping ceiling, hideous wallpaper, an ancient bed—much too small—a chest of drawers, on top of which was a water pitcher and a basin, a tiny wooden desk and a funny looking, overly painted armoire that probably had just enough room for my jumpsuit and nothing else. I slid out of my jumpsuit and hung it neatly on a hook in the armoire. Sage tenderly tucked me into bed and kissed me goodnight. He left.

I sat up in the bed and looked out the window at the vista of Florence on a bright, clear night. It was time for some reckoning. I remained both dazzled and apprehensive. So far no ill had come my way. But I wasn't catching on. I had always fancied that I was pretty quick on the uptake. This environ was off the chart. The unfamiliar here was *too* unfamiliar, the rules queer and elusive. Also, *I didn't have any pants* or a wallet; lacking such items makes me underdressed and not ready to take on the world, especially this new world. Clothes really do help.

Suddenly, my room was awash in that cold blue light movies use for lovemaking scenes. I took the hint. I reached under the covers and thought I'd have a go at a good jerk-off. No luck. I decided whatever fantasy I was caught up in certainly topped the one I would have to program in my head to beat my meat. I tossed and turned all through the night.

Sage reappeared as the sun flickered through my window. He wore grey trousers, a white cotton turtleneck and a blue blazer. He sat on the end of my bed, staring at me.

"It's like *Topper*," I said, a little impoverished, so early in the day, for a more exact reference. "The way you come and go."

"It sort of is and sort of isn't," Sage replied. "In fact, Thorne Smith was here for quite some time. A pleasant drinking companion all agreed. But just as often moody. And sometimes he'd forget the punch lines! But he's drifted off somewhere. We haven't seen him for the longest time." Sage patted my legs. "Have a decent rest?"

"It seems I am not tired."

"Not to worry. It can happen whenever you want. We're all the restless type anyway and it's so much more fun being awake and able to program our dreams while conscious. The trouble with being at the mercy of the unconscious is that it is so spotty and unreliable. Did I say most here were restless? I will now correct myself. Not restless. Chronically nervous. Restlessness tends to belong to the curious and brilliant. Nervousness is just its mass market edition."

I rolled my eyes. "Sage, you have the advantage. I'm a little slow in the morning."

"Well, just as long as you are not bored. And here's a treat. I've brought you a visitor!" Sage turned to the door. "*Marie!*"

The door opened. The room brightened a bit. A young-looking woman entered. She was slightly over five feet tall, trim, with orangey-blonde hair in a pixie cut. She wore a high-waisted A-line dress. She looked like the daughter of some Republican President. I expected to dislike her.

"Marie, this is our new friend. He hasn't chosen a name yet."

Marie pranced right over, gave me a chaste peck on the cheek and sat on the bed next to me. My petite mattress was getting quite crowded.

"I saw you at the welcoming ceremony," she twinkled. "I loved it when you requested that medley of old Negro gospels. We haven't done those for some time." I had no idea to what she was referring but had the good sense to ignore it.

"It might have happened that Sage and I did not stay for the entire program."

Marie gave me a sickly sweet smile. "I know that. But you stayed as well, and when you want to do it again, or even watch it, you'll recall every joyous moment."

I also smiled, but was curt. "Please. I didn't ask to be here. And I don't want to be patronized."

Sage didn't miss a beat. "Wrong on the first count." He pinched my arm. "I'm afraid your will to be here was so strong I had to call a special meeting. Now, there, I've just broken one of the primary rules. And, secondly, no one will ever patronize you. So you may as well discard the word and the concept. There are so many more important referents. Marie, have I made a mistake? Am I hurrying him too quickly?"

Marie's eyes sparkled and she grinned at me. "He's enjoying every bit, adoring the attention, as who wouldn't? Really, Sage, you've been at it too long. You've forgotten the absolute joy of doing something for the first time!"

Sage laughed. "Marie's right. She's very eighteenth century and has a practical sense about things. I'm more or less pre-Raphaelite, or so I occasionally pretend. Marie's wiser and more fun."

"The eighteenth century is a wonderful plaything," I noted.

"Darling," Marie was serene, "much more than just a plaything. You'll find out we have so much in common."

"That *we* again!"

Sage and Marie sighed. Marie said, "You've just joined us and we have selected you and we have welcomed you. It's simple enough. And there is no other way."

"No other choices?" I queried.

"On the contrary. *All* other choices. But you *have* chosen. And, I might add, wisely." Marie was direct.

I gently pushed back the bed cover. "Excuse me, Marie, Sage. I wish to dress." I crawled out of my bed and they watched me pull on my jumpsuit, as though amused by the novelty of an act they hadn't seen in millennia, like a young child struggling to tie his shoe.

"You have such beautiful skin," Marie purred. "It's just that sort of thing we can't really know before the arrival. It's very attractive. It will cause a sensation. By the way, what will you call yourself?"

I zipped up the front of my jumpsuit, hoping for better threads. "I still have my name from the place I left. Will that do?"

"*Anything* will do," Marie was polite. "But, my friend, we are not here just *to do*." She walked over to a chest of drawers. A bright stainless steel espresso machine appeared on top of it and Marie drew three demitasses of hot coffee. She handed cups to Sage and me. She stood, stirring sugar into her cup. "You need a name you like."

"Is Bunny too silly?"

Marie looked at Sage. Sage nodded. "Bunny is fine," Marie said. "It's lovely. Furry and warm. You and the other Bunnys can form a warren." She giggled. "And what sex would you like to be for now?"

I felt like a piece of meat at an Army intake. "*For now*? The same." I drank my espresso, put the cup down on my bedside table and sat at the foot of the bed. "I shall be known in this realm as Bunny LaRue." I gave them both a bedroom look.

"He thinks he's dead," Sage sighed to Marie. "I told him he wasn't, but you know how it can be."

"It's not precisely that," I piped up. "It's just…" I didn't know exactly what my complaint *or* state of mind was.

Marie was all comfort. She sat down next to me and took my hands in hers. "We know you're the kind of person who believes in the evidence of things. So why not do the obvious? How about a quick trip down to the Elysian Fields?"

Before I had the chance to say anything, the little pensione room melted away and Marie, Sage and I were in a large park. Babbling brooks gurgled to my left and right. Birds twittered. Clouds zipped by in the sky above.

"We don't come here often," Sage said quietly. "It upsets them."

Marie took my right arm and Sage my left arm as we walked along a dusty little path. A figure appeared ahead of us. My first shade!

"Have attitude," Sage advised. "Otherwise they'll talk your ear off."

The shade was rotund, with drooping jowls and pudgy arms.

"I think we've landed on Quean's Row," Sage whispered.

"OOOO, look who's back," shrieked the tubby shade, lunging at us. "Just one in an orange jumpsuit this time! You must be a new one. The others finally got fashion consultants. What brings you down here? Slumming again, girls?"

"Go away, bitch!" Sage snapped his fingers and the roly-poly shade was forcefully sucked backward out of our sight. It dawned on me it might have been the shade of Edward Gibbon, but I didn't get to card him so I will never know. "I may as well disappoint you right now, Bunny," Sage continued. "We actually know that you were assuming your friend, or would-be-friend, Voltaire would be amongst us. Alas, he is a resident of these Elysian Fields." Sage stared at me with wet eyes. "I just didn't want you to be shocked."

There's always been something about me that makes a certain kind of person feel protective of my perceived delicate sensibilities, which I can't figure out. But I like to exploit it.

"At this point, Sage, I am beyond shock!' I was *full* of attitude.

"They have a little club down here," Sage explained, "sort of like what we have—they think they know all about us, but of course it's all disinformation to keep them confused—and they call it The Immortals Club. How pompous! They give awards to each other. Anything for an occasion. I think Voltaire started it. You know how awful the French are about their ridiculous little literary prizes. The very core of meretriciousness. And, by the way, don't be too surprised if you see Voltaire in drag. He loves to get done up as a countess. I should let Marie handle this. She's better in this circus than I am." Sage looked bored.

I turned to Marie just as we approached a huge old elm tree under which lay the shade of Truman Capote on a chaise longue. He wore sunglasses—shades on a shade!—and fanned himself with a grass fan. He had about him a claque of sycophants as he blabbed some outrageous story about Hi Life Among The Swank Shades. He spotted us, snapped shut his fan, and pointed it at us.

"Inspectors, I hope! I just can't get used to the plumbing here. It's like the hotels in Leningrad. You turn on the shower and the toilet flushes and the sinks backs up and the turds don't go anywhere. Aren't there any good dead plumbers? I mean to take this up with the highest authorities. If this is the way they treat their guests in the Elysian Fields, they don't deserve to have any!"

Inspired by Sage's precedent, I snapped my fingers and shouted, "Get out of my face, bitch!"

Truman and his silly entourage were quickly pulled into the deep background with a harsh slurping sound. I heard him scream, distantly: "How rude! Just remember, I'll get you! Somehow!"

"Try everything, my dear," Sage advised, "because something's going to work."

"This is dull," I groaned.

"The Elysian Fields made dullness famous. But let's do visit Voltaire," Marie was perky, "and get that out of the way right up front."

"Why *is* Voltaire down here and not with us?" I demanded.

Sage winced. "Everybody asks. It was a tough call, to be honest. There was some discussion, but it came down to this: François-Marie is just a bit too much, how to put this delicately, of a self-publicist. That's not automatically a killer quality. But it's a heavy co-factor. And," Sage paused, lingering, "there's one faction that's militantly against him. That's what sealed his slot down here, among the grey dull dead."

"Does he mind?"

Sage cackled, somewhat too meanly, I thought.

"As a matter of fact, I come down here rather a lot," Marie confided, "even though Sage reprimands me, just to hobnob with the lot of them."

"It's true," Sage agreed. "Marie flits back and forth. She's backgrounding some scenario for the French Revolution. She uses the Elysian Fields as a research library."

"I enjoy their stories," Marie said, "though much of what I hear falls into the category of apocrypha. When it comes to the important things in the eighteenth century, one must scrape the barnacles from the truth."

Sage sneered. "Dreary self-regarders. Most of them. They wear their self-importance like cheap jewelry. It's like living in New York City in the literary world in the mid-sixties. Their envy poisons everyone and everything."

We made our way to a smart garden house. We walked around it to the back and found a long table set up for a feast. Around it sat numerous shades, eating, drinking, gesticulating.

"It's Pope's house," Marie whispered in my ear.

The shades, in a uniform take on us, turned and stared. I recognized Voltaire immediately. He looked anorexic. He wore a long, embroidered robe. He stood and bowed to Marie.

"Welcome, my dear Marie. And your lovely friends. Being who you are," his eyes were as cold as his smile when he said this, "you already know everybody here."

I scanned the baker's dozen of shades. I *did* recognize each one. There was poor little twisted Alex Pope, slumped in his chair, his glinty eyes taking in everything. Next to him was Suetonius, busy eating. And, clockwise around the table were Gibbon, bloated and full of himself—looking daggers at Sage for having shouted him away— the two Goncourt brothers, Dorothy Parker sucking on her wine, Oscar Wilde, Boswell, prim and polite, Colette, sitting in profile to us, Elsie de Wolfe, all angles, Robert McAlmon, and Ambrose Bierce. The one on the end was probably Firbank.

"And, now, Marie," Voltaire continued, "would you be so gracious as to introduce us poor shades to your august friends?"

"Dear amigos, most of you must know Sage, as we are now to call him—"

It was Wilde. "You still owe me forty quid, bucky. Not that it matters." Everyone ignored the outburst.

"Please meet our latest acquisition. He calls himself Bunny."

Voltaire oozed right over. He took my hand. I could feel his touch and not feel it. I was impressed and chilled. "Please sit next to me, Monsieur Bunny. Marie, you must also sit with me."

Servants appeared with more chairs. The shades rearranged themselves so Marie and I could sit next to Voltaire at the head of the feast board. Just as I pulled my chair into the table, I noticed a mustachioed man in an orange jumpsuit appear at the corner of the house. He saw us and quickly disappeared.

I leaned over to Marie. "Was that who I think it was?"

Voltaire heard me. "Mark Twain. He's strange. I can't figure him out. He never stays to chat. Just drifts in, soaks up what he wants, and then flees."

"He's temperamental," Marie confided to me. "I'll fill you in later."

Voltaire turned to me with an open face. "You're not by chance a religious, are you?"

I smiled. "My knees crack when I kneel."

He chuckled. "Pain should only be enjoyed by those who truly appreciate it. The pontiffs I knew were always men of pleasure."

Sage sat at the other end of the table, between Dorothy Parker and Wilde. He and Wilde were deep in some private—and, it appeared, rather tart—discussion.

I was new to the game, but not inclined to let on. "I insisted on meeting you, brother Voltaire."

"It's a constant stream. But I never tire of it."

"Is this," I indicated with a sweep of my hand, "the core of the inner circle?"

Voltaire smirked. "Just the riff-raff who show up for free eats. But enough of us. We must talk about you! Monsieur Bunny"—Voltaire leaned in close to me—"you are clearly privileged. How I admire your station in this strange turn of things."

I suddenly felt the power of Sage's cold stare. *A warning?* There was chatter in my head I couldn't decipher. It quickly passed. "I was always curious as to what you and Mr. Pope discussed on the visit you made to England when he received you at his home. In fact, years ago, I wrote a play about it, making it all up, of course."

"Alas, it was rather a formal visit. He showed me his gardens. He talked of literary things. My English was poor then; his French not much better."

"I had imagined it was a great dish fest."

"I'm sure your account of it is much more fun. Some pleasures are always saved for those who come later. As now." He touched my brow. "How I admire your perspiration. It's just a small thing, but—"

In a flash, Sage was by my side. He gently lifted me from my seat and said, "McAlmon would adore a few words with you."

I walked halfway down the table and stood beside McAlmon. I could hear Sage hissing at Voltaire.

"My boy, I want to thank you." McAlmon's famous drawn face and sharp nose lifted as he grinned.

"*But for what?*"

He took my hand in his. "The obvious. For caring. It's such a rare action among our lot. Caring as advocacy. So much more profound than that academic *soi-disant* caring."

"Do you write here?" I was sweet.

"Well, it's tough. I get the rare impulse and when I act on it, it's like *abcherynaddyloonrw%l# ...*"

"Excuse me?" I wasn't sure I had been listening.

"There is the permission, for which you must wait, and then the heavy hand of the record." He looked around. "Which we can't change."

Marie was suddenly by my side. "Time to go, cupcakes," she purred.

"Come back and visit me sometime," Voltaire was at my other side and whispering. "*In private!*"

Sage and Marie each took one of my arms and before we had even turned around the party scene disappeared in a blur.

We found ourselves in a sweet little Japanese garden.

"You see. As I told you," Sage said, "we only upset them. Voltaire, in particular, still can't accept his fate. He always wants to know more about us. The shades can understand to a certain extent. But it's to no one's advantage for them to get a greater wisdom. It will only make them more miserable and breed resentment. It is my job to promote happiness. Though, clearly, Voltaire is one restless rat."

I was confident. "He has all eternity!"

"Perhaps. Perhaps not. But the point is," Sage was firm, "we don't want the rules to break down. *That* can only lead to chaos."

As I have always had a fondness for a certain amount of chaos, I found this attitude provocative. "I have to learn a new set of rules?" The prospect annoyed me.

"Actually," Marie sighed, "you pretty well know them by now."

We came across a group of shades. They were debating the intricacies of capital financing.

"Dead bankers," Sage noted. "Nice chaps, but lethal when they get onto golf. Though you'll notice over there they've done quite well building The Elysian Fields Country Club. We *saw* them do it but haven't quite figured out how they managed it. They have their little secrets too, if somewhat grubby and narrow. Nothing is supposed to happen that much down here, at least not on this scale. It's actually quite plain inside, reflecting the tastes of its makers. And it's restricted against Jews and Blacks. These dull prejudices, happily, are nowhere in evidence within our realm. But that's the Elysian Fields for you—more of the same."

"They're not like us, then?" I probed.

"Oh, Bunny!" Marie laughed and pinched me. "When will you stop being so generous? *Of course they're not like us.* That's the point!

That's why we're where we are and why they came *here*. It seems self-evident. All that boring class consciousness, status obsession—just too retro. But they're stuck with it. They think they're modern. In fact, they're just tired. And as we are in our timeless state, we are above their bug-in-amber museum display. Just how it is."

We walked past the Country Club, along the asphalt highway and came to a terribly '50s-looking Dairy Queen.

I needed to know. "Are we inventing this as we go along? Or is this Dairy Queen really here?"

"A double chocolate madness, Bunny?" Sage asked. "Or a simple strawberry surprise? And Marie? The same?"

Sage eyed me with delight. I got the chocolate. Sage didn't seem to pay for the iced treats we three were enjoying. A sucker for details, I wanted to get a peek at the coins of the realm.

We continued walking in bright sunlight. Cornfields filled the vista to the horizon. I thought it was thirty years ago, and I rolling through Illinois on a bright August day, with nothing but corn in sight. I lapped at my chocolate madness. It was cold on my tongue, but as I held it before me, it didn't melt in the warm air. I looked obliquely at Marie and Sage as they licked their cones.

"Marie! Quick!" I snapped. "What do you see hereabouts?"

"I see," she caught herself and looked at me and then looked again at the landscape, "fertile corn fields, endless to the eye, waiting for the harvester's reaper. I hear the sounds of crows, crickets and cicadas."

"You're a liar," I said, as sweetly as I could.

"Please," Sage said, polishing off his Dairy Queen treat, "let's not start. I suspect Bunny is agitated by his experiences with the shades. Visiting the dead, especially the energetic dead, is always an ordeal."

"Are we still in the Elysian Fields?" I asked.

"I don't think so," Marie sounded vague. "I've never seen the sun so bright there."

"It doesn't seem that bright to *me*," Sage was crisp.

I turned to Marie, hoping for better luck. "OK, we've done the Elysian Fields. There wouldn't be a Hell, would there?"

Marie and Sage swapped anxious glances. Something was up. Marie relayed the news. "Actually, Bunny, there *is* a Hell."

I sighed, pleased.

"To be precise," Marie continued, "there are *many* Hells. Sadly, for those who want such a place, hard as it is for *us* to fathom, each invents his or her own Hell. And such energy they bring to the enterprise! All very compartmentalized and vivid in the details. By inclination, we generally avoid such places. It's like a triple horror feature at the local twin drive-in on Saturday night."

I was astonished. "*People actually enjoy it*?"

"I hope so," Marie was serene. "I'm sure you are wiser than I am, Bunny. There are instances when I never attempt to divine motivation."

"Would you like to visit the various plantations in the circles of Hells?" Sage was challenging me.

"*Right now*? No, not yet, though I am curious. What kind of famous people are in their various Hells?"

"Funny you ask," Marie squinched up her nose at me. "That's what Voltaire always wants to know."

"He hasn't been, then?"

"Unlikely," Marie seemed hesitant. "I don't think he can. And, anyway, most of the shades are absolutely terrified of going there, afraid they might fall over the edge and land among the truly damned, whence no escape."

Sage continued. "Voltaire is particularly intrigued by the religious in Hell. He has a list of Jansenists, as well as a few Jesuits, that he has given many among us who visit him. He wants one of us to photograph them in their various agonies. I think it's all in poor taste, but, again, I try to get away from judging. The popes he doesn't much care about. Actually, most of the popes reside in the Elysian Fields, and some of them give the most fabulous costume parties."

"Many of us troop down for the annual Papal Ball," Marie confided.

"And listen to their endless Papal Bull," Sage quipped. "They never lose it. There are worse things. In our state of affairs, we can be beyond quotidian moralism, though few really opt for it in their first few years. Our kind still enjoys intrigue. Revenge for our crowd is such a tawdry and, in imagination, such a full activity."

I thought this a strange comment. I have always regarded revenge as delicious—hot *or* cold.

"Can we move on?" Marie was frisky.

"Bunny, the question is to you." Sage sounded paternal.

"Why, of course, Marie, anywhere you would like."

"Nothing eighteenth century, please!" Sage put a hand to his forehead. "It's like fly paper. We all tend to stick there."

Marie rolled her head and took my hand. There was a sudden discontinuity, an event becoming all too familiar.

We were on the backlot of a Hollywood studio. Everything was in color, so it must have been the very late 1930s. As we walked along rue d'Eddie Cantor, a handsome man came flying out of a studio doorway. He dashed through the foot and auto traffic.

"*Judy!*' he shouted, running up to Marie. "Mr. Mayer is *furious*. You're really going to catch hell this time." The hunk eyed Sage and me in a very queany way.

Marie, as Judy, did introductions. "LB can wait. Have you met my friends?" She turned and pointed at me. "This is Erik Satie."

The hunk's eyes widened. "Erik! So nice to meet you. I'm a great fan. And congrats on your contract at Warner. It's a real cushy tit."

Turning to Sage, Marie said, "Of course you already know Orson Welles."

"An honor, Mr. Welles." They shook hands. "But like I said, Judy, Mr. Mayer has to see you. About the contract screw-up, rescheduling or something." The hunk fled.

"Fine mess you've gotten us into, Ollie!" Sage said, scratching his head and staring at Marie.

Marie, suddenly clad in a little girl jumper and with ribbons in her hair, looked ready to level mountains. She marched us right into the sacred inner sanctum of Louis B. Mayer.

"Is there a purpose to these forays," I asked. "Or is everything just a lark?"

"Darling, don't be a journalist," Sage sneered. "At least not just now. This could be fun!"

I adored all the late 1930s clothes. The men seemed so much larger; the garments were cut loosely, giving the males amplitude. Also, people smelled different. Louder. Sharper. Raspier.

LB sat at his desk, taking his good time to even notice us. When he finally raised his head and checked us out, he seemed annoyed.

"Whatever you're thinking about steamrolling Judy's ideas," I told LB in a firm tone, "*just cancel it.*"

"*And who are you?*" LB looked at me as though I was the tiniest piece of lint.

"Heads of Europe call me Bunny. You may too. In fact, I may be a spotter for the First National Bank of Boston, which, a few years from now, just may save this junk mill you call a studio."

"You got an appointment?"

"Baby, sunup to sundown, it's nothing but appointments."

"Look, Judy, I don't know who these clowns are, and I don't care. This is between me and you. You're under contract, young lady. And

I don't know how in god's name you talked me into this. You must have bewitched me. This *Tale of Two Cities* project is already fifteen months past its release date. I've lost Coleman and you talked me into making you the lead and now you want to pull out the guillotines! *Oy!* The only reason I'm eager to get on with this, in whatever shape, is because that asshole Skouras would love to steal the property away from me. *But taking out the guillotines!* Judy! Where's the drama if they don't face the guillotine?"

"It was my idea, LB. You loved it, remember. The French Revolution as a musical? The tunes and the dancing will carry the plot." Marie-as-Judy flirted shamelessly. "I know it will work."

"It stinks of box-office, LB," I said, full of blowsy self-confidence, as though I had been graduated from Harvard.

"Who asked you?" LB snarled.

"Wait! There's more!" Marie was on a roll. "You can put *Anthony Adverse* into production now. I've given it a whole new point of view."

"Why have I let all these projects be stalled?" LB kept making fists. "You've changed, Judy. There's something different about you." He eyed me and Sage coldly. "I think you've learned the business too quickly."

"I just think we need to showcase the French Revolution with a better profile."

LB pushed some papers on his desk. "Well, it doesn't matter now. It's locked in. Shooting starts tomorrow. I've got David Rose to arrange some of the big numbers. But I'm warning you, Judy, you and the other kids better dance your hearts out on that tennis court oath number. Because if you don't, I'll stick you in the corny *Oz* picture that already stinks of disaster but I can't get out of it." He shook his head. "To think of all the money I've already spent building those guillotines! Now get out of here." LB waved us away.

We left the office, did a slight twirl and spun into a spray of white light. When it passed, we landed in a quiet dell. We sat in cute metal garden chairs, overlooking a leafy vista as a soft breeze brushed our skin.

Sage looked a little rattled. "I understand your agenda, Marie, but I can't figure out how what we just did fits in."

"I just thought it would help. Working at it from the back as well as the front. Undoing the harm of post-facto propaganda."

"A novel approach."

"The whole point is that I can't permit *A Tale Of Two Cities* to get made as it was. Now, if I *really* succeed, then the book will never be written in the first place, but until then, I thought this was worth a try. Now, posing as Judy Garland, I've gotten Mayer to hold off production for at least three years, nix the guillotining, and do the French Revolution as a dancing musical."

I felt I should have had my agent at this discussion. "I'm lost."

"Don't feel bad," Sage explained. "Marie has one overriding goal while among us: to remake the French Revolution without the Terror."

"I think it's beginning to fall into place. *If* I can get Diderot back from Catherine's death palace, and return him to Paris, get him just enough honor and glory, I think I can make him the first President of the Republic and effectively forestall the Terror forever!"

"It won't be easy, my dear," Sage sniffed.

I was pensive. "*We* can change history?"

"We can try!" Marie was enthusiastic.

"We have this power?" I was flush with possibilities.

"You demand simple answers, and rightly so." Sage took my arm. "You see we are here because we have in fact this curiosity with human affairs. And what is history but this mass webbing of human affairs, intrigues, scheming, power grabs and the occasional grand experiment? Marie, darling, excuse us." Sage rose and I followed him. We walked through the edenic dell arm in arm.

"Bunny, this isn't easy to explain. You will learn The Way the longer you are one of us. Yes, we have the ability to go anywhere that humans ever were, and we can try to do things in the manner in which we, with our experience, curiosity and humanism, would have had them done. But it doesn't always work out as we want. Small things, yes. For example, Marie changed a ball gown for Madame DuBarry from a pearl grey to a brilliant scarlet and it caused a stir at court. This was of small import, but it was simply and effectively done. This triumph gave Marie hope for her bigger plans. We are all vain and architects on a grand scale."

"A French Revolution without the Terror would change the modern history of the world." I gnawed, engrossed, at the top of my Bic pen.

Sage smiled. "Precisely. But the idea is always bigger than its execution. Marie *is* marvelous but a *bit* of a sentimentalist. She expects revolutions without terror. Poor child must have grown up a Unitarian. But we all wish her well."

"I'm dizzy thinking what I'm thinking."

"Enjoy it. Because you see, you may want to tinker one way, but another of our colleagues may be tinkering in the exact opposite direction without your knowing about it. Even with all the information we have access to, you can't know everything. As clever and determined a bunch as we are, there's no guarantee even for us. Oh, I've seen some things actually transpire, and we can walk through some examples later, though, frankly, I myself have become bored with this particular hobby. I have to deal with these creatures who think they can just do *anything*! Well, more often than not, they run into some really awful, but rock-granite character who won't budge no matter who is pulling the strings. Like that horrible Johnson fellow."

"Lyndon?"

"No. Sam. The English one."

"Surely, we are all now demi-gods." I struck a profile. Sage looked at me as he had no doubt looked at other puffed-up profiles.

"Sadly, Marie and her toy revolution will make all gods into rather shabby things, and I say this with great affection for both Marie *and* the French Revolution."

I was heady with the possibilities. "I have my work cut out for me."

"Early enthusiasm. I understand it. And, yes, have a plan. But may I offer some free advice? Select your goals wisely. Start narrow and find out what works. Don't necessarily follow Marie's example. She really has bitten off a leathery piece to chew."

"Where have *you* been active?" I queried.

"Oh, you ask too much." Sage laughed. "Well, there's this place that takes so much time and attention. As to my hobby, I work to put in place funding schemes for artists. The real solace-givers to any society."

"Pedestrian work?"

"It is. Getting rich people to set up foundations before they know about them, getting changes in the tax codes, getting governments to take care of writers—well, it's meetings, more meetings and, Bunny, there comes a time when you can no longer face going to yet another meeting."

"Big yawn."

"So I take my time. I have all eternity. One mad thing I did do was get the Dadaists to hold a show in Paris in 1927 of work which purported to be from the pornographic collection at the Vatican. All fakes, of course. It was wonderfully funny. All this fake lewdness. It was a scream. The pope couldn't win on that one. The history of it is just being written. Massive scandal. But, here's the down side to even such casual meddling: I'm not sure what the fallout from the event will do and which folks it might help. Though my intended target was religious hypocrisy. There's always been a lot of that around. Trust me."

"I get your point."

"One must be very judicious in one's tamperings. The longer I'm around, the riskier I see it being. I'm increasingly content just herding our strange flock. In case you are in need of more warning, I should mention that a few from among our brothers and sisters have gotten so involved in their little historical intrigues that they've lost the power to return and we can no longer rescue them. Take poor Mary Renault. Once she understood her powers, she encamped in ancient Hellas. She was determined to keep Alexander alive. She slipped just a little too far over into that world. Last report we had was that Mary was trapped inside the body of some Phoenician slave who's chained in the rowing deck of some trireme on the watery wastes somewhere. Just too awful."

"We're omnipotent, yet still limited in our powers?" I arched an eyebrow.

Sage sighed. "You have the gifts of a public relations accounts officer."

"Give me time. I'll be stunning."

"Delightfully, time is what we have lots of around here. Speaking of which, I think it's time to mosey along. I will leave you to your own judgments, good or otherwise." Sage faded away.

I looked around the dell. I strolled through it leisurely, past a series of what appeared to be scrim-type sets, with creatures busily scurrying about. Tech crews hoisting scenery about. Writers yakking about careers. Loners drifting through odd patches of fog. I recognized some and nodded to them. I decided immediately what needed to be done.

The windows at Monticello were open and the warm air lightly tripped in. The place looked much more ordinary as an actual residence than it did as a national treasure.

Thomas Jefferson looked at me, completely calm, as though every day a stranger suddenly showed up in the seat across from his desk.

"May I ask your name?"

"Mr. Jefferson, I am Mr. Bunny LaRue."

I thought it might take him a minute or two to catch his balance; I was wrong. Jefferson had the gift to get the conversation going. "Franklin got the French all excited with his air baths," Jefferson said to me, closing a ledger book. He'd been jotting something down, the chronic note-taker type. He stood and shook my hand. "Actually, I think old Ben was just trying to blow the stink out of the room. The French don't bathe! And what they do regarding their sanitary behaviors! The most hoity-toity dukes and duchesses just go out and drop their turds in the gardens at the Tuileries. That's one reason why the French court moves around so much—the parks get too filled with shit!"

"The whole country's a toilet, alas," I quipped. I sneezed into my tatted hankie. Allergic to my powdered wig?

Jefferson stared at me. Hard. And very skeptically. "Now, Bunny, you say you are from…"

"Massachusetts. Boston."

"Strange that no one ever mentioned you to me."

"My fame will come in another time. After which, it will be universal."

"But, then, Massachusetts turns out so many odd fellows."

I couldn't get over that Jefferson was so tall and so thin. He looked rather sickly. What was his diet? Who cooked for him? The red hair, the freckles, the boyish frame, well, he wasn't my type at all. Brainy. But sneaky!

"In fact, it was while I was in France, just recently returned," Jefferson continued, with the manner of one accustomed to being listened to, "that I did some sketches for a water-trap, mechanized water-closet." He opened one of his notebooks and showed me some rough drawings.

"Fascinating," I said, totally bored, "but it will be Thomas Crapper in England, in the mid-nineteenth century, who will be the first to get a patent on such a toilet."

Jefferson looked at me queerly. "It must be your schooling up there in Massachusetts. I can't understand a word you've just said."

I saw the limitations.

"Mr. Jefferson, let us leave the plumbing aside." I gently closed the sketchbook. "I am here on business."

"Of course."

"About the new national government."

Jefferson held up a hand. "If you are here to represent the faction out to tear apart Washington's administration, forget it. You have no popular support. Washington is untouchable. The farmer-general tending his crops and livestock. The father of a country. Though childless, he has sired a nation."

"Actually, Mr. Jefferson, I think you'd make a swell President."

He smiled. "My Martha would have agreed with you, but she is no longer with me. I suspect George's Martha wouldn't, though I do not know. George is the military hero. I'm the man of ideas and diplomacy. What I do is important but hardly as glamorous as all those military victories."

"Yes. New York. Valley Forge. Ticonderoga."

Jefferson chuckled. "It's the victory in the war that people will recall. The various battles will be quickly forgotten. Can there be anything less interesting than a battle?"

"As a matter of fact, yes. *Treaties*." Jefferson ignored the slap. "What concerns me is the future of The Republic."

"All conscientious citizens are concerned."

I looked at myself in the mirror. I liked the tight pants, the silk stockings, the body-hugging coat and the linen shirt with the decorative sleeves. The loosely-cropped wig sat neatly on my head, though I did wonder what the wig thing was all about. To achieve the appearance of authenticity, comfort clearly was no object. The shoes pinched.

I opened a leather satchel I had brought with me. "It's about the religion issue." I leafed through some papers. "I must admit I possess a special historical perspective on this matter and I greatly admire what you did in your Constitution for the Commonwealth of Virginia back in seventy-seven."

Jefferson smiled. "It wasn't easy."

"Precisely. The religion clause. Disestablishing the church in this state."

"Can there be anything more hideous than the Anglican establishment? Those bloated lifers with their snobbery and their royalism?" Jefferson's words were enlivened by his antipathy.

"You're perfectly right. Horrible when they have the sanction and the money of the state. But, as a matter of fact, most of the Anglicans will soon reform."

"Yes, I know. I watch these oily creatures as I would any prospective pestilence. Back in eighty-five, they regrouped as the American Episcopal Church. A change in name can't fool me. They remain a stinking bunch of quasi-royalists. Happily, the worst of the scum fled to Canada after we won the war. Poor Canada. Such a crippled land to be infected with such a pox of privilege and superstition. Soon, Canada too will need a revolution."

"In two hundred years, Mr. Jefferson, these same Episcopalians will be rather enlightened, *as churches go*. Quite progressive in fact."

Jefferson scowled. "Please, young man, I can't understand you if you persist in mumbling like that. Make your point."

"We must put the new federal government on record in favor of disestablishment."

Jefferson waved a hand. "Good as done. Madison and I have it all planned. Congress at this very minute will consider enacting twelve amendments to the Constitution. These seemed to have been left out of the first writing, for which I blame myself, lolling as I was with the turd-laden French." He smiled.

"Those scribblers late of Philadelphia needed your touch."

He shrugged. "Now we make up for it. Madison will get these twelve amendments through the Congress. I call them 'A Declaration for the Rights of Man.'"

"Actually, Mr. Jefferson, I've seen the draft of the proposed amendments. There seems to be a bit of lack of focus. Why not drop the last two, make it an even ten and call it, simply and tastefully, 'A Bill of Rights'?"

Jefferson gave me a cold look and said nothing.

"Actually it's the First Amendment I'm keen on," I continued.

"Oh." Mr. J didn't seem to be in the mood for free advice from yours truly. "We think it handles the problem well enough."

"For *now*, perhaps." I had to be careful here. "But what about the future, when we will see the nation infected with new religions, old cults and cliques of hysteria and unreason?"

"It matters to me not whether my neighbor worships twenty gods or none."

"Well, you should get over that pose right now!" I was curt. "Because those with their twenty gods, or twenty cults each with one, fill up the neighborhoods with their temples, their chanting, funny processionals, their mean prejudices and conflicting morals. It's a recipe for instant civil war."

He had heard me clearly talk about the future. He looked at me with his head at an oblique angle. Then he waved his hand. "The religion issue is to be settled this way. Then it's done with. We have too many other internal problems that command our energies and attention. We must admit new states without giving in to any imperial impulses, though what with the way Burr carries on, who can say. Others lust after Canada. For all I care, let miserable Canada be the home for filthy royalists, religious leeches and the detritus from a degenerate social system. I prefer making for *our* people a national identity and creating a truly educated class of Americans."

I couldn't resist. "A time may come, Mr. Jefferson, when there are more towns, cities and counties named Jackson or Lincoln than Washington or Jefferson."

Jefferson gave me another sharp, oblique stare. "You have odd information. Who might such a Jackson or Lincoln be?"

"Future heroes of The Republic."

"We will have great need of them, no doubt." Jefferson walked to a sideboard. "Some sherry?"

"Of course."

He poured the wine into two finely cut crystal glasses and handed me one. "I must confess, I have never been a great admirer of the Puritanism in my brothers from Massachusetts. Sam Adams, full of fire, was just incapable of what we here in Virginia regard as some of the pleasures of civilization. It must be your cold climate and relative poverty."

"The ban in Boston on live theatrical performances will be kept in place while Sam Adams is governor and not repealed until eighteen-three."

Jefferson looked at me with piercing eyes. He had understood me perfectly. "Put him together with his cousin John, and you've got two bitter prunes. The last tribe you'd want to invite to a social. Mutilated by their constrictive religion."

Bored with dishing the Adamses, I changed the subject.

"I had the pleasure of meeting Voltaire once," I said.

Jefferson sparkled at the sound of the name. "It's one of my great regrets, not meeting Voltaire. He was dead for six years by the time I arrived in Paris. Franklin had stories about him—everyone had stories about the great Voltaire—but dear Benjamin, late in his life, drifted between the real and the invented, the old writer's lot, and you never knew what to think. Where did *you* meet Voltaire?"

I was cagy. "It was at a dinner party. Filled with noisy people. I was fascinated."

Jefferson gave a deep sigh. "Poor Voltaire. Dead and buried in obscurity. Oh, well. Such is fate. Though I have a late report that Diderot has returned from the court of Catherine to Paris. Terribly ill, but busy with French affairs. He's the other great writer I regret not meeting. But I shall write him this very day."

I was confused. Diderot returned to Paris? How did he escape his demise in one of Catherine's old drafty, dank castles in Petersburg? Had Marie somehow managed to bundle him back to become President of the Republic? And did the First Republic even exist yet? I felt emboldened.

"I must return to the reason for my visit. Your first amendment doesn't go far enough. I will give you an example. Because of the weakness and the unwillingness of the federal government to make individual states accept its authority on matters the federal government has already resolved, the Commonwealth of Massachusetts will be the last state to disestablish religion."

"*When?*" Jefferson shot back.

"Eighteen-thirty-two."

He winced. Then stared at me with some curiosity. "I knew immediately because of your teeth. You are not of this time, are you?"

"As a matter of fact, Thomas Jefferson, I *am* from another time. I wasn't sure you would understand me if I just blurted out the news. You see, this is my first time out."

"I hear you clearly, young man. Go on."

I gave Jefferson a brief history of the future, assured him he'd become President—unless someone meddled on Burr's side—and that he would be regarded well until the Sally Hemings story hit the headlines, detailed the Civil War—I got more sherry after I told him about the Emancipation Proclamation—and described the growth of the industrial corporation.

"A long way from your vision of an agrarian Republic. The great immigration, due in time, will bring all sorts of people with their various religions, which will complicate things. The folks already here will invent yet newer superstitions. Some of their churches will come to look like the great industrial corporations. Many will have their own school systems which will breed prejudices, hatred and undemocratic values. Some will advocate reestablishing their religions to the state. In some states, like my own, churches will exert political pressures to outlaw and punish competing views from groups they dislike. I hope you see that it's not going to be easy. We need a remedy, something done now, at the start of the Republic."

"These corporations you talk about are just monopolies come again. Everything we have done in the past fifteen years has been to prevent this kind of centralization of power."

I moved right in. "I propose this. Regard churches and religions as corporations. Treat them, as we will in the future, as great concentrations of economic and political power. Make them pay taxes. Make them obey the law. Regulate them as we do other businesses. License them if necessary. Most of all, *write it into the Constitution!*"

"Well"—Jefferson looked down—"if something so simple as a little regulation can lessen or prevent these vicious things from happening, it is well worth trying. A benign way of putting restraints on the fanatics."

I cracked my knuckles, satisfied.

"Now that we have solved the religion problem," I was firm, "I want to discuss your position against sodomy."

Jefferson's face flushed and his eyes became dots. He looked like an angry teenager. "A vile, unspeakable practice."

"Now, now, Thomas Jefferson, why be hasty? If you agree we must unlink church and state, why should the state be in the business of enforcing the morality of some of the loud-mouthed religious?"

"Sodomy degrades human relations—"

"It's simply a matter of taste."

"—that must remain criminalized."

I sighed. "Your Enlightenment, Mr. Jefferson, seems to be a rather limited affair. Above the waist only. And angled mostly for the womanizing sybarites."

We glared at each other, Jefferson clearly unpleased with his momentary display of unreason. I reopened my leather satchel and withdrew a video cassette. I handed it to Jefferson. He turned it around and stared at it.

"What's this?"

"It's a video cassette for your VCR, which won't be invented until near two centuries from now. No matter. It's called *4-Fisted Friday* and the story is that this Lon McAllister look-a-like gets fucked by an entire fraternity on a hot summer afternoon. Look, *no more questions.* Just deposit it with your collection once you set up the University of Virginia, and then forget about it. When they discover it years from now, it will shock historians, *if they can play it,* and give your image a whole new effervescence."

Jefferson, completely puzzled, slid the video into a desk drawer. The quiet of the salon was stirred by the approach of a carriage. The horses trotted on the gravel drive to Monticello. We watched from the window.

"This surely is Madison now," Jefferson told me. "You must meet him and explain that you are from another and later time."

"I think not." I was adamant. "I've already created enough confusion for now. But I *must* know, will you and Madison do something about the religions?"

"We shall do what we are able to do." Jefferson looked distracted. "Answer me one question, Bunny,"

"Yes, sir."

"Have you, in your time, somehow conquered death?"

"No. Not at all. But we have made it possible for the great majority of people to live longer through medical advancements."

"Then how am I to understand your appearance here before me now?"

"If I believed, I would attribute it to divine powers. Lacking belief, I cannot give you an answer. It is just some weird and wonderful power I have come into."

We heard the carriage door slam, and saw Madison heading to the front entrance.

"I must leave. Goodbye, Tom." I closed my eyes.

Everything became white.

The whiteness faded into familiar forms. I was in a toney, serious bookshop, wandering among the free-standing display units, which were made of oak with a bright finish. Beneath my feet, the carpet was a plush burgundy with a springy nap. All the books were displayed face out, and the selection featured elegantly printed and bound volumes on all sorts of diverse subjects for the curious and well-educated. A Vivaldi thing wafted through the air. I seemed to be alone in these sumptuous surroundings, until I spotted a body, clad in a loud orange jumpsuit matching the one I was once again wearing. The body was darting around a display designated Eighteenth

Century English Paintings.

I put my hands on my hips and bellowed, "CLEMONS!"

Twain, crouching, turned around and peeked out from behind the books. "You called?"

I smiled. "I'm pleased it's you. Shoplifting again?" I winked. I waited for him to make a move. "Well, you might be at least polite enough to come over and say hello."

Clemons stood up, stared at me, walked over and put his arm around my shoulder. We walked to a section marked Literary Biography.

"Actually, Bunny, you caught me here as I was trying to brush up on some of the things they've written about me." He gave a deep and sinister cackle. "Some of it is just awful rubbish."

"Given our powers, we can easily change that. You want to arrange it that there will no biographies at all?"

Twain looked horrified. "Don't be stupid, Bunny! Anonymity is the true hell for an exhibitionist. Let them scribble away. My rep can stand a lot of assaults. Some of it may just turn out to be mildly amusing."

"My dear, you should read what they've written about Walt Whitman since his death." Though I was never a great fan of Walt, his post-mortem career struck me as a kind of bellwether to the fashions in literary taste-makers.

"I've actually watched the career of that old fraud quite carefully." Twain seemed competitive.

"Where is Walter, by the way?" I asked.

"Off munching leaves somewhere in a verdant corner of Poet's Grange in the Elysian Fields. He don't cotton to visitors. I've tried to see him. Doesn't like any company, unless they are teenaged working-class boys. Every once in a while one of those poor flies will drift into his web. Once a year, you see him handing out gloves to the tram conductors who drive the streetcars marked 'Elysian Fields,' delivering the new dead."

"Strange man." I shook my head.

"Deserves everything they write about him. I've always been a man who believed in getting out and making one's image well known and taking every advantage." Twain smacked his lips. "And destroying what's in my way."

"You would have done well in the nineteen-twenties."

"I agree. Only I'm afraid had I lived that long, I would have been thought some hideous relic of the past. Sort of like Henry James, whom I rather liked at a distance, though never publicly. The twenties belonged to the young. And rightly so. After the Great War. New technologies. It was like your sixties in that regard. A decade you recall, Bunny. Lots of fun, I hear, though a time I rarely tune in."

"To be young in the sixties was very heaven." I was silky and sublime.

"And now *all* is heaven!" Twain twinkled. "Don't your tits tingle?" He gave me a squeeze. We stopped and Twain picked up a lovely volume on colonial houses of early America. "I watched your tête-à-tête with cranky old Tom Jefferson," Twain said softly while leafing through the book's pages. "For a new one, you did rather well."

"Let's not kid each other, Twain. I saw you lurking at the lunch at Pope's when I met Voltaire. But you fled before we could meet."

"Too true! I admit!"

"*You fled!*" I was accusatory.

"I'm told I hog public appearances. It's part of the baggage. Actually, I didn't want to interfere with your first audience with those in the Fields. First times should always be special."

"You make it sound like fucking."

"At the Pope gig, I was casing you. The word on the grapevine was that you would be tough stuff. I figured I'd just check out the new meat on the block."

"Given where we are," I announced, "I needn't thank you nor wonder why you're curious."

"Pure self-interest, though the matter of 'self' remains dicey. Now, having gotten a glimpse of you in action, I've decided I had better adopt you before you adopt me."

"Which I had every intention of doing."

Twain put the book about colonial houses back on its shelf, in its correct space, which says so much. Authors are sensitive to such matters. "The edifices of the past, like the past itself, need so much updating. The ripe antiquity of modernity." He reached over and gently closed my eyelids with his rough fingertips.

When I opened my eyes, Twain and I were sitting in a smoky tavern, in a booth. We both wore period clothes, something from the years around the turn of the nineteenth century into its successor. I preferred the drag from my drop-in on Jefferson, but I was getting used to the various costume changes in my new adventure.

"George, a shot of whiskey for me and a draught for my friend." Twain signaled the barman as he shouted.

I looked around. The other men—it was all men—were dressed in heavy suit coats and trousers. All wore hats, though some of them had their hats on the bar next to their drinks. One awful thing I had forgotten about this not too far past: *you had to wear a hat.* I'd soon change that!

"An old haunt of mine," Twain confided. "I come here frequently just to gather some wool."

"A nice place to mix up conspiracies," I mused.

"That too." Our drinks came. I tasted my beer. It was delicious, full-bodied and smooth. "By the way," Twain continued, "the famous Free Lunch is at the bar. Hard-boiled eggs, pickle, rye bread and real butter. It's fed working men, nutritiously, for decades."

"I'm still curious," I said.

"The condition of our kind."

"Are there many writers in our little fraternity?"

"Writers? Well, yes. Just about all writers, I think. But the word fraternity is inexact. It's about forty percent females and the rest is of the male persuasion, as I see it. I don't think anyone really knows. But some of the women complain. Demanding *more* dead women writers. And why not? Perhaps that's something you agree with and will do something to bring about. Bring over more dead feminist writers and jazz up the place. Come to think of it, Sage might have a master list of the crew. *Why writers*? Because if they're any good they are such meddling and self-inventing creatures. Some spark survives death, it seems. The ambition, I suspect. We do get the stray politician, set designer, all very literate, and surprisingly even a successful New York hairdresser, who coiffed all the au-courant. What do you call them in your age? Stylists?"

"Hairbenders."

Twain chuckled. "But, I'll tell you. Since I've been here, and I can't recall how long that's been, something close to forever, I'm often surprised at the choices that have to be made."

"Like?"

"That a bore like Ouida would be among us while poor Wilde is stuck lolling in the dull Elysian Fields. It doesn't seem fair."

"Is there so much difference between our clouds and the grey Fields?"

Twain looked astonished. "Yes! We have mobility. They don't. Secondly, they are all dead. Not *all* of *us* are. *You* for example have been brought over in mid-life and still have a being in the quotidian world of..."

"Nineteen eighty-five."

"Hmmm. Nineteen eighty-five. You can go back any time."

The noise level in the tavern surged to an unbearable level and then receded.

"And after I go back, will it be possible for me to return right here with you?"

Twain looked perplexed. "Uncertain. Also not a looming question for most of us, who like me, came over after death. Just got reconstructed somehow. In fact, most of us don't ask. That's your role. It's hard to get so many dead writers to discuss anything substantive. They're all wading in the harmless. Our one hairbender is busy all the time and pushing the hottest gossip this side of the tombstone. Most peculiar. When some are deposited here, they develop whole new personas, quite unlike what was expected. So they become irrelevant, unless they turn dangerous, like Pound. In such a case like that, they are made to go away. Don't ask. Others just flower in weird and wonderful ways. Like Marie. We really don't know who she was when alive or why she was brought over. Perhaps some minor female writer. Perhaps 'Anonymous.' That's my guess. She could be a grim social worker who somehow got slotted wrong after death and wound up here with her agenda. At some point, you stop wondering and enjoy the spectacle of it all."

The handle on this place was not going to be an easy grip. "Isn't there ever a meeting of all who are here? Or some little guide book to give some history and explain the lay of the place?"

"To the first question, no. The only unanimity around here is that everybody hates meetings. As to guide books and histories, yes, alas, scores and scores of them. All fiction and fluff. Just gibberish. Though the one by James Branch Cabell, rumored to be ghosted by Nathanael West, is quite amusing."

"Sam, what's your hunch?"

Twain sipped his whiskey. "Actually, I think there are fewer of us here than the impression gives. Some of the folks have, strangely, just disappeared. Not the bad boys like Pound, who was just cast out, to popular acclaim, but the others—we have no idea where they went. I've never figured it out. Once, at a cocktail party, I cornered Sage and his friend Peter—I don't think you've met him yet but you will, and I warn you, he's a worm—and the two of them mumbled some blather about everybody being free to go wherever they want. My guess is these guys give the heave-ho to some marginal ones to instill terror in the rest. It seems to work, though it's frustrating at times. Most hang pretty close to the home fires."

"Everything can change so quickly when we want it." I wiped beer foam from my upper lip.

"Yes. That's one reason I've built my little world in it all. I move out on my own when the occasion merits it, which is not often. I mix less and less. The others, with a few delicious exceptions, bore me."

"Your projects?"

"Much like yours, Bunny. Revamping human society. Particularly the American."

"Any luck?" I drained my mug.

"It's a lot harder and more annoying than I'd like. Few around here share my list of preferences. Which is why I'm counting on you." Twain gave me a whiskey-soaked, leering grin. I was taken. "We seem to have similar tastes."

"In hatreds?" I twinkled.

"Yes, of course. *And* in visions." He picked at his teeth. "There's so much that one not only wants to change but *to get in on*. The whole progress of transmitting information. My god, what I could have done with wonderful typewriters, typesetters, computers, word processors, web printers and everything else. I'll tell you right now, Bunny. The hardest thing for us to change and even *get around* is technology. It has its own immutable progression with which we cannot tinker. Most frustrating. We are restrained, as far as I know, to changes in consciousness and the whims of human designs, though this itself is a very grey area. It's a mighty challenge and requires great gifts of imagination *and* a certain finesse."

I was all confidence. "I have a blueprint in my pocket, or perhaps in my cortex."

"I suspect it's a copy of mine."

It was music to my soul. I ran down the litany. "Put the religions in their place—churches are businesses and faith is a pathology—change the kind and quality of education, stop the wars, attempt a nation without slavery—"

"Slavery is the most evil institution of human invention and, I fear, the most universal. Particularly ugly in America because it was one race against another. Next on the ugly list are the various religions."

"Boil. Season to taste. Then chuck in the toilet."

Twain smiled then looked away. "No one likes to confess his failures, but I did try to keep that bomb from going off at Haymarket. It just ruined so many things, and the anarchists took the rap. And then there are trade unionists, who—"

"May we join you?"

I looked up and there in the smoky haze and noise was a tall, passably elegant man with a full head of silver hair.

"Why, Peter, what a surprise." Twain's voice was full of false jollity. "I was just telling Bunny about you and the weight you throw around here. Peter, Bunny. Bunny, Peter. Oh, and who's that behind you?" Another man stepped out from behind Peter. He was dark, shorter and wore his clothes badly, though still sexy in a long-past-the-flirt-stage. "Bunny, this is Peter's companion of the recent ages. We call him Mede. We suspect it's short for Ganymede, alas, now all grown up. The little sprites always do. Peter treats him well, and

Peter always has one in his orbit. Poor Mede. It's tough in life when you peak at eight."

After shaking my hand, Peter and Mede slid into the booth. Mede, who was eyeing me, had heavy black hair on the back of his hands. He clothes fitted him very tightly and he radiated dirty sex. A tough-looking piece of rough trade. The waiter appeared with drinks for all, as though accustomed to the traffic. Mede's leg rubbed up against mine under the table. I rubbed back, figuring what the hell.

"I suspect Peter would have checked you out somewhat earlier, Bunny," Twain continued, mildly put-upon, "except you are a mite advanced in years over his priority interest. It's the boy dick he likes. Mede pimps for him."

Peter gave me a gooey smile. "You must ignore Twain on matters of the heart, Bunny." He was syrupy. "Twain's all brains and no sentiment."

"For which I have always counted my blessings." Twain lit a cigar.

"Bunny, you and Mede will be great friends," Peter enthused. "*This* I know. You have so much in common." Peter put one arm around Mede, who was trying to feel me up under the table. "Mede is by nature sympathetic to someone like you, Bunny."

"You know, Bunny," Twain rolled into a story, "none of us has ever been able to pinpoint *who* Peter actually *was* in his so-called real life, in that other region. We just all assume he's just some sort of spy or provocateur sent from another dimension."

Peter laughed. "I was asking Mencken about this. He's convinced I was a Greek minister to Cyrus. Might have helped set up the Persian Empire. It was terribly successful, you know. And lasted rather long, as these things go."

"Personally, I suspect you ran the bazaar in Alexandria," Twain was snippy. "That thing lasted somewhat longer than Cyrus's tatty empire. And more suits your disposition."

Peter gave me a faux-severe look. "Such a cat today, Twain. Get yourself a boyfriend and drain some of the venom." Peter winked at me.

"Bret Harte and I once did the peg-houses in and around San Francisco when we were young. I was not particularly taken with our effort. Bret found it more agreeable. He'd fuck anybody. All those young men sitting on those pegs putting out for the grossest of god's creation. I've never thought young men were very adept as sexual prostitutes. Only those amongst the literary can be successful whores. Male *or* female."

"Sorry to hear about it." Peter hadn't listened to a word. "I've never done Frisco, now or back then. Much too busy here receiving the greats." Peter turned his brilliant smile on me. "You're enjoying yourself here, Bunny?"

"I want a lot more poop on this joint." I gave him my tough guy profile and a sneer.

"Everything shall be yours." He was pure virgin olive oil.

"Mencken is here?"

"Yes, but reclusive."

"John Horne Burns?"

"No. Alas. I wanted him but he got shifted down into the Elysian Fields and was clearly not happy about it. He's heard about your arrival here and is expecting you. Don't keep him waiting. You'll cheer him up. If anyone can."

"Joan of Arc?"

Peter actually sniffed. "Not a writer, a subject for the writers. Furthermore, we stay away from national hero types. Such long shadows! We tried one once, and I can't even recall which one it was now, but the sad creature had nothing to say to the writers, and all it did was strike postures, and who cares about that? So it finally slinked off to Dinosaur's Den in the Elysian Fields, which has a vast bosom.

It's what we call where the soi-disant great ones hang out. Who was that hero, Twain?"

"Santa Ana. Maybe Napoleon. Didn't last long."

"We're here for the writers," Peter puffed up like a peacock—perhaps he *had* set up Persepolis—"and though all are welcome here, only the writers feel truly comfortable. The others find their own kind." Peter gave me a wink and Mede squeezed my thigh. I seemed to be a popular personality.

I went for the hard one. "If I am here and still living at that party I crossed over from, does that mean I will never die?"

Peter plunked his elbow on the table and put his chin in his hand and looked perplexed. "Oh dear, what shall I say to that?"

"The truth, Peter, will, for once, suffice." Twain was cold.

"As a matter of fact, I was talking this over with Sage," Peter sounded flippant. "In terms of restructuring the process here, just to handle these kinds of questions. You know, to expedite administrative procedure and increase happiness quotients. I suggested a Customer Service person. Someone like Adrian, who's just super at answering the tough nuts, and never means a thing he says, but, and here's the beauty part, *so convincingly!*"

Twain's stare was hostile. "You're sick, Peter."

"Who cares, Twain? I'm off duty now. Mede and I were just on our way to dinner. Something at Delmonico's. Don't give me that look. I've locked the pearly gates so no riff-raff will float in and spoil your lovely set-up." No male bonding between these two. Peter sighed. "There's only one thing that bothers me about Delmonico's. They serve such *huge* portions."

"You've never left a pea on your plate!" Twain was tart.

"It's a fact. But at my age, one struggles to stay in trim shape." Peter winked at me again. I was beginning to feel like a cheap prostitute; I was getting tired of this silly chit-chat.

"What *has* happened to Henry James?"

Both Twain and Peter were silent, exchanging glances.

"Well, it's odd," Peter admitted. "James's career has been peripatetic. But it's always refreshing that somebody actually cares. Another inquiry for Customer Service."

"I didn't say I *cared*," I was curt. "I just want to know. Is he here or below?"

Twain's tone was reserved. "What I know is that James was brought here and then, by what I assume was a decision on the part of the executive committee that Peter and the other lugs direct, poor Hank was expelled and cast down into the Fields. As I understand it, the first and only such change of decision. Needless to say, Henry was livid."

"But not really, Twain. Don't exaggerate." Peter looked peeved. "You'll only scare darling Bunny and darling Mede. James got all those lovely flowers and sympathy cards and is now quite settled in at an address in one of the swankier districts in the Elysian Fields. I saw him recently. He's not bitter at all. He lives in an exquisite mansion. He wears the most charming lady's pantaloons and entertains from among the finest of history's society. Not a bad deal, all in all. Some have gotten much worse."

"Fine for him, perhaps. But *you* wouldn't take it!" Twain challenged.

"*And why should I?*" Peter closed his eyes and gave a shrug. "Happily I foresee no such situation where it might happen to me. Now, really, we must go." Peter rose. Mede goosed me one more time under the table before he got up. "Bunny, you're enchanting. Let's tête-à-tête soon. *Alone!*" He glowered at Twain. "And, Sam, as always, I recommend meditation and an hour a day of sun worship, with the appropriate sunscreen, of course. It'll perk you right up." They were gone.

"I see the mutual admiration club never took," I said.

"I am amused by Peter," Twain said. "He's such a privileged snot. And, in his favor, he does it rather well. Most don't. No one has passed on to me his full dossier and without that..." Twain waved a hand. We finished our drinks. Twain pulled a timepiece from his vest pocket, popped it open and inspected the hour. "Let's not be late."

"I march with the late who are never late."

"I savor every triumph. You will join me on this one. It'll be stunning. Which is why that cold clam Peter came by just now. He knows what's about to happen. All of us do, if they care to look. It wasn't just out of curiosity that Peter dropped by; it was his homage. You and I are about to claim a joint coup."

"Do tell." I was all ears.

"Even better. I will show you."

We walked from the tavern across a busy street. Horses, and horse-drawn trams, and piles of horseshit were everywhere.

"We are in ...?" I asked.

"Boston. 1904. The federal courthouse."

We approached a stodgy building, not yet the WPA-Stalinesque edifice I would know from a later time. Protestors marched in a line in front of the courthouse under the stern eyes of a phalanx of over-dressed, whiskered Boston Irish cops. Several protestors recognized Twain, screamed his name and spat at him. Their wads fell short and landed on the courthouse steps.

"The religious are, ultimately, so rude," he quipped.

We entered and walked to a third floor courtroom and sat on a bench near the back. The courtroom was packed to capacity and heavy with the smell of too many people wearing too many clothes.

"Today is the sentencing," Twain informed.

The judge entered, a bushy-faced, portly older man. We all rose. He sat, pulling about his black robes, coughing into a hankie. We sat.

"The convict will rise," ordered the judge.

A stooped little woman, wrapped in mounds of clothes, pushed back her chair and stood facing his honor.

"Mrs. Mary Baker Eddy," the judge droned, "you have been found guilty by a jury of your peers in this court on all counts against you. The jury has found that you as a person and as head of your organization did willfully and knowingly conspire with others in your organization to avoid paying federal taxes on money earned by yourself and others in your church. The jury did also find that as a fact your organization did willfully and knowingly conspire with others in your organization to avoid paying federal taxes on money earned by yourself and your church. And that you organized and consented to this fraud. Is there anything you wish to say to the court before this court passes sentence on you?"

"This is too wonderful!" I laughed to Twain.

"Shhh," he hissed. "There's more."

Mrs. Eddy turned to scan the crowd. She rose and stepped towards the judge. "All I can say, Your Honor, is that I believe that I have executed my duties as I rightly understood them. In compliance with my congregation and heeding the laws of my government, I pray for mercy and ultimate vindication."

"You may pray all you wish, Mrs. Eddy. That is your specialty." There was laughter in the courtroom. The judge scowled. "But I'm afraid your failing to understand what the government requires regarding religious organizations has led to your convictions. Ignorance of the law is not a defense. But this is not relevant in your case. You well knew the law and deliberately and very cleverly tried to avoid the law, hiding behind the mask of religion. This is a serious offense, Mrs. Eddy. And I am not inclined to be sympathetic. The great Founding Fathers of this government adopted a benign and generous position as to religious expression. Many religions operate in our society within the law and have found a comfortable place for themselves. But all religions, as required by the First Amendment of our Constitution, must be licensed by the federal government and be taxed in the manner which Congress has deemed fair and appropriate. You have deliberately and repeatedly defied the intent of the Fathers, the will of Congress and the will of the people in the acts of your organization. I therefore sentence you to twenty years incarceration on each count, to be served concurrently. I also sentence you to fifteen years for each count of fraud, also to be served concurrently. I sentence you personally to pay one hundred thousand dollars in fines and court costs, and I sentence your organization, The First Church, Christ Scientist, to pay seven hundred and ninety thousand in back taxes, with interest, and additional fines and penalties." The judge banged his gavel.

Eddy sprang at the judge. "You can't do this! It will ruin my church!"

"Guards! Remove the prisoner!" The judge bellowed

Mrs. Mary Baker Eddy, stooped, broken, dressed in black, wearing an elaborate hat that seemed to have a stuffed bird on it, was taken by two male guards from the courtroom as she burst into spasms of wailing. News reporters fled the courtroom to file their accounts. Spectators buzzed then left, the show being over.

In a few minutes, Twain and I, and a lone, and rather hunky, court officer, who eyed us with interest, were the only occupants of the courtroom.

I laughed. "Now comes the bad news. You're about to tell me this was just our complete invention."

Twain, paternal, patted my arm. "We'll pick up the late edition after another cocktail—such a lovely word, cocktail. I don't think it was around when I was your age. Now, we might think about calling a good real estate agent, putting out a bid on Eddy's church properties, as I suspect they will soon go up at auction. Some say they just might build a Symphony Hall out that-a-way, so it might be a good investment. Culture always brings in the marks."

Twain took my arm as we descended a staircase. "It's all true. Mr. Madison was real tight in his writing or, as *we* know, his *rewriting* of the First Amendment. These multitudes of religions are now licensed by an agency controlled by the Congress. They pay to get their licenses to carry on and like corporations they are bound by the rules and some minor obligations. Paying a minimal tax for their right to carry on madly. Mother Eddy thought she was smarter than the game. Dumb duck. It was you, dear Bunny, in your chat with old Tom Jefferson, who got this thing into place." Twain grinned at me, pride all over his face. "When I wrote my exposés on that old fraud, I banged away about how the Christian Scientists, arrogant as the day is long, hadn't paid a plug nickel since they bought ground for their great temple here in Boston. Now, Eddy will die in prison and her church will go out of business. And if that is not enough good news, the federal indictments are out for the Mormons."

I was ecstatic. I had just wiped out one entire church with an appropriately bold and quick intervention. It seemed so easy. I hoped popes and pastors around the world were quaking in their boots. Though, more likely, I suspected most were pleased to see a competitor go out. It didn't matter to me. Soon, all the dominos would go down.

Still arm-in-arm, Twain and I exited the courthouse. The wall of the religious, now out for blood, surged at us. The handsome Irish cops kept them at bay, perhaps as delighted as we were, but for different reasons, at the demise of Mother Eddy's odd heresy. We headed into the rush-hour throng of a busy industrial Boston.

"You know, Clemons, I have this urge to go back over. Just to touch base."

"I'd counsel against it." He looked concerned.

"But I feel I *must*."

"We all control our own peregrinations hereabouts. But let me not cavil about this. Let's at least get settled in a tavern. Then you can go if you must."

We turned the corner and entered a bar, sat on barstools and ordered drinks.

"How exactly do I get back over?" I had no idea.

"To that familiar trap? Just think it real hard and wish it." Twain squeezed my hand. "I'll be waiting here for your return."

"It's a deal."

I closed my eyes and thought real hard of my work room in my Boston flat in the mid 1980s, located only a few miles and several decades from where we sat. Distances can be such trouble, except on those rare occasions when they aren't.

I opened my eyes. I sat at my typewriter, the dreadful wallpaper before me. The cat meowed at my feet. There was one thing I had to check. I reached over to my shelf of reference books. I pulled down a volume of U.S. documents. Suddenly, I felt a cold shadow across my shoulder. I looked around and saw a blur, semi-formed and grey, move past me out the door. The cat followed it making cat noises. I peeked out the workroom door and watched the grey blur open a can of cat food. I shivered.

I opened the reference volume to pages on the U.S. Constitution and the Bill of Rights. I read the First Amendment.

"Congress shall make no law interfering with the free flow and exchange of ideas. Nor shall Congress make any law respecting or establishing any religion. The Congress, as representatives of The People, shall respect the various manifestations of religion on the following terms: religious organizations shall petition the Congress for a charter to enable each religion to legally practice its beliefs. Congress will have full and complete powers to set the specifications for these charters, which must be uniform for all religions. Any religion in non-compliance with the terms set by Congress will have its charter revoked and be subject to prosecution under the laws of Congress."

*There it was!* I had told Jefferson, and he and Madison had cooked up a semi-ideal solution. O, happy world! Bunny was loose to rectify the errors and oversights of modern history. *Watch out!*

The grey blob reappeared and *sat right on top of me!* I felt a heavy mass overtake me and I feared I might be absorbed back into the dull world of daily life. I found myself immobile. Apparently the grey mass, which must have been the real-life me, felt similarly ill at ease and quickly rose, leaving me alone. I rolled a piece of paper into the typewriter and tapped out: "I was here—*in both places at once!*"

I then got out of the chair, went to a corner of the room, located a small keepsake, a steel penny from 1943, put it in my pocket, closed my eyes, rolled my head, and dreamed of sitting next to Twain in the bar.

Even before I opened my eyes, I heard the bar chatter, smelled the cigar smoke and the stale stink of alcoholic beverages. I popped my eyes open. Here I was, once again on a barstool next to Twain, who had a sour look on his face. On the stool to my other side sat Sage. He also looked dyspeptic.

"I am being excoriated by Sage," Twain mumbled, "for allowing you to go back over."

"Twain had nothing to do with it." I was firm. "It was completely my own idea. I had to check something."

"Twain knows the rules," Sage was tense. "We don't crack the whip around here very much, Bunny. But what you did was *very* risky. We might have lost you. And then the plan would have been ruined."

"I *didn't* linger." I waved to the bartender for a fresh drink.

"Not the point at all." Sage was surly. "There's a probationary period here, as you pretended not to know. I mean, why would anyone *want* to go back over so soon after arriving? It defies logic!"

"Sage wants you more under his control," Twain observed.

"It's just that you don't know the risks involved."

"None of us does," Twain snorted. "Especially in Bunny's case."

"Please translate for me." I was adamant.

"Well," Twain offered, "you're in a rather delicate situation, Bunny, as you are the first person who we've crossed over who hasn't actually died over there."

"I know."

Sage continued. "And we don't really know how things will transpire in this experiment. We want to play you very conservatively."

"You make me sound like a device, which, of course, I hope I am. To my own intentions and ambitions." I wanted to sound smug and succeeded.

"Point being," Sage was terse, "don't do it again without checking with me. *Got it*?"

"I shall be monitored. This takes some of the glow off this adventure." There was no response from either of them. "Why don't you just tell me the formula? *There's always a formula.*"

"There is no formula," Twain said sadly.

"The writers die," Sage sighed, "and they come here. That's it."

"*Or* they go to the Elysian Fields, *or* to their private hells." I was on top of it.

"Actually, Bunny," Sage seemed remote, "it's not that simple. Some just stay dead and don't go anywhere. That's the first stage of the selection process. The diplomacy of it all." Sage swilled his drink. "I've made my point. Now I must go. Just promise me one thing, Bunny. You won't do it again."

I held up my right hand. "Promise!" I was so two-faced I even surprised myself.

"Trust me. It's the best for all of us, certainly for me." Sage was gone.

"He's *so* self-satisfied." Twain lit up a cigar. "Though you seem to have located a loose nerve ending."

"He's hiding something."

"I suspect he has plans for you. You are his new toy."

"Oh, great. I wind up in what I think is heaven, and it turns out to be just another job."

"The pay's crummy but the perks are nice."

*"All I want are answers!"*

"You must ask the right questions."

"Would Sage really be heartbroken if I crossed back over and never returned?"

"I don't think heartbroken is the right word. But I do think you'd spoil whatever little game he has going, about which I am still in the dark." Twain stared at me. "Would you really want to go back *for good?*"

It took me no time. "Of course not. Just because I'm pretty doesn't mean I'm a fool. Since I, apparently, am the first being to inhabit both spaces, it is a mighty temptation to live in both spheres, just for the novelty of it."

"You'll get over it. It's much more fun here. Though we are missing the youth, perhaps a cohort of the human race to *your* tastes."

I reached into my pants pocket and found my steel penny. I twirled it in one hand. Twain was intrigued.

"What's that?"

"A penny. Made of steel."

*"Money made of steel?* Marvelous! The metaphor of the culture as currency. Just perfect!" He took the coin and examined it.

"It was during the 1940s and a great war. The government used all the copper for the war effort. So pennies were made of steel. Just for one year."

"Still Lincoln, I see. You'd think if they had changed the metal, they might have changed the icon. Carnegie or Rockefeller would be more to the point."

"Robber barons and mass murderers, though in fact great parts of our national culture, just don't seem right for the money. But you touch on one of my favorite topics, Sam." We ordered another round. "It's the currency. Since the federal government standardized the money, it's been so boring."

"I think that was the idea. After all those wacky state bills, it was time for something staid and comforting."

"Nonetheless, so dull. Let's change it!"

Twain sipped his beverage; it was clearly the last thing on his mind.

"Until Sage has more use for me, I think I'll take up a beautifying project. Make the money more attractive."

"You propose?"

"Subversion of the engraving contracts."

"Anything specific?"

"I want to find Saint Gaudens."

"He's already done a coin."

"Yes, I know. But now I want him to do a three dollar coin with Jackie Kennedy on it. And I want a seven dollar bill done by Warhol. I want Gerald Murphy to do a whole line of modernist money for use in buying collectibles." I carried on. It was strange, though strangeness was no longer unexpected. We ate, we drank, and yet I never felt full, bloated or drunk. And no money ever changed hands. We constantly got what we wanted, as though running up some monstrous tab.

Twain finished his drink and wiped his lips.

"I think," I continued, "I'll use this project to help in going back and forth to the Elysian Fields, which I'll have to do to commission some of these designs."

"Tell me, what's the big picture?" Twain eyeballed me.

"For starters, to prepare the way for bringing over Voltaire from the Fields to our more festive venue."

"It's a great idea, but I must inform you that it has been tried before. With no success."

"I'm sure. Poor ambitious bunnies. But *this* Bunny can do it! You see, I have the advantage—still mortal but at the same time eternal. This is a unique hand I have been dealt. It's certainly worth a try."

"What will you do if Sage or Peter gets on your case?"

I smiled. "My first line will be 'I was brought here as your guest and if this is how you treat your guests, you don't deserve to have any.' And if that doesn't shut them up, I'll threaten to take them back to that dull party, this time as *my* guests, and make sure they will die for good, once and forever, and never be heard from again."

"The big guns approach."

"Call me Time Warp Tammy. Tell me if I'm wrong, Twain, but I just don't trust the little clique that runs this joint."

"I'm with you. Details upon request."

I took Twain's hand. "Let's smoke 'em out and take over this paradise."

"To what end?"

"The obvious ones. Change history, remake the human race and try to save it from its certain self-annihilation."

"Are you certain that's not Sage's goal?"

"*Who cares?* Anyway, he doesn't strike me as the kind of guy who can pull it off. He looks—how to say this—'over-qualified.' He's like the goo-goo liberals. Nice smooth talk, no action and turns out a smart report, then washes his hands of the whole affair. I've got his number." I rose. "I'll see you in a bit, Sam. I'm on to business."

I flew from the saloon. And, willy-nilly, after traipsing through some oddly ill-organized vistas of eras, ran into Billy Blake on the perimeter of the Elysian Fields.

"Stop right there!" I screamed. Manners didn't matter in the Fields. "Got a minute?"

Blake had a crazed look in his eyes. "Not now, Bunny! I'm deep into a scheme."

"Anything of import?"

"I'm trying to get acrylics in use by the mid-eighteenth century. It will change painting, and then I can—"

"Forget it, Louise." I knew the rule about technological innovations not crossing over.

"I don't care what the barriers are. I think I have a fabulous way around it. Plastics in Manchester are going to be the boom industry by the seventeen-sixties. Trust me on this one, Bunny." He winked at me.

"Good luck, kiddo. Meanwhile, I want you to knock off a job for me. Like doing some paper money for the United States of America."

"More horrible little green things with surrealism for the mass market. Not my style."

"Oh, ducks, but it is! I want a star-shaped seven dollar bill done up in amber and azures. With pictures of sprites and fairies on it." I could tell Blake was suddenly interested; his eyes lit up. "And once you get the steam going, how about a three dollar fold-out piece featuring Dolley Madison in bra and panties holding up the globe. Shay's Rebellion on The Ultimate Coupon, and the Eakins boys pissing number on the back of the new quarter."

"You're twisted, Bunny, but I like it." Blake looked fascinated. "Give me a week."

I opened my wallet, found a strip of tabs in a plastic bag, pulled off a single and pressed it on his tongue. "Here, Ginger, swallow this. And have a ball with the currency thing. Now I've got to find someone who can print the C note on Spandex."

I gave Blake a quick peck on the check and twirled around. *Was he reliable?* You just never know with that type. Would I ever see him again? A week would tell.

I opened my eyes. I was at the front of a pasture that was the great common for the shades of the Elysian Fields. As always seemed to be the case, the sky was grey and the wind cold and snappy. I seemed to be wearing my orange jumpsuit once again.

The weather notwithstanding, many shades reclined on beach towels under the mean skies, wearing skimpy outfits, as well as the latest in fashionable sunglasses. They seemed to be reading either trashy celebrity-type magazines or bibles. *If, in fact, they were reading at all.* Some called to me by my name. I ignored them as I quickly crossed the pasture. I walked past several two-backed beasts that were humping hither and yon. I was certain one involved was the shade of Tennessee Williams. I didn't stop to watch. I couldn't care less.

At the end of the pasture was the main town in the Fields. A spry, neat little town in fact. Real civic pride. I strode through numerous streets, admiring the façades of many different ages, filled with folks of all colors, cultures and languages—there was even one little Cherry Grove–type shack labeled "Thimk Pimk"—when by sheer luck I arrived at the pseudo-provincial residence of François-Marie Arouet, known to all as Voltaire, another lovely creature of self-invention, *the one way.*

I opened the cute little gate, which came up to my waist. I snapped it shut behind me. I padded up the tile path. The exterior of the house was all white, though looking a sad grey in the existing light. I rapped the little knocker. And waited. Minutes later, the door was slowly pulled open. There stood Voltaire, dressed in a loose white shirt, tight trousers and slippers. He wore a big ruby brooch shaped like a snake. He looked thinner than even Jefferson! It appeared that people from History had an eating disorder!

Voltaire gave me a heavy once-over. "Please. Come in."

I entered full of confidence. I looked around the foyer and then peeked into the salon. It seemed to be organized clutter. Publications piled up. Stacks of books on the floor.

"I've been making some notes on Ovid's *Ars Amatoria* and scanning some late twentieth century pornography. I fear Eros is not very meticulously cared for in the modern world. After all, what's *hedonism* without the *head*?"

Voltaire escorted me to a fluffy little chair. I sat. He brought out a carafe of wine and two glasses.

"I drink all day. My friends are scandalized. Particularly those inclined to Protestantism. I was saddened very early on, Bunny, to find out that bourgeois morality had such a grip on the denizens of the Elysian Fields. I do what I can to educate them, but it's an uphill struggle." Voltaire rolled his eyes. "Can you imagine it? There's even a prison here! Happily, I have never seen the insides of it, except, of course, as part of a support group that Jane Addams has put together. Baskets of food and such. To think that death would turn out to be just a recapitulation of the same old wars! Our race has such limited imaginative capacities. Isn't that sad?"

Voltaire had seated himself across the room from me. I rose, joined him on his divan and sat real close to him. We stared at each other.

"Good news, my friend. I have decided to whisk you away from these humble digs and have you join me and the others in the celestial stratosphere."

Voltaire crinkled up his thin face. "This is odd. Between my last two meals, I have had a couple other visitors proposing the same. One, a woman, Lillian Hellman. And this scruffy Italian, Pasolini. Both wanted to just pick me up and take me away. Pack my bags and just go. Imagine the nerve!"

"The impulsive type, I'm sure."

"I reserve judgment."

"You declined?"

Voltaire smiled. "Of course."

"My proposal is somewhat different. I can succeed where no other can."

Voltaire pulled back and looked concerned. "Familiarity is such a powerful force. I've rather gotten to like it here."

I scowled. "Don't lie to me, François. You have envied our powers from the minute you discovered what made us different. Players with the ultimate power. It's right up your alley."

Voltaire sucked on his lips. "Do you do drugs?"

I thought the question impertinent, though I was not about to tell him so. "Yes. At times. If they are good."

"There's a lovely variety available around here."

I said nothing.

"There are these powders made from organic materials, exotic leaves from around the Fields and the chemists here do the most amazing things with them. Alas, there are times when we get ration cards—though it's never explained exactly why and no one questions it—but there are always ways to get anything you want. The Fields, for some of us, seems to be a *very* administered place. Not at all as you might imagine it."

"All the more reason to come with me. Try out your powers in a place worthy of them."

"So simple!" He mocked me. "Just like that," snapping his fingers.

"Then plan on leaving. Twain and I will arrange everything, down to the slave girls throwing the rose petals in front of you on your arrival."

"I've brought some change here, some increase in amenities. A number of the shades are quite appreciative. Not many seasons ago,

I was presented with this Certificate Of Appreciation"—Voltaire pointed to some scribbled rag that was framed on the wall—"and that can mean so much."

"Save it for the tear-duct crowd, François. *I'm all business.* When you leave with me, you can lark about and change history. Forever. Correct all those things, big *and* little, which need your attention." I raised an eyebrow, figuring someone so thin must have a taste for revenge against all the bullies that tormented his life.

Voltaire popped open a small jewelry case and removed a green leaf from it and gently placed it on his tongue. "Purely medicinal," he said, smiling as he chewed. He munched for a bit and then daintily spit out the remains into a napkin. "I have my spies in your heady stratosphere, Bunny. And I get regular reports. I know you are new there, still stretching your wings, an inexact metaphor, but what's the rush to drag me up there with you and all the others?"

"First, you want to be there. Second, we need you. Third, only I can make the transfer. Fourth, you have to help us break up the little cabal that spins the heavens."

"*Godbusters?*"

"It's Sage and Peter. The iron fist in the velvet glove routine."

Voltaire looked stern. "I happen to know those gentlemen. They pose as The Big Bosses. They may well be. They come down here and bait shades like me. I find Peter particularly sadistic. Imagine a mind that would seek pleasure in tormenting shades!"

"Sounds like one of Mussolini's goons."

"The breed is present in every society, in every regime, rewarded by governments of a benign stripe or the boot-lapping vicious."

"I offer you all history as a plaything." I thought he might be pleased with my frivolity. "Or, if you prefer, an engine."

"I'm still listening. Where's your hard sell?"

"Smashing religions, ending slavery, though that looks to be a tough one, curbing nationalism, ending the mass slaughters, and changing those small important events so crucial to us and the slope of human development."

Voltaire did something strange with his mouth. "It sounds like hard work."

"When it stops being fun, I'll be the first dropout."

Voltaire relaxed into the divan's cushions. He picked up a little puff, on which there was embroidered a scene of black-clad religious types tossing books into a roaring fire, and stuffed it behind his back. It was clear that the mild drug was relaxing him.

"I detect the whiff of self-interest here. It is sometimes a wholesome and healthy aroma. You say you are in two places simultaneously. An interesting, if perhaps stressful, situation. But since you remain alive in the world of the quick dull, you have a concern in remaking the actual world so your living will be protected as long as humanly possible."

"Nothing ignoble in that."

"I'm not suggesting it. But you hardly expect us jaded dead to care."

He had a point, not an important one, but a point. I didn't miss a beat. "Unless the juices of both vengeance and justice—often connected—still tempt one."

"You and Twain offer me some guarantee?" Voltaire was every bit the tough customer. "That once I relocate into your realm, *if* that is what I decide to do and *if* it is something that can be done, that you won't make me sign some sort of contract or join up with some sort of crusade? That if I elect, I can just run off to Venice, set myself up in a fabulous palazzo and be *the* social butterfly."

I liked him. "If you do, my dear, I will be the first to barge through your door and be let in on the good life. 'Til then, there is much to be done."

Voltaire stood. I rose too. He took my arm as we walked to the front door. "I like what you say, Bunny. But your plan is vague. When you return with a solid proposal, we'll discuss the options. I like having options; funny that way, isn't it?" We stopped and Voltaire gave me a queer look. "I'm curious about your exceptional powers." He leaned over to me and whispered in my ear, "These are very curious places where you and I reside."

After he closed the door, we two strolled across a meadow.

"I think it is time you visited John Horne Burns. He occupies the house right over there." Voltaire pointed. "I just adore him, though I suspect it is not reciprocated." He sighed. "The Irish-Americans are the toughest ones to love. I think they like it that way. Sometimes they just won't let you through." Voltaire leaned on me as we crossed the field. Was he being too hard on Burns? Though I could feel his arm in mine, it was a ghostly and prickly sensation. We came upon a cottage. Burns was in the yard, at a table, dressed in chinos and a loose white button-down shirt with a cigarette burn near the front pocket. He sipped a cocktail, sucked on a Lucky Strike and scribbled on a legal pad.

"I've brought a new friend!" Voltaire was Welcome Wagon.

Burns looked up. "You must be Bunny. Voltaire promised me he'd bring you around." Burns shook my hand. "Please sit down."

The sky was lightening, though still pretty much its ubiquitous grey. Burns looked smaller than I had expected, which is often the case when you meet someone you think a giant. His body was tight, like a bantam weight boxer. The drink only made it all the tighter. I would have to study how drink changes the writers, though, for most, it is all too apparent. I sat at his patio table. Burns poured me a Bloody Mary; Voltaire declined.

"A pleasant residence," I noted.

Burns smiled. "It's fine. Last night I made it into the NBC studio when Toscanini did his *Don Giovanni*. It was marvelous."

I leaned over. "Excuse me?"

Voltaire touched Burns on the arm. "Bunny doesn't know. He's from the other realm, or, more truthfully, at least to his own account, two other realms."

"Oh. I see. Another meddler."

"Be kind, Burns," Voltaire was snippy. "Bunny has great ambitions."

"They all seem to." Burns put down the pen he had been toying with. "You see, Bunny, you and *your* crowd think they can change things, or so I hear. So you call up these scenes in order to pander your influence, if that's what it is. For Voltaire and me, it's different. Our powers are much more limited. For us, history is like going to the movies. You *have* been to a movie, *haven't you?*" Burns looked intently at me and arched an eyebrow. "We can will anything that has happened and then witness it again and again. But we cannot participate in it or attempt to change it. As soon as *we* try to meddle, we get grounded and it's no more movies for a very long time."

"Who revokes these privileges?" I was curious.

"Don't know. Whoever gives them, I guess. We'll never know. And I don't ask any more. I watched them building La Scala not long ago. It was inspiring."

"I particularly enjoyed the beheading of Charles the other evening," Voltaire chuckled. "Regicide is such a good *viewer-oriented* activity."

"You watch these events and have no impulse to intervene?" I was cold and rational.

"It has atrophied. And no longer exists, Bunny." Burns seemed uninterested.

"I would like to change this."

"To give us your powers?" Burns was snide.

"Yes. Exactly!"

"Good luck. Just don't come to my door for your experiment.

Things are fine for me just as they are."

"Not to worry, sweets," Voltaire was saccharine. "Bunny wants me as his first project."

"Knowing you, Frank, you'll go for it."

"You judge me too quickly!" Voltaire protested with a sly grin.

I rose and shook my host's hand. "I'd love to come back when there's less urgency and just chat."

"Urgency is not in my vocabulary," Burns said. "Chat is."

I leaned over and whispered in Voltaire's ear, "Soon." I quickly kissed him.

I closed my eyes and concentrated.

I opened my eyes to find I was sitting on a vinyl stool in a busy diner at lunch hour, a steaming cup of coffee in front of me as I scanned a newspaper filled with the oddest jumble of stories: Henry James opening a Communist Party conference in Tibet, Emily Dickinson apprehended for a string of church torchings, Zora Neal Hurston and her gang proclaiming themselves the new government of Paraguay. It was a very sick omen. I looked about. I didn't recognize anybody. This was not where I had planned on being. Had I got caught in some time discontinuum where all the outtakes go? Where the crazy ideas that didn't take off are secreted away to spin out their own twisted existences?

The counter waitress approached me. She cased me hard.

"Seems there's a phone call for you. Most irregular. You can take it on the pay phone just inside the swinging door to the kitchen." She threw some shoulder action at me.

I was baffled. I slid off the stool and squeaked past two more waitresses as I slipped through the greasy swinging door. On the other side was a video editing studio. I was surprised. This seemed unusual. The studio was dark. There was Sage, all by himself, sitting at the console. On a bank of monitors, hung in a row above him, he played the videotape of my just completed interview with Voltaire. He stopped the tape, rewound it and then played it again. He looked over his shoulder and spotted me. He patted on a seat next to him. I sat on it. I had no idea what he was up to. *Or what I was up against.*

"I like it. *Mucho*," Sage said, with a shit-eating grin on his face. "This part in particular, when you try to get Voltaire to make a decision and he does his leaf-munching routine." Sage cackled. "Oh, this will be a great hit on the circuit. They're just going to love it."

I was furious but didn't show it.

"Don't feel badly about it, Bunny. It testifies to your determination and your *earnestness*. Anybody in our realm worth his or her salt tries to sweet-talk the great Voltaire into joining us. It's the oldest game in town. And each and every comes up with A Plan. After visiting the great one, and getting hit with his very sublime wet blanket, most abandon the idea. And V. stays, perhaps quite happily, in his dell down below." Sage turned down the audio on the tape.

"Yes." I was firm. "I suppose all you say is true. But I think I can actually wangle it."

"I know. I watched your pitch. Red rover, red rover, let Voltaire come over! Quite good, actually. Something new to his tired ears. Your duality may have an advantage. Which we just don't know yet, *do we*? One of the reasons I brought you over. Anyway, good luck with your project."

I stared at him. He seemed, at that moment, his most ineffectual, diddling with the knobs and pods of the video toy. "You haven't any plans to try to stop me, have you?"

"Why would you even imagine it would occur to me to try?"

"I think you're an oily old creature."

"Well, that's one of the nicest things I've heard said about me in over a decade. I'm not at all evil, Bunny, as you may be inclined to think. But I do have my own interests to attend to. With all these wildly ambitious creatures running about, you must forgive me if I haven't the time or interest to follow your little games. I keep my eyes on things, in a scanning kind of way, and I counsel caution when it seems necessary. That is all. It has turned out not to be very easy. I thought I was supposed to be retired. The rest of the time is mine. For rest and relaxation. *Not* scheming. I'm post-scheming. Why must you beings project what is so clearly your own ambitions *onto me*? I've never understood it." He was the huffiest I had ever seen him. Score one for me, I thought, even though I was sure Sage was a veteran actor.

Sage saw my skeptical look. He gently drew down two pods on his console board and drew up two others. On a monitor, to one side, a face flickered into a familiar and recognizable form. The face looked distracted.

"Sorry to disturb you, Henry, but could you join us?"

The image of the face floated out from the screen, followed by a ghostly body which quickly became corporeal. I didn't even need funny glasses; this was real 3-D.

It was Henry Adams.

"Henry, this is Bunny."

"Yes. I know. I read the press releases and hear all the gossip. A pleasure, Bunny, to meet you at last." He leaned over to shake my hand and then sat on the edge of the console unit.

"Do you want to do the honors and explain a few basics to Bunny?" Sage asked.

"It's like this, my friend," Adams was dour, "It's not nice to play with the dead. One might normally think that it doesn't matter and,

I suppose, in the grand scheme of things it doesn't. But in our microscopic way of going on, it clearly does. More than just upsetting the shades, it can set off some of the more unstable in that group. *It disrupts our delicate equilibrium.* It throws things out of balance. That's why Sage and the others in the leadership have provided us with so many different, healthy and useful activities."

"What can that possibly mean," I snapped, "with so many of us trying to reinvent or revolutionize our worlds and others before it?"

"It's difficult to explain." Adams looked down. "And anyway, what you are curious about are the quick little time-dated things. *Our* peace needs to be a little more long-lasting."

"If you're suggesting that we are expected to be quiescent, I simply cannot accept *that* line."

"No doubt," Adams mumbled. "Let me approach it this way. Even here, we mostly keep to ourselves. I, for one, would just love to get closer to Erasmus, but he keeps to his set and we have only a correct acquaintanceship. It's all a matter of cohorts; some are more expansive than others. And those who choose to dabble do it in their approximate real-time life."

"I saw Suetonius at Pope's little luncheon for Voltaire."

Adams sighed. No doubt he thought I was intractable. "Things are different in the Elysian Fields and the wits are a club unto themselves with the most severe entrance requirements." Adams wagged his head, clearly a gesture of contempt.

"I've learned folks in the Fields have their own powers." I was smug.

"I wouldn't really classify it as a power," Adams wanted to be precise. "It's like going to a museum. The passing parade of history and entertainment. And as we all have learned, through long and painful experience, entertainment is just a diversion for the dull, a vast throng."

I went on the offensive. "You mentioned the leadership of the heady realm." I looked at Sage and Adams. "Who is in this clique? *I'd like to know.*"

"Your expectations are hierarchical, Bunny," Adams was brusque. "And off the mark. To my information, there is no high command."

"I don't believe you for a minute, Henry." I eyed Adams coldly. "Do you meddle, yourself?"

"When I got here, there was so much I wanted to do. I tried to prevent the Civil War. Now that's just what an apprentice needs to take on! Somewhere, in these vast video archives over there," he waved to a floor-to-ceiling bank of tapes, "is a record of me imploring the South Carolina legislature to reject secession. I look so ridiculous. The famous charm of the Adams family only goes so far. Our Southern cousins seemed to be immune. At any rate, my effort didn't work. Actually, earlier, I tried to prevent the election of Lincoln. Can you imagine? That was particularly risky because, had I made it come to pass, it would have changed my own life in the quick world. But I figured it was worth a try, just to prevent that great and horrible war. I got some votes thrown to Douglas, some to Breckinridge, having to bribe some of the finer element in the Electoral College, which reveals the depths one will go to for a noble effort. I think I would have tried anything to prevent the inevitable. Alas, the coming conflict *was* inevitable, not even subject to our great meddlings. I had wasted all that effort for naught. I think I learned something from that experience."

"*Nothing* is completed wasted," Sage was schoolmarmish. "And particularly for us."

"Since then, I've been interested in the development of education in America, Bunny. Doing small things. Getting districts to set up quality schools as quickly as possible, rights for teachers, putting a liberal curriculum in place. Terribly tiresome. But terribly important."

"Sage and his writers' funding schemes. You and your education projects. Where can I find the grand gesture to change history?" I challenged the masters.

Adams and Sage looked at each other. Sage spoke. "Wherever it is, it has eluded us both. But don't dismiss us completely, Bunny. We may just surprise you yet."

"Twain and I got Mary Baker Eddy sent to the big house and ruined her so-called church"—I snapped my fingers—"*just like that!*"

Adams actually smiled. You could see the dominance of the cold genes in his chromosomes. Jefferson was right, not a fun clan. "Beginner's luck, Bunny. But a bold and successful move. I hope this will now keep her remains out of Mt. Auburn. We never really felt she belonged there. You have my congratulations. And that of many others." The smile on his face turned into a severe frown. "But, since you have not deigned to be interested in your handiwork since your lightning strike, there is an update on the Eddy zap. Remember, nothing remains as you want it when others are interested. The tides shift all the time. Two federal courthouses have been bombed. Six people seriously injured. One federal attorney barely missed being assassinated. Police suspect Eddy is running a terrorist campaign from her prison cell to win her release."

"Well, good!" I was delighted. "Let the Christers take the heat instead of the anarchists. A healthy change in things."

"I see you take the long view," Adams was wry, though content.

"My advice, offered for free," Sage said, still playing with the video mixer, "*is leave Voltaire alone.* He doesn't want to join us anyway and, even if you should succeed, he'll just be another pain in the ass."

"For *you* perhaps. Not for Twain and me. And besides, aren't you the stern nanny? First you berate me for crossing back into my real-life time. Now you warn me off my Voltaire Project. Why did you bother bringing me over here? To start a stamp club?"

Adams seemed interested. "I'm still trying to get that great early issue from Albania of King Zog and Queen Hog!"

"I'd rather conspire with Twain and Voltaire to prevent the writing of the New Testament." I snapped.

"*Really*?" Sage seemed suddenly vivacious . "I've always rather liked the New Testament. It's sort of a breath of fresh air after the *rigors* of the Old Testament. All those costume changes."

"An anti-MGM, I see," Adams quipped. I gave him points.

"You are both such cranky old conservatives. Where's your spunk?" I gave a long sigh. "To me, it's just gas from the swamp."

"As you will." Adams slowly seeped back into the video monitor and faded away into a blizzard of screen snow.

I walked to the screen just as his image faded away. "Bye, Henry. Nice to have met you." I walked over to Sage. "Make a copy of that video for me, will you? I'd like to keep it for use when necessary."

"So modern. Documents on call."

"And why not? I never know what I may need for my future wars. Now, one more question, Sage. Which way to the piss-pot?"

Sage pointed to a corner. "It's behind the door marked exit."

"When I bring Voltaire over, we'll have a lovely reception. I'll be sure to invite you." I twinkled my ivories at Sage. I sashayed to the metal door on which was painted EXIT in a bright red. I pushed the panic bar and passed through.

I entered a nice study that reeked of familiarity. A wooden desk, a typewriter, filing cabinets, a silly old telephone. A nesting place for any busy writer. I spotted a pack of cigarettes, took one, lit it, sucked on it and let go a cloud of smoke.

"You handled those icy monsters well."

I turned. It was Twain, walking out of the closet.

"Does everybody spy on each other here?"

"Pretty much. It goes with the territory. And the natures of the beasts in the bestiary."

"Everybody always knows what I'm doing?"

"It's the best lesson of the late twentieth century, to behave as though you think you are always on television because, here at least, *you are*! Any of our grand community can tune in anyone at will. Cocktail parties around the realm are laughing at this minute and deconstructing the tape of your interview with Voltaire."

"I didn't like walking cold into that little session with His Highness."

"Sage? Well, no one ever does. But it happens time and time again. Nonetheless, you are not to let his feeble protestations stand in your way. I mean, it's pathetic. He brings in Henry Adams to be his *muscle*. It's ridiculous!"

"I wish I could actually dislike him. It would make things so much easier. He does have his charms."

"Never bother disliking anyone ever again." Twain was instructional. "It's a vulgar human emotion, best rid of. And barely useable as a plot device in any level of affairs."

I didn't really care what he babbled about. I was lost in thought. My plans had set.

"Secondly," Twain continued on a more pleasant note, "the significance of your being in real-life time and here simultaneously has finally sunk in among the leadership caucus. They are fascinated but apprehensive. You need to tip over their cart very quickly. But very carefully."

We were on the same beam. I was agitated and ready to move. "Look, Sam, are you with me on this one?"

"All the way." His eyes sparkled with the pure joy of a devilish conspirator. I leaned over and whispered in his ear.

"OK. *Here's my plan ...*"

It was simple enough to set up. I bought a plot in The Elysian Fields—cost me a pretty penny too, *who knew?*—and hired a developer to build a lovely ranch home right next to Voltaire's white French provincial abode. My place was all aluminum siding, vibrant 1950s bathroom tile, big windows, two-car garage, plastic pink flamingos on the lawn, sprayed with a glow of pink spot lights. There were tiny low level illumination lights on the gravel walk to the big front door which featured a knocker *and* doorknob right in the middle. *Très chic!* The lawn was all sod with a smart little hedge trim around the perimeter. The backyard featured a patio with serious cook-out equipment as well as picnic tables and benches. Construction went quickly. My project was the talk of Poet's Corner. Shades came by and gawked.

Voltaire kept his distance, which I understood, though I could see him peeking through his curtains, keeping a sharp eye out at all times.

Came the night for my house warming party. I festooned my new residence with strings of gay little Japanese lanterns. I hired smart waiters from the best agency in the Fields to handle the catering. They wore red vests over silver shirts, with sateen tight trousers which tapered to the ankle. They wore pointy-toed mid-top shoes made of shiny black leather. They circulated with drinks—Manhattans and Martinis only!—and canapés of processed cheese on crackers and slabs of tomato aspic as finger food. I threw open the doors to the haute trash of the Elysian Fields.

Truman Capote was the first to fly through my door, a not unexpected event.

"Dearest Bunny," he gushed, "I feel right at home. The suburban motif is *just* perfect. The shades are *so* embarrassed by the fifties, and I keep trying to tell them it wasn't that way *at all*. So, here's to your good work." The weasel flew in to price all my precious *objets*. I met all the guests at the door. The Duke and Duchess of Windsor were suitably elegant. Tennessee Williams hung out on the patio and told racy stories to a bevy of thin, svelte foreigners.

I took a minute to admire myself in the full-length mirror. I wore a broadcloth, loosely cut blue shirt, a skinny black leather tie, baggy blue jeans with rolled bottoms, penny loafers with *real* pennies in them, and I had my hair pomaded into a fabulous retro DA. I had also painted a small star under my right eye.

My new house was mobbed. The shades did the cha-cha until my poor roof shook. I was DJ. I played Connie Francis and Little Richard records. Cut with a little Elvis, a tad of Brenda Lee, and Patti Page of course, and the Four Preps. Pat Boone somehow didn't make it onto the playlist. The waiters were constantly being groped by some of the drunken shades. It was my first experience of watching those in the underworld at play *and* inebriated, a condition many of them reached rather quickly since it was on my nickel.

Eventually, as I had anticipated, Voltaire, completely sober, drifted my way. I welcomed him as I had the others. I got him a non-alcoholic drink and let him mingle and make his usual catty remarks, which the good folks so enjoy. Tiring of that, he slowly wended his way back to me.

"Quite the successful debut, Bunny." Voltaire was crisp. He kept his eyes on the crowd. "Not many meddlers have actually chosen to take up residence with us in this grey, pedestrian Elysian Fields. We are honored." He gave me a little bow. I saw the Duchess of Windsor watching us with envy dripping from her eyes.

"Oh, I don't plan on becoming a voter here," I was unctuous. "Just sort of a hide-away kind of place. When things get too hectic."

Voltaire gave me a gooey smile. "So *many* pressures."

The two of us were then caught up in a swirl of celebrities—it looked like Brenda Frazier and her crew—and handed flutes of champagne, which turned out, to my surprise, to be a lovely fresh and very dry vintage from the Fields itself.

The party carried on, as parties, good ones, do. I put on *The Greatest Hits of Johnny Mathis*, turned down the lights and watched as the shades paired off for some slow dancing. I took Voltaire downstairs to see my fabulous new "rec room." We slinked down the narrow stairway. I reached for the light switch, found it and threw it on.

"What's *this*?" asked Voltaire, looking around at my complete entertainment complex.

"Oh? That? Just your basic ping-pong table."

"What do you do with it?"

"Simple. I'll show you."

We batted the ball about for a few minutes. It was a very boring exercise, but necessary. I was starting to get nervous.

"Look, François, I didn't invite you down here to teach you the mysteries of ping-pong."

"Nor, I suspect, to have sex." He arched an eyebrow.

"Sex with a shade?" I mused. "I'll have to think about that. I might even be willing to try. But not now. Actually, there is an embrace I would like to demonstrate just to get your reaction."

"I didn't say it first, for which I regret, but I do get the credit, once a philosopher, twice a pervert."

"In that case, Mr. Philosopher..." I took Voltaire by the arm and led him into a dark corner off the rec room, which, and I was supremely pleased with this, was decorated with garish posters of Miami Beach and Disneyland. Very quickly, I surrounded Voltaire with all my limbs. I put my arms over his head and shoulders. I put my legs in front of his. He made no resistance to this rather odd exercise. We became as one, though not for sexual release, but for a grander and longer-lasting mission. And I closed my eyes, focused all my energy and hoped this plan just might work.

When I opened my eyes, both Voltaire and I were snugly ensconced in my humble apartment in Boston in 1985. My real-life time self moved about with some curiosity. I could see myself clearly on this visit. I assumed I was just as likely as clear to his vision.

"Just dragging anyone home at all hours, I see!" My real-life self was catty. "I happen to have dinner guests due in ten minutes."

"Whatever have you done with me?" Voltaire, poor dear, was shaking.

"*Please! Everything will be fine!*" I was single-focused.

"If you want to stay for a drink, fine. But that's it!" My real-life self was polite but firm.

"Drinks, yes." I said, just to get rid of him. He padded to the kitchen. I heard ice tinkle into glasses. Good. I quickly turned on my old 1962 vacuum-tube monster black-and-white TV. A snow pattern filled the screen. "Just stand here, my friend," I said softly to Voltaire. I positioned us both in front of the TV screen. "OK," I shouted, "take it away, Twain!" I closed my eyes and rolled my head.

When I opened my eyes, I stood next to Twain in the video studio wherein I had last encountered Sage. Twain sat at the controls, looking a little baffled, and who could blame him. On a large monitor was the image of Voltaire, looking even more befuddled.

"Remember what I told you!" I was sharp. "Throw the forth pod over on the top deck." Twain moved the lever up. Suddenly the image of Voltaire moved past the screen of the monitor and materialized right before us, just as Henry Adams had. This was the corridor, perhaps one of many. Voltaire, looking a bit shocked, simply stood before us, a dazed Venus on a somewhat porous half shell. It didn't matter. *He was here, and my plan had worked.*

Twain sighed. "Well, that was easy."

"Welcome, Monsieur Voltaire," I bowed deeply, "to your new home."

Voltaire stumbled forward a step and then braced himself against the console. "I'm afraid I'm a little dizzy."

"*Only a little?*" Twain was quick. "It'll take a lot more than that to do well here."

"François Arouet, known to history as Voltaire, you have been crossed over from the Elysian Fields into this realm of the..." I was suddenly foggy.

Twain recovered for me. "To the realm of not only the true immortals but, as your gang calls us, *The Meddlers.*"

Voltaire quickly scanned the studio and then sat in the most comfortable chair. "I'm not so certain this is something I would have wanted, *if actually asked.*" He gave me a snide look.

"You are a charming, but bad, liar, Frank," Twain was sweet. "Many have planned this and even consulted you on it. Bunny, here, executed it."

"And a rather exhausting experience it was," I piped in. "That little leap frog number. Jumping to real-life time. Then to here. It was a gamble. But it paid off."

"I'm rather old," Voltaire sighed. "It takes some adjustment."

I stared at him. "You've got five minutes. I'm counting. Then you and Twain and I must get down to business. We'll start with the religion problem."

Twain was lighting a cigar. "I never figured out why the monotheists thought they were on to something. It gave them such a thrust to their moralism." He puffed and then let out a cloud of smoke.

"Are we still out to crush the infamous?" Voltaire queried. "And, by the way, on the single god issue, what makes you think the Catholics are monotheists? Their Godhead has many facets, or so I was once instructed."

I couldn't resist. "Like *The Three Faces of Eve*?"

"I am unfamiliar with that product," Voltaire mostly certainly lied. As he had had so much time in the Fields, he must have watched every movie ever made. "Now, as to my new universe. There are amenities here?"

"Darling," I cooed, "I'm still discovering them."

Voltaire rose. "In that case, I think I'll stay."

"A wise choice," Twain said bluntly.

"Twain, I hope you will set up François nicely. I must be off on urgent business."

"What's the rush?" Twain was critical. "You've just done something that will rattle the crusty elite here. Don't you want to hang around and take their measure of it all?"

"I'm off to Chicago at the turn of the twentieth century. I want to fix it so Wrigley's gum gets poisoned. To end, at the very beginning, the hideous habit of chewing gum."

"So far, baby," Twain was sassy, "you're battin' a thousand."

I understood this to be a sporting metaphor.

Downtown Chicago was a bustling place. It seemed to be sometime in the late 1890s. It didn't matter. I took a horse-drawn trolley to the Wrigley plant. There was a change in shifts, workers coming in and workers going out. The giganticness of high industrialism shocked me. The noise. The bulk. The inattention. The squalid conditions.

I had the potion in a packet in my pocket. I swirled right in with the workers on the new shift. I grabbed some card off the bunch on the wall and punched it. I was in! As to my potion, I had decided on a noxious mix of a concentrated mescaline and a forceful stomach-heaver, so people, having chewed on this brew, would trip and then puke, not a combination to endear customers to a product.

I walked through the factory full of authority. I was stopped twice by Pinkerton guards. I was huffy to them, and reminded them that I was from the Inspectional Services Division making sure about quality control. This seemed a foreign concept to them but impressed them nevertheless and they let me by. I rushed to my task at hand.

After much prowling, I wound up in a large open area where a vat of gum-like substance was being mixed by this huge rotating blending arm. Sugar, flavoring and other ingredients were funneled into the mixture. As it came out of the vat, it was dried and cut into blocks, unlike what I expected. Busy making meaningless notes on a clipboard, I slowly made my way to a metal walkway near the top of the vat. Sneakily, I dumped the bag of toxins into the mess. Quickly it got mashed into the concoction. I slid away and left the factory. For just a moment, I felt like I was walking on air.

After I passed through the gates of the factory, I made my way to the offices of the Chicago *Herald*, a sensational tabloid of its day. I demanded to see the city editor. I was pointed to a back desk. I found him puffing on a cigar, shirt open, a dismal fan above him blowing around the wretched air.

He looked up at me, surly to the tits.

"You lost, fellah?"

"Hardly. I have a hot story for you."

"What's your name?"

"LaRue. Bunny LaRue." I slurred my pronunciation of Bunny. Big butch men get upset when they meet a man named Bunny.

"What can you do for me, Buddy?"

"It's some terrible news. About the gum coming out of Wrigley. It's the ingredients in their new formula. It makes people sick."

He rolled his eyes. "Yeah. Yeah. So what's the big news?"

"Poisonings. Panic. Mayhem. Scandal." I raised an eyebrow. No response. "Here, let me write the story for you."

"Sure. Be my guest."

I sat at a desk next to his and tapped out the story on an antique typewriter that was of a baroque design. Ten minutes later, I handed him my copy.

"Hold on to it for a few days. When people start coming down sick from the gum, you can run it. Paint it yellow. Run a big editorial. Scream holy hell. It'll be a feather in your cap. Trust me."

He chewed on his cigar, true to type. "Sounds strange. But I'll keep it on my desk."

"You do that."

He eyed me top to bottom. "We get all types in here."

I left the newspaper office and walked around Chicago. It was gritty and boring. I hated it. I crossed back over to my real-life time and went into my apartment. I ran into myself as he dined off a TV tray.

"Don't ask me to share. It's leftovers and there's nothing left in the fridge. You're on your own." He/I continued chomping. I ignored my other self and left him watching *Solid Gold*. I went to my typewriter, knocked out a more detailed version of the news story I had just written, made multiple copies of this document, returned to turn-of-the-century Chicago and mailed each and every to the major newspapers in the country.

I flashed forward two weeks. I took a cheap hotel room in The Loop. And waited.

Three days later came the jackpot. A *Herald* headline screamed: CHEWING GUM SICKNESS: Hundreds Felled! The story was pretty much my release, gussied up, of course, with touches of local color, interviews with relatives. A day later, it was national story, lurid interviews with the victims of the gum sickness. Some legislators in Illinois announced there would be a probe. The Attorney General jumped in. Lawsuits were threatened. Lawyers swarmed. Sales plummeted. After three months of bad publicity, Wrigley announced that the corporation was abandoning chewing gum production and going into the breakfast cereal business. RIP chewing gum.

I was satisfied and returned to my heady realm.

I decided to be grand. I was aboard The Twentieth Century, which I checked out from stem to stern, a rather impressive and dressy way to travel. I adored it. The train pulled into an art deco station. Slowly, it came to a complete halt. I disembarked.

Twain waited on the platform, dressed completely in white, a devilish grin adorning his mouth. No one I had ever met did it better. The train inched out of the station, a blast from its horn, and a sooty spew of coal ash rising just above us; Twain's poor white suit!

"You will exhaust even those from among the brave of us, Bunny," he said. "Everyone here watched every second of your exploits on their screens."

I took his arm. "I feel I am just coming into my own."

The railway station melted away. Twain and I approached a verdant campus, with ivy-covered buildings surrounding a neatly trimmed common. I hoped I wasn't about to win some treacly award.

"Let me bring you up-to-date." Twain seemed calm. "While you dawdled in Chicago, busy destroying the chewing gum industry—and, by the way, I had shares in Wrigley—the shit has hit the fan here.

Things are not in a pretty shape. It's time to do some fence-mending on the home front."

"What is it *now*?" I was not in the mood.

"First up, Marie has been arrested by the Committee on Public Safety and she's unable to get herself out, for whatever reason. She's in some hideous revolutionary prison, charged with some vague anti-revolutionary charge. We're going to have to spring her."

"No problem. What else?"

"I suspect Peter did this as penalty for your bringing Voltaire over. That's Peter's mentality. And then there's Voltaire. He refuses to eat. Hasn't even touched a lettuce leaf. He's bunking in Mencken's abode and is being stubborn as an old goat."

"Just cross-over shock, I'm sure."

"And I ran into Sage, Peter and Mede on the Rialto yesterday. All three of them were fit to be tied. I suspect they had just come from a meeting. Mede spread the rumor that 'The Council' was soon to put the entire eighteenth century off limits."

"Let them try!" I scoffed. "*What* council might this be?"

"I actually don't have any idea. Mede wanted me to believe it existed."

"Yeah! Only in his mind. But if it does exist, let's crash it and have some fun."

"Expose them!"

"But, before we do, let's go shake Voltaire out of his maudlin self-pity or whatever funk he's in."

We strolled off the campus to a cute row of brick houses. We climbed the stoop and knocked. The door was opened by Mencken.

"We are not receiving." His bushy eyebrows were meant to convey terror, but we weren't buying.

"On the contrary," I sniffed, sliding right past him, "how can you turn away Samaritans on a noble mission?"

Voltaire sat in the parlor in an overstuffed easy chair. A bottle of cognac was on a table at his side."

"Enjoying yourself, Voltaire?" I was businesslike.

He stared at me. "In fact, I am pretending to be in a state of time shock."

"To which you are well entitled," Twain said, "providing you don't get carried away with it."

Voltaire smiled. His thin lips were unconvincing. "Just trying to fathom the lay of this new land."

"I actually envied your position in the Elysian Fields," Mencken sighed. "It had stability written all over it. *Here*, you just never know what's going to happen next."

"I still feel like a guest," Voltaire grumbled. "I can handle that for a week or so, but not for all eternity! Like being seduced, a position not much to my temperament." He glanced nervously over his shoulder." It was clear he was in some stage of minor discomfort or was marvelously faking it; with a pro like Voltaire, you just never can tell.

"I take responsibility," I confessed. "I thought you might take to this place more quickly than you have. What you need is your own home. Something roomy, nicely lit, gracious and with all the amenities."

Just then, Sage strolled out from the kitchen with cranky-faced Peter by his side. They looked like they wanted to bust up the place. Both glowered at me.

"You have ignored the stress you have induced, Bunny," Sage said firmly.

"These are big changes," Peter echoed, the perfect toady.

"We're thinking of returning Voltaire to his happy domicile in the Fields. He was so popular there." Sage was sickeningly sweet but severe in his tone.

"Over my dead body!" I was firm. "Voltaire's transfer is a *fait accompli!* Irreversible. End of story." I turned to Voltaire, who was secretly adoring all the attention. "Have you any wish to go back to your digs in the Fields?" I asked him.

Voltaire rolled his head and rubbed the back of his neck. "It's hard to make a fair evaluation after so brief an acquaintanceship. Now that I'm here, I may as well stay and see the sights. Anything less would be unfair to my new hosts. I like to have some respect for the efforts of others. I know from my own experience: *work is work!*" He eyed Sage and Peter with obvious suspicion. It was nice to deal with someone who had been around the block. I thought, as Voltaire stared at Sage and Peter, that they must have reminded him of the screws at the Bastille.

"We've already taken a vote," Sage was grabbing at straws. "They want Voltaire back in the Fields by a two-thirds majority."

"And what about the *other third*?" Voltaire was, correctly, curious.

"Come on, guys! Polling the dead?" *Hadn't I left Chicago?*

"With Voltaire gone from their midst," Peter pouted, "there is a vacuum in their society. He is so desperately missed."

"My dear! So sensitive all of a sudden!" I tried to be rude but was it worth the effort? "If you want that slot filled, I would suggest you or Sage rush down below and lead the shades. Either one of you will be fabulous."

"This is not a frivolous matter," Sage sputtered.

"We agree," I said.

"These things have to be cleared!" Sage snapped.

"The rules change with the weather around here," I sniffed. "I'll wind up as queer as poor Alice on the *wrong* side of the looking glass."

"We could make you a traffic cop," Mencken proposed. "Give you a smart uniform, dark glasses and shiny boots and let you direct the trafficking of the images, from substance to representation to its double to its façade."

"I think what's wrong with this place," I said, trying to hide my exasperation, "is that no one seems to know who pulls the strings on this show, and those who should know are too mousey to find out or, perversely, won't tell."

"No one has ever before complained about their powers or access." Peter smirked at me. I hated him.

"I will come to the next Council meeting then and expect to be a voting member." I put them on notice. "I want to bump pussies with the gods of this strange domain."

Sage was suddenly nervous. "Not possible, Bunny. It doesn't work that way at all. You have it conceptualized all wrong. In time you will come to understand." He clammed up.

"We'll see about that!" I was all attitude and self-confidence and why not. Once I got my hands on the throttle…

"No! Please!" Sage held up one hand as a warning. "Don't force this, Bunny." Sage seemed near tears. "It can only get ugly and put everyone in a really foul mood, and that takes a long time to clean up."

I felt like I was locked in a confab of therapists, ready to gag on their mephitic cant. "Pshaw," I hissed. "You have nothing to fear but the exposure of the truth. I snapped my fingers as Sage and Peter looked at me with faces of pure horror.

I guessed I was on to something. But *what*?

Suddenly everything was a glare of intense bright whiteness, just the worst visual for a constant drinker like yours truly but, happily, it quickly passed. Most things do. I found myself settling into business.

It was a large and busy powder room, something out of a Harlow movie. All black and white with the most expensive shades of grey. A phalanx of painted faces floated from plush chair to chair in a din of high-pitched screeching and, what seemed to me, mean-spirited cackles. I heard the march of satins and crinolines like cannon fire. I sat in the inner sanctum where the women of the elite put on their many faces for the battles. The atmosphere was a cloud of powder, streaks of the loudest lipstick, terminal doses of the stankiest *parfums* and veritable artillery of coiffures and killer perms. In a sudden rush, there was an exodus of The Platoon Of Ladies. Back to the wars.

As the quiet settled, I found myself seated at a vanity, looking into a make-up mirror surrounded by little incandescent bulbs. I wore a simple cotton work shirt, a neck scarf, bleached cotton trousers and loafers. Such attire would not get me a date in this milieu.

Across the room, sitting at their own vanities and staring at me in their own vanity mirrors were two plump and very serious-looking women. We stared at each other in our respective mirrors.

*Was this it?* The heartbeat of the heavens? The counting room of the cosmos? The locus of the hocus-pocus? The music being piped in through unseen speakers bleeped a tinny, barely recognizable version of *The Threepenny Opera*. Their fragrances reached my nose. It wasn't overpowering but it wasn't subtle either. It was probably pricey and from the twenties and, like most fine drugs, sold by the ounce.

I knew who they were, of course, part of my new job assignment: Fanny Hurst and Edna Ferber in a rare joint appearance. They were dressed to the nines, lacy flourishes and long gloves. This must be serious.

"The reports on you are disturbing, Bunny." Ferber spoke first. "For which we don't hold you entirely accountable. Sage must bear some responsibility for his failure to familiarize you with our acceptable rules of conduct and etiquette, as well as the norms of social conventions here."

Hurst gave me an executioner's grin and continued the reproach. "It is in everyone's best interest, ultimately, to stay within our established guidelines. Edna and I have worked long and hard in drawing up these sets of rules and we both agree that we have been as fair as conditions and our interests allow." Hurst struck me as a gasbag. Suddenly she got prickly. "This *mania* for the eighteenth century! Just crashing across borders and carrying on like you do! It can't go on! *We won't have it!*" She clapped her hands just once.

"You see, Bunny," Edna tried a patrician tone, "the eighteenth century is very fragile. Like fine crystal, it must be delicately observed, reverentially handled and kept in pristine condition to pass on to those yet to come. We mustn't spoil it for the others." She folded her hands in her lap, looking like a self-satisfied alcoholic priest who had just explained the logic of a miracle to a retard.

"Excuse me. But I have no idea where persons in your situation get your sense of history. It all seems pretty clear to me. Through your glasses, it looks like some taxidermist's museum or some rich man's drying board for his dead bugs. Hanging around dead things from the past. *I want to make it new again!*"

"Actually," said Hurst, "I was planning to fund a study to find out which is more expensive—modernity or antiquity."

I had had enough of their gibberish. I spun around on my stool and looked at them directly for the first time while they continued to look at my reflection in their vanity mirrors.

"I just don't get it," I snapped. "This is the highest council in this nimbus-world. And it's got you two old hacks as the reigning deities? You sit here on your well-powdered rumps and find it fit to judge me and my goals for this place. *Is that it?*"

Edna and Fanny spun around on their vanity stools, their faces suddenly full of predatory grins, and shouted in unison: *"Precisely!"*

"I'm getting out of here, though where I wind up when I leave the Ladies' head will be a surprise. Everything in these zip codes is a surprise, especially meeting you two." I rose and gave them the evil eye. "I think you are just part of some creature's sick joke that he or she, most likely a he, is playing on me, and it's not funny. It's annoying." Before I left, I stopped and stared at them. "And by the way, thanks for the free advice." I walked to the door, gave them one last look, wondering why they had bothered, and slipped away.

I walked immediately onto the large front porch of a Victorian country house. Twain sat in a rocker. I was still fuming.

"You have the skill of alienating people," Twain said.

"I wasn't born to it." I was curt. "It's taken years of work. But one must be selective. *And,* being where I am, I am determined to transcend simple judgment."

"Well, I wouldn't worry about it if I were you. They just think there's some mileage in this play-acting of authority." Twain looked at me obliquely. "I'm sorry you haven't figured this out on your own yet, Bunny, but just about all of this is radiating out of your own mind. Lucky you."

"My mind? *You mean what's left of it!* Look, Twain, I am not one of those writers who is an intractable solipsist, though it has occurred to me. I want the world reformed and I want to be the primary agent of its reformation. Don't put me in with the bellybutton watchers, those too lazy or unimaginative to invent a new world but, also, afraid to live in the one they occupy." I plopped onto the porch swing and swayed back and forth. I didn't mean to scream at Twain—and why had I taken up screaming at all; must be something in the air—but Twain was silent, rocking away across from me, as he lit and relit his cigar.

"Let's go for our daily constitutional," Twain said, getting up. "A little exercise will clear our heads."

We took a little walk, though I was certain Twain had an agenda.

I took his arm. People stared at us. I couldn't gauge the exact—or even the rough—time we were in but the place seemed to be some highly developed city center. And somewhere in America. *You always know.* The good *volk* glared with hostility when they saw two men holding hands or even loosely linking arms. Had it always been thus? Such a sad, occupied country.

"It's something Sage is loath to show you," Twain mentioned. "I can't really understand why. Because, for you, it's a natural."

We turned into an entranceway; it looked to be some sort of medical complex. Ambulances rushed in and out. People on crutches and people in wheelchairs came and went.

"The most difficult thing," Twain advised, with a gentle squeeze to my arm, "is the stench."

We entered the complex. Twain waved and said a cheery hello to the woman staffing the front desk. We walked down a long hospital corridor and passed through several sets of fire doors. Twain seemed to know his way around this maze. We came to a dark grey metal door. It had a tiny window at eye level. A sign next to the window read: Buzz For Admittance.

"Go ahead," Twain said, looking at me.

I buzzed.

We waited. Finally, a face filled the tiny window and gave the two of us the eyeball. We heard a click and the door opened. I thought: this must be some sort of inner sanctum. The man before us wore hospital whites. He looked familiar, a James Agee-type, but I couldn't place him.

"Sam, good to see you. You've brought a friend."

"I have. This is Bunny. I think he should know about this place."

"It's odd we don't get more visitors," our host noted. "You'd think people would get a kick out of this."

"They made the decision to keep this place out of the tourist guides. Made strictly for political reasons, I can assure you." Twain sounded in-the-know.

"I'll let you show your friend around." The fellow withdrew to an office in the corner.

I scanned the place. It was a long room with cubicles. It smelled of formaldehyde. "This place stinks of death," I whispered to Twain, wishing to be respectful, of the dead, if they were here.

"As well it should." Twain was bright. "For, you see, Bunny, this is the morgue of American writing."

"*What*?" I laughed.

"This is where the dead writing is laid out and embalmed. It's a little complicated but the corpses of creation are preserved here."

I was confused.

Twain stared at me. "Here. Let me illustrate." We walked to a nearby nook. Twain rolled open a morgue rack. It was filled with books and manuscripts.

"Here lies the entire catalogue of Faith Baldwin." Twain waved a hand over it and then lit up a cigar.

I stared at the collection and then rustled through it.

"It just sits here?" I asked.

"It's the kindest thing that can be done with it. At least on these slabs it collects little dust. You see, Sage, in his haphazard way, had planned a Museum of American Writing, but it never got off the ground. So these things just stay put right here." Twain was sniffy. "Actually, I don't object. It seems a fit resting place."

I went along the racks and pulled out other drawers. There were works of nineteenth century men and women, most of which I had never heard of. There was also the work of recently deceased writers.

"It's all the same," Twain observed. "It had no use, except, in some cases, as commercial property, and once that was spent, it came here."

"Everything equal in death."

"Don't be hasty. Some things survive with lives of their own. My works, please note, are not to be found here. Though, I must admit, I check regularly, as there is no accounting for changes in tastes."

I walked to the end of the hall. There was new construction being completed around the corner. A whole new ell with fresh plaster, paint and mortuary slots.

"What's this?" I wondered.

"Something new. The Contempory Writers' Wing."

We strolled in. The workmen were hammering in fixtures and testing the roller trays that held the work.

"It's for today's writers. Those not even dead yet but, if any good, anticipating it." Twain was my tour guide. "Though *they* are not yet dead, their writing is. So here it comes."

I ambled through the confusion. I came to a rack of papers in boxes, yet to be stacked in the mortuary trays. I fingered through them.

"I know this work! Its paperback rights went for three hundred and fifty thousand dollars just two years ago!"

"Doesn't matter." Twain lit a cigar. "It came here DOA. It used to be it was the dead writing of the dead writers. Times have changed. Now it's the dead writing of anything issued. Killer prose. Born dead."

I knew exactly to what he referred. I went over to another set of boxes and looked through the books and manuscripts, finding yet another recent commercial success. "She got a half-million dollar advance for this novel," I told Twain, holding up the evidence.

"Stone cold dead the minute it arrived." Twain blew out a cloud of smoke. "There is a pipeline. And a publishing death machine that feeds it. In any cycle, there are always two prominent literary magazines; the imprint of either one is a death certificate. They kill it, chop it up, freeze it and then package it and sell it, just like a fish factory. It shoots from its first imprint to this morgue for embalming and preservation. You see the care that is taken with it as it rests in peace."

"The Living Death Of Amerikan Littrachure!" I laughed.

Twain twinkled. "Some things remain constant. It helps me sleep at night."

We departed the Grim Reaper's harvest of petrified prose, calcified imaginations and rotting writing. Suddenly, we were back on the porch. I was in the swing again; Twain sat on the rocker and looked good in it. The sun was setting. The cicadas were a chorus.

"We can create as much as we want and even make *them* do certain things," Twain said.

I was lost in thought. "To whom are you referring?"

"Our fellow beings in this heady realm. And we can eavesdrop, a most wonderfully precise referent." Twain put his arm out before the two of us and, as though drawing in air a rectangular screen, created a space which was instantly filled with an image of Sage chatting worriedly with Peter.

"I can't hear them," I complained .

Twain waved his hand again. The sound came up.

"Clearly Hurst and Ferber didn't reach him," Sage sighed. "Which means I'll catch hell at their next soirée."

"How did it ever come to pass that those two old dames would be the doyennes of Our Headiness?" Peter was sharp. I suspected he didn't like the two of them.

"How should I be able to remember? These things just rotate through the rolls. I think I used the Doge system when I set it up, but it's all been so long ago, I can't recall exactly. They were just up this week after fifteen rounds of balloting. Who knows?"

Twain leaned over and whispered to me. "It's interactive, you know. You can talk to them if you'd like."

"I prefer to spy."

Peter, with a sweaty brow, continued. "They've already captured

Voltaire. It's only a matter of time before he joins their cabal. We've never had to deal with this hard-core activist type before. Voltaire is likely to turn into a real loose cannon. It might make for some real problems down the pike."

Sage looked very old and worried. I indulged a moment of pity for him, then quickly cancelled it. "Perhaps *we* have become degenerate. Perhaps they are the new force. Is what is old, new? Or is old just old?"

"I've been monitoring Bunny's thoughts." Peter was all business. He flipped through some notebook. "He plans to remove Hemingway from the roll of American writers."

"*Our little Bunny?*" Sage arched an eyebrow.

"Yes, and after that he plans to help Napoleon take Moscow and install his wife as chief executive and begin to revolutionize poor sad Russia a century earlier. Denying Lenin!"

"It might be amusing." Sage shrugged.

"Can you wrap them up now, Twain? I'm bored," I said.

Twain, with a flick of his hand, whisked the window away. Sage and Peter's images quickly faded to nothingness.

"They're right about Hemingway. I *do* intend to obliterate his career," I announced.

Twain was unmoved. "Everyone around here gets one free. The others cost. Just be sure you want it to be Hemingway."

"I do. But it can wait. But not for long. Meanwhile, don't you think we should help Marie escape the wretched revolutionary prison where she is presently being held?"

"Of course. But I hate clean-up work. It's her gig, remember?" Sometimes Twain looked older than was necessary.

"Oh Twain, where *is* your sense of fun?"

"I wish I knew. Let me know if you trip over it."

"Anyway, it's a perfect role for Voltaire. It's right up his alley and sure to pull him out of his blue funk."

We started out immediately and minutes later entered Voltaire's bed-sitter, temporary digs he occupied while planning his permanent residence. He was still mopey. He stretched across his bed, wearing a dowdy robe while perusing a stack of magazines from the nineteen-thirties.

"I'm fascinated with the brassiere ads," he said, looking at us languidly. "The prominence of the tits goes in and out of fashion so quickly! One minute they're taped down, the next pushed up and out like artillery."

"Wait until you get to the nineteen-fifties!" Twain rolled his eyes.

"Oh, get over it, Voltaire!" I snapped my fingers in his face. "We've got a life-or-death assignment. So look sharp! One of our very beloved, Miss Marie, who was never a famous writer, but surely the best social worker who ever breathed, is busy re-making the French Revolution but without The Terror. She got so far as to have Diderot kept alive, returned to Paris and made president of the Republic."

Voltaire brightened when he heard this, as I suspected he would.

"The bad news," I continued, "is that poor Marie is being held in a hideous revolutionary prison and apparently can't cross back any more. We don't know why. It's up to us to spring her and put her back on track. And we need you for this job."

Voltaire was out of his bed, all aglow. "What shall I wear?"

"It's come as you are, as with most revolutions," I told him. "*Even* French ones!"

Voltaire threw on some clothes. We three then held each others' hands and closed our eyes. I trusted our mutual ambitions.

Diderot looked thin and sickly at his desk. The Tuileries was filled with light and air. And an odd smell, which I ignored. The three of us were alone with him. I seemed to have on the same outfit as I did when meeting with Jefferson. I made a note to speak with wardrobe.

Diderot looked up at us, took a measure of us slowly. He smiled when he recognized Voltaire.

"Is it possible? My dear friend! What a surprise!" Diderot stood and they embraced. Two stick figures of historical dimension. "This is clearly some miracle."

"I suspect many miracles." Voltaire laughed. "But my dear Denis, I haven't come to examine mysteries. I have a direct assignment. May I first introduce you to my new friends? This is Bunny. And this is Twain." Diderot was gracious in his welcome. He asked us to sit.

"These are terrible and fascinating times," the President said. "Yet I fear I become more and more irrelevant as the events unfold. Some of the Jacobins question why a president is necessary."

"To put a check on their power!" It was obvious to me.

"Surely," said Twain, his French being much better than mine, "you can save the Republic from the harm of the Committee on Public Safety."

Diderot shook his head. "It's not exclusively an internal problem. There are forces that want to curtail the Committee, but the foreign threats only embolden the blood-thirsty militants. It's a tough balance."

Voltaire went straight to the business at hand. "One of our compatriots who, in fact, had much to do with your becoming the President—please don't ask; Marie herself can tell you—has been imprisoned on order of the Committee. We come to you seeking her release."

Again, Diderot shook his head. "My information is always out of date. And these imprisonings by the Committee are a touchy matter. You must go in person to confirm your friend's detention before I can act. But, by all means, use my name and my office to win her release.

I am fully behind your efforts."

"Enough said." Twain held up a hand. "We'll check things out and report back to you."

We walked from the President's office and headed to the compound where the Committee was holding its politicals. It was a long walk. The facility was on the edge of Paris, near an old slaughterhouse. The entire area smelled foul. Shouldn't France smell better? The noise was loud and jarring.

We presented ourselves to a revolutionary guard, a handsome seventeen-year-old gendarme. Voltaire introduced himself first, then us, and informed the guard that we were on a mission, representing the President of the Republic. Happily, the French so like titles, awards, designations, these things usually work. We were presented tri-color ribbons to guarantee our exit. We wended our way through the sad shanties and muddy pathways where those who had been targeted by the kooks on the Committee awaited their fates.

"Psst!"

I looked over my shoulder. I saw a rumpled man, wearing a filthy cloth headband and ratty clothes. He hobbled over.

"Don't you recognize me?" He grinned with stained teeth.

"You have the advantage." I was haughty and didn't favor the role.

"I am Thomas Paine and I do not like being here."

Voltaire perused him. "Nor should I, sir."

Twain was curious. "I never did understand why they sent you here."

"I fear to offer my analysis," Paine spoke without emotion. "But it seems to boil down to a case of jealousy on the part of two of the Committee members. This is their attempt to upstage me."

Our conversation became relaxed. All the while word raced throughout the compound that the great Voltaire was in their midst. A crowd grew about us, prisoners and guards alike. It was getting all too festive, something not really appreciated in detention facilities. Soon the revolutionary captain of the prison pushed his way to the front.

"What is happening here?" he barked. "Is someone causing a disturbance?" He stood, arms akimbo, confronting us.

"Creating a disturbance?" I was coy, perhaps not the right venue for this pose. "On the contrary, *we are creating a sensation!*"

"There is word going about that someone among you is posing as the great Voltaire." He scowled in that angry kind of way that can also be sexy, and he gave all of us a very mean look.

Voltaire also casually scanned the crowd, then stepped forward. "I must apologize for being unable to confess to posing as the great Voltaire. For I am he, the humble Voltaire, friend to the wronged, defender of the oppressed and seeker of light and truth among the dark forces." He lifted his arms, skinny as they were, and bowed deeply to the prison captain.

"You are a clever imposter. I have seen so many. The great Voltaire died years ago. I myself participated in the procession where Voltaire's remains were brought to the Pantheon, in a great homage from the nation to a hero."

"It was a sweet gesture." Voltaire smiled, folding his hands together. "And through ways I cannot explain, I have returned from the beyond and from other times and now judge you, my admirer, as the latchkey to these detainees."

"These scum! These traitors to the Revolution! We argue with the Committee for the use of the guillotine against this perfidy but, for some reason, they are not built. It is very frustrating."

"I'm sure it is." Voltaire reached out and touched the jailer. "But let me ask you. Had I lived, with my reputation, could you guarantee that I myself would not be here as a guest of the Revolution?"

The crowd mumbled, as crowds often do. The screw was not pleased.

"An apparition!" came a scream from the throng.

I suspected things were to get ugly sooner rather than later.

"I am here looking for a citizen called Marie," Voltaire announced very publicly to the crowd.

"*Marie!* We have legions of traitors in our custody called Marie," the jailer snapped.

"To your pity. I wish to speak to just one." Voltaire raised an eyebrow and looked about the crowd of faces.

*Our* Marie came running to our circle.

"*Bunny!*" she shouted as she ran up to me. She embraced me. Then Twain. And Voltaire.

"You will release Marie in our custody to see the President." I was polite but firm.

The jailer was flustered. "But this is impossible. She is here on orders of the Assembly, by way of the Committee."

"Do you wish me to report you to Monsieur Le President that you refuse to release this person into his custody? May I have your name, please?" Voltaire was every bit the scorned English Dame.

The jailer stuck out his chin and took a profile.

"I am Jacques LeMonte!"

"You will be Jacques LeMort if you resist Marie's release!" Voltaire's grin was thoroughly intimidating, achieved, I suppose, with much practice.

"Silly of them not to have a phone here," Twain quipped. "It could all be solved so simply."

"Alas," I sighed, "this being France, and particularly during one of its many revolutions, they probably wouldn't work just when you need them."

"I *must* get out of here." Marie was frightened, and rightly so. "And I must meet Diderot."

"You know our Citizen President?" Jacques the Jailer was curious.

"My dear comrade," Twain summoned up all his authority, "sister Marie had more to do with this Revolution than we have time to explain. She made Diderot your President! *Release her at once!* And in the company of the American, Paine."

"No! No! You demand too much! I must consult with representatives of the Committee."

"Leave those turkeys out of it!" I snapped.

Voltaire oiled over to LeMonte. "The Bastille was nothing like this at all. It was not pleasant to be there but friends came to visit and, finally, through bribes and friends at Court, I was released. Now, clearly, we cannot bribe you, Monsieur Superintendent, as this is a Republic of Virtue." Voltaire spoke in a tone loud enough for the throng to hear. He also made the appropriate gestures; actually, to my tastes, somewhat flamboyant. "But I *can* appeal to you as an enlightened Frenchman, one who wants to be part of a society that is better, more humanitarian than its predecessor, more compassionate than the cruelty of the Bourbons. You must act in a manner befitting the reputation of this great Republic!"

There was scattered applause.

Jacques LeMonte chewed his lip. Then caved in.

"It is difficult for me to believe that you are the real Voltaire. But, if through some miracle, you are his ghost, I will grant your plea. I will release Marie. She arrived here with no papers and no background. Most peculiar, though suspicious and unusual. The perfect profile for an Austrian spy. Can you give me your honorable word that she is not an agent against our great Republic?"

"I can give you more than my word," Voltaire was at the clinch point in his sales pitch. "I give you my embrace!" Voltaire stepped forward and took Jacques LeMonte into his arms, hugged him warmly and kissed Jacques just once on each cheek. The crowd was delighted and applauded. "And, now, Monsieur Citizen, you will personally escort our party to the control gate. Including the American."

Paine quickly appeared and melded into our lot. He whispered to me: "Nice move, Bunny. I would have sold an arm to get out of this dump. The trouble with revolutions is that they attract so many crazies. And I'm afraid I haven't the tolerance for the madcaps I once did."

"It's not that, ducks," I whispered back to him, "it's just these crazy fucking French!"

LeMonte walked all of us to the front gate of the prison and we five slid past the cute guard, smiles all around, and scurried back to the Tuileries.

"You're up to your neck in it this time, Marie," Twain teased.

"And not out of the woods yet," I said, testily.

"I can't wait to meet Diderot! *President* of the Republic!" Marie gushed like a teen Beatle fan about to met Paul McCartney on national TV.

"The *first* Republic," Voltaire reminded her. I did notice how full of himself Voltaire seemed to be. No trace of any gloom. *Voltaire was back!*

"By the way, Paine," I said, "we plan to take Marie back with us. Get her out of this dismal time and place. And you'd better high-tail it back to the US of A and go about becoming a citizen farmer. When Tom Jefferson, who likes you very much, becomes the President, he can throw you at the tired old New England divines. A useful role, and you'll be just perfect."

"To think it would come to that." Paine sighed.

I looked at him dismissively. Paine looked at me with a curious expression and then just bolted off, on a mad dash. Go figure.

Diderot was in a meeting when we arrived back at the palace. I don't know what he was being paid for his job assignment but, clearly, *it wasn't enough*. We were ushered in. He interrupted his conference. "Ah, my friends, please meet my colleagues from the Assembly." They nodded at us, looking exhausted and somewhat pinched about the eyes. "But this is someone new," Diderot said, smiling at Marie. He shook her hand. "Delighted to meet you."

"Mr. President, it is my privilege to introduce you to my friend, Marie. She is very dedicated to the cause." Voltaire did the honors.

Marie batted her eyes and her face flushed. She did a little curtsy, which I thought either old-fashioned or inappropriate. I wondered more and more what Marie was doing in writers' paradise to begin with; I assumed she was some whim of Sage.

"Mr. President?" Marie was all agush. "About Marat…"

"An extremist!" Diderot waved three fingers.

"Yes, but the only one who can check the growing power of Robespierre. We must keep Marat alive!"

"Alive?" Diderot cackled. "He sits all day in his bath, scribbling, like"—the President searched for the exact phrase—"like a turd floating in water."

Everyone laughed except Marie.

"This is not funny!" Marie was adamant. "*It's the future*! You must assign Marat a guard around the clock. To protect him from those who might want to murder him."

"This is not the job of the state." Diderot, still smiling, gave Marie an odd look. "Scribes must meet their own fates unimpeded. I know I have!"

Marie became frantic. I feared this role would overwhelm her. "But Citizen President, we must prevent those guillotines from being erected. The Revolution will be stained forever if the mass executions come."

Diderot became sympathetic. "Dear Marie. You must trust me. I have my own plans. Dr. Guillotin's instrument of death will never get any funding as long as I am the President. Simple as that."

"It's the horrible problem of technology," Twain whispered to me. "How can we get our busy innovative race to stop inventing clever machines of death? As well as other noxious things."

"I did a pretty good job getting rid of the chewing gum."

Twain winked at me and patted his pursed mouth in one gesture.

"Marie, darling, you *must* come back with us now," I said firmly. "*Paradise awaits.*"

She turned on me. "*I will not*! My work is here!" She had clearly been case-hardened by her sojourn in the pen. Politicals, to be effective, must never sour.

"You must all stay," beamed the President, "as my guests for dinner. The times being what they are, dinner may be a bit humbler than I would otherwise wish. Others there will be from the Assembly, with whom I must conduct some business. You may enjoy it. *The New France!*"

"I will be there!" Marie looked at us, challenge in her eyes.

"Can I count on the rest of you in our struggle?" The President was bright and solicitous. "You, Voltaire, must help me cage the Austrians."

Voltaire moved about a bit, closing in on Diderot. "We came here on a mission and we have succeeded. Now there is nothing for us to do but return whence we came. We must make our exit."

Diderot feigned shock. "My dear friend, you must come back soon. I will have great need of your talent. It is strange. I feel that neither of us really belongs here. Yet here we are. We must play our roles, no?"

"I have always played my role," Voltaire noted with a smile. "To good reviews, I hope."

The two men embraced.

Twain, Voltaire and I instantly transported ourselves away, leaving Marie to whatever happened next.

We found ourselves sitting on a huge grey-and-white-flecked sofa in a conversation pit in a wood and glass ultra-modern home. The wall before us was all glass; the late afternoon sun streamed through the smog and bathed us in its rays.

"You like it?" Voltaire beamed. "I had it built while we were off rescuing poor Marie. It has all the latest do-dads. Which I intend to have fun with—and improve on. I am mad for the idea of patents and copyrights!"

Peter appeared from the kitchen with a tray of drinks.

"I figured you boys would be thirsty after your little exploits." He handed around the gimlets. "My dear, our first PEN caucus! I think Voltaire will be just marvelous as a *nouveau-riche* upper-middle-class American. A perfect pose." Peter sat next to me on the vast divan.

I tasted my drink, and then toasted Peter. "I'm glad to see you are useful at something. At last, Peter." I batted my eyelids. "And you must get over your jealousy of my having brought over Voltaire, denying you your role as Welcome Wagon Hostess to our community's new resident."

Peter leaned close to me. "I am beyond such a dull emotion as jealousy. Voltaire and I have become fast friends. It is you, my dear Bunny, who should fear the contagion of jealousy, for I may steal your friend away from you." He smirked at me.

Peter was such an amiable, if bad, liar. It was obvious he had been sent here by Sage, Hurst and Ferber to neutralize Voltaire and attempt to sign him up for their gardening club.

"This Los Angeles–type environment has such a calm to it."

Voltaire waved around his skinny arms, a gesture of possession. Did his century fail to produce any intellectual corpulents? I should see if I could find Gibbon.

"It's hideous!" Twain snapped. "You'll tire of it quickly, Voltaire, believe me. And you'll long for the East. We all left California, never to return again."

The door buzzer rang.

Peter jumped up. "I'll get it. I took it upon myself to send out the invitations, sure you'd be starved for company once you got back. After all that dirt of the Revolution." Peter went to the front door and let in the newcomers. There was some hissing between Peter and the new arrivals. I noticed Mede right away. His companion was someone I did not know, though he looked slightly familiar.

"Bunny, you are the only one here who has not met Maynard Keynes. He knows all the others. *Even* Voltaire." Mede and Keynes sat on the vast sofa in the conversation pit. Peter got them drinks.

Keynes was a brighter physical sort than I had expected. His eyes shined with intrigue.

"Bunny," he said, while sipping his beverage, "I've seen most of the tape clips of you since your arrival. What a debut! Just everyone is talking! Poor Miss Ferber is near apoplexy. Such a good sign." He laughed. "Just be glad it wasn't Pearl Buck on that watch to scorn you. Pearl's more the rough-and-tumble type."

I had no idea what to say. "How *do* we get away with it, John?"

"*Do we?*" Keynes probed. "I suspect Voltaire won't like hearing this but, as I figure it, those originally from part of the twentieth century have some advantage, at least for the moment. Some extra power of implementation. Don't get me too deep into this, as I haven't reasoned it all yet." He looked about. "I hear Voltaire has Adorno as his house guest. Adorno might have a better handle on all this. More up his alley."

"Some say," I whispered, "that I am imagining all this."

"Oh, I hope so, Bunny," Keynes was sympathetic. "It might mean that everything will have a happy ending. But you must understand, this place is chock full of mythomaniacs. They'll say anything. *And they do!* It's the problem of the poets and the politicians; they both love to play with words. You don't believe it for a minute, do you?" Keynes squeezed me arm.

"I told Twain I hate solipsism. The bane and refuge of the self-pitying. And, worse, the untalented."

"Precisely."

"On the other hand, I'm terribly curious as to my new powers for successful *re*creation." I was direct and stared at Keynes.

"Well," Keynes said, chuckling, "I suspect they are considerable. But you must have the end in mind. But, around here, there may be no end in the frame at all."

"My goal? To completely revamp the society I came from."

"Lots of work there. We only get the one society to play with. Or so they say. And *that* one is always imposing and somewhat self-selected—hard to explain—and completely self-satisfied and eternally lumpish. Just make sure you have a lot of bandages along on your adventure."

"Bunny's energized me!" Voltaire was ebullient. "That raid on the prison was an elixir!"

"The novelty of it all will wear off quickly, Bunny and Voltaire. I can assure you of that." Mede finished his drink with one long gulp and then twirled around the ice cubes. "You should look forward to staying in more, in your fabulous new home. Watch the parade. Play more board games. Invite Sage and me over for Mah Jong."

"The excitement of it all is just another drug." Twain was dry. "It, finally, comes down to the matter of temperament."

"*And,*" Keynes added, with heavy emphasis, "Bunny has the

so-called advantage of not being dead yet."

"Which poses the necessary question," Peter jumped right in with lots of eyebrow action, always a sign of evil intent, "as to his real-time demise. After that event, will Bunny be coming across to us once again? Or will he be interred in the cold, rocky soil of Massachusetts, along with so many other great dead ones? It's an open bet."

I took up the challenge. "I appreciate the effort you make in your false concern, my dear Peter, and I'd reward you with a card to my fan club but I seem to have run out of them for the time being. Don't start wetting your chops about my prospective burial in the dull sod of Massachusetts. I prefer the brightness of incineration. One last carbon imprint."

"You can enjoy whichever oblivion you find to your tastes. No one will diddle with your fate." Peter left the sofa, tired of me and looking to get another drink. It would be so nice if Peter would get out-and-out drunk. A chance to see his real character at last.

Mede waved a hand in front of me; it looked like a nervous gesture. "I didn't like it you got rid of the gum. Such a harmless pleasure." He looked at Peter, back with another cocktail, who nodded in agreement. "In fact, Peter and I have gone back to reintroduce the American public to the joy of chewing gum. The smacking of lips will be music to your ears, Bunny. And think of the bubbles from the bubble gum! The acme of human achievement!" Mede swelled up, like he was waiting to win the Nobel Prize.

"I see!" I snorted. I was sure he had an ugly tattoo on one of his forearms; it would have been completely in character. "Then I must go back and do as I originally intended and lace that batch with cyanide and cause mass death. I don't think any press campaign can overcome a product's history of causing massive fatalities. Harmless pleasure indeed!" I smiled at Mede who, as it turned out, was smacking gum.

"You might want to speak with the tobacco lobby first," Twain advised. "They have a counter-strategy on that."

"Where *is* Adorno anyway?" I asked Voltaire.

"I have no idea. I suspect he's on the phone."

Keynes moved closer to me. "This raises a point I would like to address. You seem, Bunny, to have a flair for the marvelously political act. I understand you are an anarchist by inclination and background. Your deeds are all terribly theatrical and exciting, if not necessarily good career moves. But I needn't remind you that only *some* situations lend themselves to such a quickie strike. The way you handled your first foray, against Mrs. Eddy, was fortuitous. And marvelously successful. Showing some good strategic planning. But I would caution this—it was also a bit of beginner's luck."

"Which I hope holds. After all, I have the face for it."

Keynes sighed. I was being diversionary.

"I would suggest, and I speak as an admirer of anyone attempting such massive changes, that there should be a mix of approaches."

"Oh, here we go again," Peter sneered. "Keynes and his mixed formula yet another time. Maynard, that record must be wearing a little thin by now."

"Thank you, Peter. I realize the modern world is not much to your tastes. Actually, Bunny, I think it might be more appropriate to continue this conversation in private. There is so much I want to tell you."

"No point to that," Twain said. "Anybody who is interested can know everything instantaneously. There is no privacy any more, so why pretend? Assume we are on all the channels all the time for everyone to see, because in fact *we are!*"

"I would like some private time, away from the screens," I said to Twain. I did want to work out some plans without other eyeballs all over me.

"Happily," Twain continued, "most won't understand what you are saying. So please continue."

"Well," I said, filling my lungs with lots of fuel, "there appears to be certain areas of prospective endeavor which are resistant to our meddling. Why this is I don't know but I intend to find out. One avenue for change is the economic approach. Funding. Directing resources or denying the very same to projects we favor or disdain. Then there's the problem of meddling with technological innovations. Be nice to figure that one out. After all, I took that videotape over and gave it to Jefferson at Monticello. *How did that happen?* Haven't the mucky-mucks hereabouts set up a committee to work on that one? *I would!* Your concern with Dr. Guillotin's odd device is illustrative. Though, I think, when it comes to contraptions which promote murder, mayhem and torture even we, in our aura of omnipotence, come up against that intractable trope toward thanatos which for our race seems a top desideratum."

Voltaire looked fascinated. "I think Necker made some fundamental errors. Mostly, I suspect, as the result of political instruction. Yet financial management is closely connected to the making of the wars. And, to throw a question into the mix, is there any record of anyone being any good at long-term financial management? I'd certainly like to know."

"It's true," Keynes looked humble. "I have tried a dozen different times to reconstruct the Boer War so that the English will become predominant in order to promote, in future years, to be sure, racial equality. It was all for naught. Wars seem to be the unchangeable events for the quick. My sense is that we must try to change the earlier events which lead to these wars."

"Economic privation and the forced movement of great masses of people?" I suggested.

"And the greed and ambitions of states," Twain rattled off his list, "and the manipulation of false information, quite common these days, the projection of derangely empowered egos, the messianic impulse of evil superstitions, and on and on."

"Twain is right," Voltaire was serene. "It is a very large catalogue."

"Wars bore me," I hit a light note. "They seem, ultimately, so inconsequential."

"And, but for the slaughter and the destruction of real property, *they are*," Keynes confirmed. "Like football games, they wind up being sheets of statistics."

Twain chuckled. "As an economist, Keynes, you have the advantage. No dull figures or eye-numbing charts."

"Quite right. I leave such dullness to the coaches and the generals. As a child of the Enlightenment, and its latest upgrade, I think human endeavors should be bright, cheerful and somehow rewarding." Keynes beamed.

"I've never understood how anyone could think the fathoming of wealth, and its generation, could be dull or grim," I said.

"We are of the same mind, then, Bunny," Keynes noted.

I felt a sudden impulse to get on with urgent business. I caught Twain's eye first, then Voltaire's. "Gentlemen," I spoke to the others, "if you will excuse us." We three rose and strolled out onto the redwood veranda which still had the delightful smell of something newly built. There was a hibachi, a round glass table on some sort of swirling art nouveau base, Barcelona chairs and an array of earthen flower pots filled with sprays of 'mums.

"I think we need to conference. To lay out our agenda and establish a common style. Work out the correct voice for our up-coming campaign." I was very focused.

"Nothing wrong with my voice," Twain protested. "I've worked on it for a very long time and it seems to be fine."

"Well, Sam, since you brought the subject up," I was going to try to be non-judgmental, "I hope you don't mind my candor. You do have the tendency to drag your stories out a bit too long. That's a no-go. We must be sharp editors, be crisp and get right to the point."

"That is merely an affectation of *your* age, Bunny. That awful truncated narrative. A good, if long, story-telling has the greatest impact."

"We must keep up with the times," I was gentle, "and learn to speak the *lingua franca* of the moment, such as it is."

"Minor adaptations are all that are necessary." Voltaire waved a hand.

"But, François, in your case you must come up with new material. All well and good that so many of your lines are now considered classic, thus to be used sparingly. With each sting, they lose potency. We must write for each other. This will be integral to our triumvirate's devastating new style."

Suddenly we felt a dark shadow fall on our shoulders.

"Did someone mention the word 'style'?"

We three rubber-necked to check out the interloper. It was Hemingway. I had wondered when he would show up. That type always does. I stared at him. He was all loose flesh, hairy skin and beady eyes. His body looked like an overstuffed sausage. He wore baggy khaki pants, a loose Hawaiian print shirt and top-siders. Did he just get off the boat? And, if yes, *from where*? His fingers were stained with the ugly residue of his tobacco habit. He invited himself right in and pulled up a chair. He sat right in the middle of our little group and gave each one of us a whorish twinkle. He stank of alcohol and gunpowder.

"Style is what I am famous for," he announced, as though it was expected that all should know. "Perhaps I can give you boys a few pointers."

I was livid. Twain disgusted. Voltaire aghast.

"You stole your so-called style from Gertrude Stein and you're only half the woman she was!" I felt the truth had to be said.

Hemingway chuckled in a snide way. "If I could have de-leeched

Alice from the body of Stein, I might have gotten to fuck the old gal, which is what I always knew she wanted."

"Something a mite homosexual in that scenario," Twain mumbled.

I decided now was the time. "Twain," I waved, "come with me." We walked down the wooden stairs to the sandy beach, leaving poor Voltaire to handle the Big Guy. I figured that Voltaire, after his stretch with Frederick, could handle *anything*.

Twain and I walked arm-in-arm along the beach. I usually dislike plodding through piles of sand but *this* sand was comfortable and sensual. Things, well at least some of them, were considerably more custom-tailored in the celestial abodes.

"As to Hemingway," I said, "I simply will not tolerate his presence. He's worse than the bee in the bouquet; he's the turd in the punchbowl. I must now put my plan into action."

I waited for Twain's response. There was none. Not even an arched eyebrow.

"I shall explain. It's not just for his bad writing, his perverse sensibility, his disgusting slaughter of animals for so-called sport, his posturing, his twisted egomania and his rudeness to others that I dislike Hemingway," I stated crisply.

"Though, I suspect that for the others, that might be enough." Twain seemed to be simpatico.

"It's his manipulation of class consciousness and exploitation. He gives middle-class boys with pretensions the bad name they so richly deserve."

"Please explain."

"Well, you see, everything Hemingway did was gauged to get him that one slot ahead."

"Bunny! This is America! Nothing wrong with that."

"Of course. But once he moved up and on, he would cut those who had helped him or were still below. He wasn't very good to his harem of wives, either."

"He comes from a family with an odd history. Be hard for him to escape it."

"Still, there's no excuse for it all. And I have made up my mind. I will delete his fame from history. Fasten your seatbelt and watch."

I transported myself to Paris. The year, as I figured it, was 1924. I sat on a chair outside the Le Dôme Café. Robert McAlmon spotted me, came over and straddled a chair. I drank coffee; he ordered a glass of wine.

"So, what do you think?" McAlmon asked eagerly.

"Of the Hemingway manuscript? Very plain. There's nothing there. Either one of us can spit out a window and hit ten people who have more talent. The stories lack content and the delivery system lacks style."

"He's a very eager and determined young man."

"That will pass. Maybe. Does he put out? Though he's not my type."

"Say what you will. I've already made the commitment. Contact Editions will publish this manuscript as *Three Stories and Ten Poems*. I will confess that I made my pledge to Ernest late one night when I was a little tight but I intend to stick by it."

"Couldn't he knock out a couple more stories and a few more poems? Fatten up the product a bit?"

"It is what it is, Bunny."

"I understand. But I have the most awful thing to admit. I've lost Hem's manuscript. Someone must have walked away with it from my flat."

McAlmon looked ashen. "Oh my god! That was Ernest's last copy. He said he sent one to New York but it was never received and he has no idea where it is."

"Nothing so stupid as a talentless writer with not enough copies."
I raised my coffee and saluted him. The beginning of the end.

"*What* will I tell him?" McAlmon was crestfallen.

"Tell him to fuck off and lay the blame on me."

"Easy enough for you to say."

"Or do him a really big favor. Buy him a rifle and tell him to give
it a really good blow job and take the load."

McAlmon laughed. "OK. He's a genuine shit. It's still rude to
destroy his manuscript."

I lowered my eyes and took on a faux-naïve pose. "Bob, I didn't
destroy it. It got lost. It did the world a favor."

"You talk like the Spanish. *It* got lost. Poor little manuscript, the
author of its own fate. Just up and wandered away. Drifting through
the boulevards of Paris, never to be found."

"Here." I reached into my coat pocket and pulled out an envelope.
"Give this to Hem. It explains everything so that he can never blame
you for this incident. It's on my account, and I'll be out of here in
two minutes. I also recommend he sail off to the United States and
take up sports broadcasting on one of the radio networks, soon to be
invented. I think he has a great future covering football and baseball
games over the ether. Like Dutch Reagan, he can make it all up!"

McAlmon took the note and gave me a skeptical, and somewhat
sad, stare. I rose from our session and was gone.

I returned for a pit stop in my real-life time. I strolled to the
Boston Public Library and scrolled through the microfiche catalogue
under "Hemingway." There was listed the armful of biographies. I
jotted down the numbers and went to check them out. I flipped open

the more serious of the lot—imagine someone so desperate as to want to write a biography of Hemingway. In one, there was the passing reference to an early lost manuscript, a collection of stories and poems. The rude, and inaccurate, biographer fingered McAlmon as the male-factor. More interesting, at least to me, was the account in another biography, even more devotional to Hem—though I did notice it did *not* come with a barf bag—in which there was a quote, unattributed, by someone who claimed to be an acquaintance of McAlmon, who laid the blame for the loss of the fabulous manuscript on someone referred to as Bunny LaRue. An asterisk after this assertion led me to a footnote; the footnote informed me that there was no evidence that such a person named Bunny LaRue ever existed. I thought I should have felt vindicated. *But I didn't.*

I felt awful. I disposed of the crap and poor McAlmon gets the heat. O, the perfidy of the idolaters! Hemingway's wretched career lumbered right along despite my best intentions.

I knew what I had to do.

And I had no qualms about it whatsoever.

The wind was brisk off the Boston Harbor. The limousines pulled up and disgorged the respectables. It was a gala evening. Black tie for the men. Elegant evening gowns for the women. News cameras whirred.

The Kennedy Library was awash in a flood of soft light on its promontory of land on the Dorchester coast.

The fourth floor of the library was filled with giddy noise from the celebrants. Wine flowed. Laughter rippled. Reminiscences were passed from grey locks to dye jobs to bald pates. Madame Onassis made a lovely speech. The widow Hemingway touched everyone with her salient comments. The curator noted how the Hemingway Collection at the Kennedy Library was the work of over two decades and included hundreds of donations from many scholars who were dedicated to the master. No expense had been spared to gather every extant Hemingway letter, bar tab, original manuscript, hunting license, scribble, etc. There even seemed to be some old Dick-A-Belts. The curator claimed there were eight complete novels yet to be published, providing surprises and delights for the Hemingway fans and a treasure trove for Hemingway scholars. The air was mephitic with the tyranny of this career and all agreed that Hemingway would long be offered as *the* primary modern American writer.

*Not if I had my way.*

I stood there, in my smart tux, all smiles, milling about, drinking, carrying my swank leather executive case. Many asked what I had in it. I smiled and was coy; I told them that my contribution to the Hemingway collection would be its *pièce de résistance*, to be donated privately after the gala. I pretended I was shy. People winked at me and were just delighted. Why are they like this? *I'm not.*

The crowd finally thinned. They stumbled out, as this type does, eager to head on to the next sensation. I was among the few who remained. I already knew about the construction of the Kennedy Library, its flimsy structure, paper-thin walls, its slip-shod safety defaults. Their cheapness would only make my job that much easier.

As the hangers-on swilled what was left of the alcohol and then toddled out, I opened my case and sprinkled the floor with kerosene. It was intended to be the accelerant. I then placed a two pound bomb, filled with explosives, in the stacks, at the very core of the fabulous Hemingway collection. Strangely, none of those still left on the scene, who were probably too blotto to be sensate, paid any attention to me at all.

I gingerly pawed through a drawer of documents. I found

Hemingway's original draft for his speech on the occasion when the folks from the Nobel committee deemed to present him with their award. I rolled it up, lit it with my Bic lighter and then tossed it into a puddle of kerosene. I stayed for just a second or two to watch the flame. The fire was so perfect, and so *energetic*, I sensed fabulous success. The flame wended its way along the trail of liquid. I quickly departed. I passed by a few guests who chatted away before climbing into their limos. I walked around them as I headed out to Morrissey Boulevard. I stood on the far side of the boulevard and waited.

Suddenly, there was a massive explosion as the entire fourth floor of the Kennedy Library and Museum turned into an inferno. Glass shot from the windows of I. M. Pei's dainty little edifice. The jets of fire sparkled against the dark Atlantic. It was yet another Kennedy Tragedy. How sad!

I walked back to my real-life flat in Dorchester—took me a half-hour, but I rather enjoyed the stroll, must have been the adrenaline—entered and turned on the right-wing all-news radio station. *It was the only story.* At eleven o'clock, I turned on the local TV news channel. I thought the newscasters might cry. The story of the Kennedy Library "tragedy" ate up the news hole, with poor sports and weather getting just a minute each. The bubbleheads on the TV screen interviewed the types who had been at the event. Some of them looked pretty bedraggled. Happily, there were no witnesses to the perpetrator of the incident. Madame Onassis had no comment as the camera caught her racing into the entrance of the Ritz Hotel.

One bubblehead said: "At this time, it's hard to estimate the damage, but the fire captain in charge of this detail told me that, unless there is some kind of miracle, the entire Hemingway collection will be consumed."

I poured three fingers of Chivas Regal, which my real-life self kept in the cupboard. I sipped it neat, a tribute to my daring. There's nothing like the sense of complete satisfaction. I backed up a half-hour and watched it all over again. My real-time self came in, watched the news with me.

He looked at me, both pleased and distraught. "I hope I don't get pinched for this job. I suspect they have a short list of suspects."

I smiled. "Not to worry."

The phone rang. He took the call in the hallway. I was party to both ends of the conversation, though I still sat in the deep armchair with cat hair all over it. Where *was* the cat? It was Empress Carlotta on the horn. He'd just heard of the Hemingway nightmare and seemed amused. This was a good omen. I hoped for other good reviews.

I was tired, exhausted beyond belief. It was the first time since crossing over that I was fatigued. I chalked this up to being in real-life time and, thus, subject to its inexorable ebbs and flows. I was nodding off. Just then, Miss Maxine, my cat, did show up and jumped into my lap. She looked up at me with her big green eyes, perhaps confused—or perhaps delighted—by having two identical owners. I wonder if the cats ever took to domestication. I missed the pets in meddlers' paradise. I'd have to do something about that. My eyelids fell one more time as I drifted into sleep.

When I opened my eyes I once again found myself on Voltaire's swank LA-style veranda, feeling thoroughly refreshed.

Twain slouched in a bean bag chair, wearing a white cotton suit. He was reading a New York newspaper from the time of The Great War.

"Where's Voltaire?" I asked.

Twain dropped the newspaper. "He got bored in your absence and went off on some errand of mischief. He seems to have taken to the customs of the country. Oh, and by the way, Edna Ferber called. She sounded very distressed. She asked to schedule an appointment with you as soon as possible."

I clucked my tongue. "Twain, I have decided that there is no such person as Edna Ferber. The performance of the so-called Ferber was executed by Peter or Sage done up in drag to dump on me the matronly guilt number. It won't work."

"Have it your way. I should let you know that there's been a lot of breeze about your burning the library. Bunny, please recall: you're dealing with writers after all."

"The folks will talk. They *love* sensations." I was dismissive. "I will admit, it was not a pretty job. Many hearts will be broken. But, alas, this is the way of the world. What I did can be excused on two counts. First: this fetish about libraries! Saving all this crap. You showed me the mortuary wherein there was warehoused the crap of the scribblers. As to that library I brought to ruin, just a pathetic adjunct to one odd family's cheap political ambitions, and I use the word cheap in its truest sense, slipshod construction, corners cut every which way all in order to crank out a suitable lure for the rubes. Then to tack on the Hemingway crapola—a whole floor!—is just another slap in the face. Twain, you simply cannot imagine the suffocating tyranny of Hemingway at mid-century, when American culture was being programmed to be its most repressed."

"*Oh yes I can!*" Twain hissed.

"Something sorely in need of an antidote. And a dose of humiliation. Good for the soul. Negative energy can, through will and imagination—plus our fabulous powers—have a liberating, or at least, cleansing effect."

"Shall we try it on the early Christians, say from the fourth century on?"

"Too much work on too little talent. And too far out of our way.

*What would we wear?* We now know that we are more potent when we stay closer to our own time base." The early Christians would simply have to wait, the poor dears. "Besides, Twain, you and I are still barely dipping into our agenda: Reforming America!"

"Lovely America," Twain sighed while scanning the vista through Voltaire's huge glass panes, which seemed to adjust to the bright light, getting darker. "Always so inchoate."

"And so pliable!" I added.

"You asked after Voltaire. Well, the good news is that Marie actually showed up at the door. She looked like an urchin. She went off for a hot bath, this while you were busy splashing the kerosene on the library floor. She came out wrapped in a fluffy towel and Voltaire made her a hot toddy. They went at it in French. I tried to keep up, but they were going a mile a minute. I picked up some news. Apparently events in the French Revolution, at least from Marie's point of view, are going well. Our friend is now an important advisor to Diderot, still the President of the First Republic, even though Marie confessed that she thinks he patronizes her. The guillotines haven't gone up. Marie is busy trying to work up some action with the Turks, to get them to attack Austria to keep the Austrian troops from moving against the Republic. She's adamant about keeping Marat alive. She talked Voltaire into going back with her. He signed on. His job was to waylay Miss Charlotte Corday and take her to lunch and fill her noggin with visions of her future sainthood if she turns her life to serving the poor. This may not save Marat from some equally grim fate but it will keep Charlotte, a dim bulb in even the most generous interpretations, from her unsavory rendezvous. Marie, meanwhile, is going to work on both Marat and Robespierre and she means to lay down the law. Nothing more formidable than a middle-class American university graduate with a sense of urgency and a personal history in which no one has ever said *no*. Perhaps we should have left dear Marie in that wretched prison. More middle-class types in the slammer would do wonders in shaping up those bizarre institutions."

"Perhaps that's why we're all here. To repackage history with a more alluring hook for the fussy carriage trade."

Twain laughed. "That may well be. Alas, I've never been sure of my class. Or classes. Upper-lower-middle seems exact if not wholly representative. Class in America is such a moveable feast. And, anyway, writers worth their salt must succeed in being déclassé."

"You know, Twain, I still haven't met many of my brothers and sisters here in paradise."

"Understandably. How could you?" Twain looked at me like I were a dunce. "You've been so busy. Cocteau has approached me several times when you were off on your errands. He's eager to dine with you. There's Nathanael West, C. Wright Mills and this crazy guy named Dicky Farina who's a bit of a loon, but he throws the most marvelous sixties parties. We'll have to go to one sometime and unwind."

"Sad to admit, I usually find most other writers terribly boring."

Twain gave a deep sigh. "My sentiments exactly. Which is one reason I cornered you for myself before the frou-frou set had a chance to devour you. *I need company.*"

"Listen, Twain, I have a couple things on my mind."

"*Only a couple?* Must be a thin day. I could charge by the hour. A fifty-minute hour."

"Do you think we should try bringing more live ones over?"

"Now *you're* lonely! It's like all the teenagers having babies. They can't stand adults, so they make babies to have someone they think will be nearer their age to play with. Bunny, *are you bored with the dead?*"

"No, not really. I thought I'd try it as an exercise of my powers."

"Given the headache you have already inflicted on those who attempt a genteel equilibrium around here, I would be agin' it."

"Fine. Enough said. It was just a thought. Secondly, it's bothering me that so far all my efforts—Marie's too—have been aimed at reworking the past."

"Much work to be done."

"I seem, now, to be an expert in the past. I'm finding it a tad boring. It's like sandbagging against the inevitable tide. It's response rather than initiative."

"You want to move on?"

"*I want to invent a new government for these United States!*"

"This is the wrong venue for that. You'd have to be back in your real-time life to pull something like that off. And, over there, you won't have your sorcery."

The sun dropped in the sky in a way I didn't understand—it just *dropped*! I felt frustrated, as though I were on the brink of a great, novel project but uncertain which way to go.

"If it makes you feel any better," Twain advised, "I'll take the conventional view. The past is prologue. Angle its use to your best advantage. Few here, if any, have dared meddle in the future. Given their condition, I think the future is pretty much a foreign concept. This may be your exclusive proprietary. But dicey ground to tread."

"It's just that I can't keep on looking backward, seeing the wrongs and go larking about righting them to make all of history more streamlined to my tastes. I want to start construction on the forward vector, on which my imprint will be indelible, against which others must react in perpetuity. I still have a live, active body in *that* time"—I paused, calculating, checking my watch—"about to *not* celebrate the new year of 1986."

"The past *is* a mess," Twain said, softly and with sympathy. "Humans are, often, but not always, a frightful and destructive lot. *Even* from among the comfortable and compulsively tidy bourgeoisie."

Voltaire wondered in, looking bedraggled, like he'd had a long day at the studio as a stunt man in some Errol Flynn pirate movie. He wore a tri-corner hat, a simple shirt, tight trousers, stockings, shoes and black gloves.

"*Such work!*" he complained, peeling off the gloves. "That Corday woman can talk you to death *and beyond!*" He winked at us. "But I pulled it off. And Marie now owes me a big one. Charlotte has turned to the Stigmatine Sisters for a life of prayer and service. The great Jesus dumping ground."

"Go clean yourself up, Frank," Twain said casually, "and put on something loose but swank. We three are going to party our brains out."

Voltaire unbuttoned his shirt. "A quaint but useful phrase. And I am starved for social life." Voltaire went off to his toilette.

I changed into a black leotard, crawled into a big French sweater, also black. Put on a beret at a jaunty angle. Slipped on my RayBans and a pair of cruddy old sneakers. I could have been a tourist sight in San Francisco's North Beach circa 1959! Twain popped into a djalaba and a pair of flip-flops. Voltaire soon reappeared garbed in his countess drag, with a smart blue satin turban that gave him the suggestion of The Exotic Orient.

We left Voltaire's ranch house on foot. We walked about a half-mile until we reached a block of Manhattan brownstones. No one noticed us, in that New York way—it is *they* who want to be noticed! We stopped in front of one very grand home, with marble stairs leading to its two carved wood front doors, dark stone façades and two ample windows through which we could see a crowded party already in progress.

"It's our Official Happy House," Twain informed us, "and thus usually pretty dreary. Always something going on. With a thousand different motifs."

We opened the door and walked into the grand foyer. It was a mad crush with everyone in costume. I spotted Sage standing on the stairs. He was dressed in a leopard skin outfit, chatting away with someone I was sure was Victor Hugo unless, of course, someone else had come dressed as Victor Hugo. Voltaire let out a scream and disappeared into the throng.

"Let's go upstairs," Twain suggested, taking my arm. We made our slow way up the crowded stairway, smiling as we brushed past Sage and Hugo. Though after we had slid past them, I heard someone hiss the word "arsonist." Was this directed at me? I would never know. And, frankly, didn't care. *Everyone's a critic!*

We turned right at the top of the stairs and walked into a dark salon. Heavy black curtains were drawn across the windows. Black lights, four of them, shone against the walls, giving a weird effect to the psychedelic posters hanging there.

"My dears," cooed a female voice behind us, "it's about time you made an appearance. We've all been waiting. And it's especially rude to keep the dead waiting."

I turned.

It was Natalie Barney. She gave Twain and me a chaste buss. "I was afraid you had decided to snub us, Bunny," she said, walking me across the room. "Just like Balzac. He's turned into such a reclusive old barnacle. You just never can predict these things. Now. Come over here and sit with me."

We came to a long sofa and sat at one end. The air was dense with smoke and trippy music.

"We've been fascinated with your exploits, Bunny, since your arrival. So much energy and concern! But after all that excitement, you must settle down and enjoy the company our lovely world offers."

"Natalie," I said firmly, but sweetly, removing my RayBans, "I've decided to reinvent The Future!"

"Such fun!" Barney squeezed my arm. "I hope we can all

participate. Just make sure you put in lots and lots of exquisite look-ing women."

"There are some, I fear," I whispered, "out to stop my project."

A figure in a linen shirt and linen pants appeared before us. "To reinvent The Future, you will surely need this." He held out a long pipe. It was Cocteau, as I knew instantly.

"Dear Jean, *what* are we smoking tonight?" Barney seemed amused.

"Just the best opium available, from the marvelous corner of the Elysian Fields. It seems my dealer is being deported to Hell, poor thing. So he had this Going-Out-Of-Business sale. I got my stash for practically nothing."

Cocteau sat on my other side. He gave me a coy look and placed the pipe near my lips.

"Thanks, Jean, but no thanks." I gently pushed the pipe away from my face.

Cocteau shrugged. "My drug of choice seems to be out of fashion for the moment. Everything is fast now. Fast drugs. Fast jokes. Fast affairs. What is the hurry? I must hold my own and wait until my preferences come back into vogue."

"Jean's been writing again!" Barney announced brightly.

Cocteau smiled. "Yes, after a very long while. Something com-pletely in a fabulist mode." Cocteau lit and sucked hard on his pipe. "And full of raunchy sex."

"Did you manage to arrange your winning the Nobel Prize yet?" Barney turned to me. "Jean's intent on dressing up his real-life repu-tation with some grand award."

"It requires such work!" Cocteau was glassy-eyed but no less coherent. "There are so many small-minded people to persuade. As to my prospective prize, no, my friend, not as of yet. But," he cackled, "I did fix it that Sartre will win the Stalin Literature Prize. That should put him in a pickle."

"Aren't we vicious tonight?" Barney seemed delighted.

Cocteau leaned close to my ear. "You *must* come to see me. A smart lunch. I'm on the rue de Sebastian Melmoth. Just around the corner from here. Terribly fashionable. We have *so* much to discuss."

"It's a date. Now please excuse me. I'd like to get a drink."

I rose. I left the two of them chattering away. I drifted out into the hallway. Sage grabbed me and introduced me to Peggy Guggenheim, who was dressed and painted as a Mondrian. I was sweet but moved right on into the room opposite, which had a bar. It was actually the mansion's ballroom, vast beyond belief, lit by a clutch of gaudy chandeliers. Hordes danced to an orchestra. Couples whirled by, dressed as empresses, wild animals, ghosts, odd flora and fauna, kitchen appliances and sci-fi monsters.

I fought my way to the bar and asked for a white wine. The bartender was an extraordinarily good-looking young man, bare-chested, wearing a leather vest, a tit ring and leather pants. We stared at each other as he handed me my wine. As I turned around, I bumped into another man. My wine splashed all over the two of us.

"Clumsy of me," I said. "My apologies."

"I like the leather bloke." It was Joe Orton.

"Who wouldn't? We could have a three-way," I suggested.

"Or as many as we like or want, Bunny," Orton twinkled. "Strange that way, isn't it? What some guys prefer. It'd be nice if he was only fifteen and I could stuff him."

"All tastes are a reflection of ego, usually malformed ones. Actually, I find too much diffuse energy in orgies. Nothing is ever quite right." I took a napkin and wiped off his clothes.

"Bunny, you could be my brother." Orton stared at me as I attended to his clothing.

I looked into his eyes. "I suspect I am. But since I've made mush of our drinks, let's go back to the leather bloke and get refills." We did.

Orton and I drifted away from the crowded bar, out of the ballroom and climbed the stairs—every stair just packed—up two more flights. We entered a quiet, bright room done up in Louis-Fifteenth-Lite décor. Upton Sinclair was holding court in one corner. We went over and said our hellos. I noticed that it was a mixed, and somewhat bored-looking, lot. I recognized James Thurber, Klaus Mann, who looked impossibly glum, John Howard Larson and Zelda Fitzgerald. And Ramón Sender. Orton and I settled on a divan in the opposite corner and sipped our drinks.

"I like you," he said. "You've shaken up these bloated old shits."

"Just my stretch exercises," I assured him.

"I've taken a few spins at changing things myself. Nothing really grand, mind you, just a few get-even things. And a broad stroke or two."

"Well, good for you. Any luck?"

"The whole bloody society's so rotten, I barely know where to start. Then we wind up here, with all these powers promised and no one gets off his bleeding bum!"

"After my first burst of enthusiasm," I admitted, "I'm a little asea myself."

Orton looked severe. "No, don't give it up. Never look back. Just go after 'em. You know, there are so many diversions here, it's easy to do nothing but go to dumb affairs like this and just gab and gab. Resist it. You're an American. You have your Sage, who I think is a phony old bird. I have Bernard Shaw as my mentor. Being Brits, we're supposed to clear it with him when we go off on our missions of merciful destruction. And he stiffs most proposals. Silly nationalities. Who'd think that they'd wind up applying *here*? But if you try to get around the old goat, it's a bitch, with endless meetings and reports. All very discouraging. You Yanks have it much easier."

This was news. And I was shocked. "We are restricted by our national origins?"

"It is our fate, you, perhaps, excepted. You will have to find out. I was all set to blow up that shit Mosley and his wife at a fascist rally back in the thirties. Shaw got wind of it and cancelled it. I tried going ahead with it anyway but wound up at Ascot in high season and just got arrested. Whatever power you've got, go full steam ahead before they decide to lower the boom."

"Joe, I would like to go back and prevent your murder."

"Sorry. It's been tried. Turns out it can't be stopped. There was even a pool of talent working on that one. Came to nothing. Just a brick wall. It's a mystery. Move on to other things."

"OK. I want Napoleon to take Moscow and put his wife on the throne."

"Ooooo, good one." Orton seemed amused. "A great idea. Get the Russians into the western system a century earlier. But it sounds like an item on the doubtful list."

"What do *you* think should be the priorities?" I was curious.

A burst of laughter came from the Sinclair claque. Upton wiped his lips, delighted with himself.

"Two things. Get the god-damned population down. Stop this frantic breeding. And somehow alter human aggression. Just reinvent the entire species. Some new track for evolution. Bigger brains or smaller brains or delete the opposable thumb or something. I've leave that all to you. I've gone for the easy, precise and funny jobs. I had Churchill fart, real loud, while on TV. That was fun. I had the Duchess of Windsor take a fourth husband while still legally married to the third. It was Onassis, by the way. Though I later heard that Miss Guggenheim undid that one straight away. There's so much contrariness here. It takes ambition, imagination and forcefulness to get anything done. *Without* interference from others! Types like your Miss Ferber. They sit in front of their screens all day and night, scanning the bands, looking for the meddlings they find objectionable so they can defuse them or counteract the results. Just too ghastly."

I finished my drink and pondered things for a minute, depressed. "They don't have *sports* here, do they?"

Orton tossed his head back and laughed.

"Well, people play a lot of board games and some cards. We have our allotment of gamblers. Tacky little dice things in dark alleys. These birds mostly talk and talk. Just sit on their rears and gas. That's the irony of the whole thing. Bunch of writers, most of them, and have written all sorts of things. Here they are now and all they talk about is what they would do *if.* That big if. The poison of philosophy if you're asking me. Just rubbish. Why not just ditch the gab and go out and do it? You're OK, Bunny. So's Twain and Voltaire. Fun, too. The rest are just useless. Myself included. Just wanking for the gutless."

We were summoned from our reverie back into the ballroom. Madame de Staël had organized this monstrous gavotte, a dance I thought I knew nothing about. The situation being what it was, however, I danced it perfectly. At the end, I would up paired with Nancy Mitford. She wore a half-face mask with colorful plumes rising from the top.

"You are a delightful partner." Mitford was all smiles.

"And aren't we lucky the bosses didn't put the eighteenth century off limits for scavengers like us?"

"Ha, ha," she tinkled. "Never believe anything anyone says around here. They learned their manners at the court of the Sun King—*on a rainy day*! All blowsy nothing. And, by the way, thank you, darling, for bringing Voltaire across. You have no idea of the signification of what you've done." Suddenly, Mitford caught the attention of someone across the ballroom and she was gone.

I went back downstairs, feeling like a beat Beat. I hung around the grand foyer for awhile. One creature in an elaborate costume lit matches and threw them at me. If this was the extent of the opposition, these pathetic gestures, I was determined to be even more serene about my forthcoming upheavals. Carl van Vechten stumbled by, in a wine haze, and gave me a quick embrace.

"Ready to go?" It was Twain, looking impossibly bored.

"You bet."

We smiled our way out. We slowly walked down the stoop and willed it to be a lovely spring morning—I think this act was on Twain's part, though I had no objection—and it was rejuvenating.

The thought flashed on me. "No one ages here."

"Only when they want. And only a few do. No accounting for taste in these matters. What I still find amazing is that in a place like this where nothing really *does* matter, so much pretense survives. Most of these folks are a willful and, to my tastes, a somewhat narrow lot." Twain bit off the end of a cigar and spit the tip into the gutter. He was rather good at it.

"It's not just that there is this tropism to suffocation that I've seen," I said. "So many of these folks seem to be actually frightened of *something*. You would think, as I have, that those who no longer have to fear the Grim Reaper might be free of this restraint."

"Perhaps you have observed something I cannot see." Twain smoked, actually sucked very aggressively, on his cigar. I feared this habit might kill him, a moot point.

"It's that drawn look on their faces, as though they are still wearing their death masks."

A red-breasted, perky robin hopped across our way and cocked its pretty head at us. We continued on.

"I willed myself a home while we were at that sordid soirée," I announced. "I've been here for what seems an eternity and I don't have proper digs. Time to settle in. Will you accompany me to see how it all turned out?" I sounded as giddy as a young married man who had gotten his first mortgage, the word itself meaning *dead work*, or something close enough, always that dead hand.

"My delight." Twain took my arm and gazed at the sky.

We walked another mile or two. We came to a bright neighborhood where the two-lane asphalt road had sandy shoulders. The white clapboard saltbox was mine. I just knew it. Very New England on the outside. Very moderno-comfo on the inside. Modest, functional and accommodating, it was just what I wanted.

I opened the screen door and clicked open the handle of the lovely hardwood door with the triptych of windows, set at varying angles at eye level, and we walked right in. It smelled so familiar. The furniture was blond; lots of pastel-colored cushions decorated the chairs and sofas. The tables were all highly polished wood, both dark and light. The rugs looked to be genuine Persian, but I would have to decide if I really needed them. They seemed an extravagance. My bookshelves went from floor to ceiling, a handy stepladder in position. I would have to check out the volumes, to determine which could stay and which would simply have to go.

Twain ambled over to the bar set up in the den. He checked out the labels of the finer brews, selecting a rare whiskey. He then opened one of my cabinets, stuffed with serving ware and glasses, two of which he removed and filled with the drink. He gave me one and we retired to the living room. We sat in comfy chairs. We willed it to be lingering afternoon light, as that is the best occasion to enjoy chat while imbibing a big glass of rich, deep copper liquid.

"Everyone's still so coy with me," I said. "Even you. Can't I make a footprint around here?"

"Peter and Mede have your number. But, of course, they don't count. Sage probably doesn't care. For the rest, you have created sensations which, even if they don't like, they also enjoy. They are waiting for your next spectacle, many hoping you'll make a bungle of it, turning you into the cautionary tale for our brave little community."

"Look, Clemons, haven't you ever wanted to go back and prevent your brother from dying on the exploding riverboat?"

Twain stared at me and furrowed his brow. "Ah. Well, once you are dead, these corrective measures lose their urgency. Having said that, the answer is yes. I think about it all the time. That and other options."

"Then why don't you just go ahead and do it? Marie is changing history as we speak."

"*Trying to change history.*" Twain swirled his whiskey in his glass. "You have the eagerness for such projects. I no longer do. And I will tell you why. There was something that I did execute. I had a friend named Jake. From the California days. He joined the Union Army when the war started. He was shot and killed at Gettysburg. That didn't seem fair to me. He was very young, one of so many. I went back and, since it was my time, it was pretty easy to pull off. I had him reassigned and kept him out of Gettysburg. He survived the war. Got married, had a family, started a little business in Kentucky. One night, two bandits invaded his house and slaughtered the entire family. Not just murdered them but butchered them all. It was horrible and gave me pause."

"And *you* feel responsible?"

"I didn't at first. But what do you think? Of course, I came, in time, to feel that it was completely my doing."

"It made you reconsider your abilities?"

"Not my abilities. My *applications*. It's easier to play with people you haven't known well, no matter the breadth of empathy. And, yes, it does give me pause now. Take those yo-yos at the party. I've tried, time and again, to discuss with some of them the import of what must be done. But they just yawn and have none of it. It's the innate conservatism of those who have a good thing. Though, strangely, so many revolutions come from the top. Look at Marie's! Most of our colleagues, alas, seem to be an inert mass. Thus our world. You seem to be the exception to the rule. I hope you prove that this pattern needn't be inevitable."

"I suspect it is. For the dead, a predictable fate." I paused, eyeing Twain cautiously. "You know, Sam, I find Sage sexually attractive. Just my type."

"Good for you. Go fuck him." Twain examined his fingernails.

"It just might come to that. We'll see."

"Necrophilia if he's among the dead. Deity-fucking if he's a god. You score points for novelty either way."

I smiled. "A new sensation. I will let you know, if you are interested." I stood. "Twain, I'll see you out. I'm exhausted. I must sleep."

"I understand."

We walked to the door. Twain squeezed my arm.

"I'll come collect you after you've rested. It's a concept I've completely forgotten—being rested." He departed.

I locked the door, an odd reversion to habit that had no place here, except that it was familiar. I crawled into my bed, made the sky dark, turned on my little bedside reading lamp and picked up an old and slightly shopworn copy of *Alice Through The Looking Glass*, an edition from the nineteen-twenties, one with heavy cloth covers and gossamer tissue overlaying each of the color plates. The print was large, done on letterpress and the margins were wide. The story was, as always, fascinating and I cared so much that I quickly dozed off. *Poor Alice.*

I dreamed. It didn't occur to me that this might happen. This was before I came to program my dreams, which it turned out was a lot of work. I still worry about some critter assassinating me while I am in the sticky embrace of Morpheus. Given my rep in this realm,

I doubt even Voltaire could spare me *my* Charlotte Corday. *The dead are so jealous!*

My dream was your basic anxiety attack, me rushing madly about, up and down endless flights of stairs, through a house full of empty rooms, teeth falling out, all the classics. Now I prefer to dream in the mode of Mildred Pierce, wherein I play Eve Arden's role. It's a great concept and I've sent a treatment to Mank but I haven't heard back yet.

When I woke up, I was sweaty. Just yukky. I wobbled to the can. I looked in the mirror. *I saw the face of Edith Sitwell!* It was hard enough for her to live with, unbearable for me.

I wiped the mirror with a towel. Edith was gone and my own bright peach tones came into focus. I dawdled at my toilette and finally felt ready for the new day.

The phone rang. It was Voltaire.

"Meet me at the Taj Mahal in half an hour." Click.

I did. I got there a little early, as is my nature. The elegant monument to heterosexual married love was still under construction. The poor slavies were lugging the slabs of marble and alabaster on little rollers, just too painful and fascinating to watch. I was inclined to decorate with graffiti but decided it was too small an act.

"I think everyone should have a hobby," Voltaire said immediately upon arriving. "But for Mumtaz Muhal, it was—how would modern therapists describe it?—a wee bit on the obessional side. Romantic love can veer off into such an ugly, deformed passion."

"Given the twentieth century's innovations of devices, what have we to measure against the edifices of the classical age?" I was quiz show host.

Voltaire mused. "*Le pneumatique?*"

"Hoover dam!"

"Hoover be damned!"

"J. Edgar probably was. That particular circle of Hell where evil queans like him are sent. Next to the broiler occupied by Roy Cohn."

Voltaire was chipper. "Shall we schlep down and find out?"

"Sorry, Frank, I'm not ready to traipse through Hell just yet." The idea put me off. "The day's young. Hell is more appropriate for the evening."

"Fine. We'll both go and do a quick little census and publish a smart monograph, 'Are The Damned Damned Enough?' It will create a sensation. Do you think they allow cameras in Hell?" Voltaire held up one arm. On his wrist was attached some smart little mini-camera device. "Just the best invention of these new times. Click, click, click and you can do with them as you please. Who'd bother getting a signed release from someone condemned to Hell? No amount of humiliation is ever enough!"

"We clearly can't be heavenly enough or in too many ways." I watched as a slab of marble was hoisted onto the structure. Testaments to love looked to be hard work.

"The idea of power is to invent yet more ways of having and using power. It's a specialty of the species, no matter the political regime." Voltaire waved vaguely at the temple, where people were being worked to death in homage to pure love.

Voltaire seemed to be right almost all the time. *How did that happen?* I fell into the pattern of letting him have the last line. *He had so many!* It's a position we ancients must adopt when dealing with our race when it was younger. And, besides, I could later steal his best material from him. Stuff this good is meant to circulate.

"India is so hot, and so foreign," Voltaire sighed. "And this endless cringing servility. You get the feeling that there isn't even any chance for change. Let's move on."

In our next stop, we were on a brick walkway alongside a cute little canal. Gondolas and party motorboats glided by. The men were relentless in inspecting the two of us. I was undressed a dozen times. The men were dark-haired, handsome and full of a studied overt sexuality. Both Voltaire and I started preening and carrying on, loving the attention. The air was full of the salty sea breeze. We turned to cross a steep pedestrian bridge. We laughed and swaggered, like young sailors trying to get picked up. As we reached the crest of the bridge, we ran into Sage, Mede and a young man who was accompanying them. They were the picture of disgusting self-satisfaction.

"Out for your daily constitutionals?" I asked.

Mede ignored my inquiry. He grinned at us. "Such *really* terrible news. I'm sure you've heard by now."

"I *thrive* on bad news," Voltaire batted back. "So cut the act and let's have it."

"It's Rousseau this time," Sage passed on the news. "He went back over. Into the nineteen-eighties. You know how he's been these past few decades. A little strange and *very* aloof. But he cooked up some crazy plan about posing as a CIA agent to get in on some drug deal and whatnot. Just deranged. I suspect"—Sage gave me a long look—"he's been watching too many clips on the screens of the exploits of Bunny here and got some sense of re-invigoration of his rusty powers."

Mede cut in. "And you know, Rousseau hasn't crossed over in who knows how long. Just the laziest, and the most fraidy cat, among the sybarites."

"All true," Sage continued, "and unlike riding a bicycle, one *does* lose the knack." He nodded at me. "At any rate, he mis-aimed his trajectory and target. He *did* land in the eighties, but not among the CIA crew or the drug dealers. He landed in the body of this incredibly over-weight anti-porn crusader in the United States. I think somewhere in New York."

"It seems to be permanent," said the new face.

"Which," I asked, "the fat or his fate?" I wanted to stain Sage's little bad news scenario on this old bridge. "Pity it wasn't de Sade who went over and got stuck. He's more the type. It could have been a melding of interests and perhaps instructive to that old lech."

"Oh, I've been rude," Sage was suddenly hostess. "Bunny, Frank, this is Lenny. He's just joined us. By which I mean *us*. He has graphic artist skills. I'm putting him in charge of designing our new community paper we're starting next week. Lots of celebrity interviews and lots of nudes, which is Lenny's forte. Good for sales." Sage gave me a big wink, which made this exchange even cheaper.

"I don't believe a word of it!" I put on a heavy attitude to see how it would play. "You've made it all up."

"Oh, ye of little faith," Sage reverted to old material. "Mede, reveal to the disbelievers."

Mede casually waved a window in the sky immediately in front of us. Into sharp focus came this vision of sweaty jowls, blubbery arms, flapping cheeks and a mouth as big as the Grand Canyon. The creature who owned all these remarkable features pranced back and forth before a podium, wearing a mu-mu, a tight mu-mu.

"Sisters! We know porn causes rape! But these men, with their evil penises and their murderous erections, each one a phallic weapon of terror and oppression, are using their eight-billion-dollar porn industry to shove eels up our cunts. It is war, sisters! Total victory or chains and eels pushed up our cunts. Then the beast runs and hides behind the Constitution. You know what I tell them? They can take their First Amendment, oil it up, get it real greasy, have them bend over and they can shove it up their assholes! Because we are angry and right is on our side. We'll burn down the bookstores, torch the movie theatres and smash their evil porno empire."

"*Please!*" Voltaire snapped, putting his hands over his ears. "Nix the audio. She's an instant migraine."

"They'd put her in a straightjacket," I suggested, "if there existed one that would fit."

"I feel sorry for the eels," Voltaire quipped.

Our featured personality on the screen went on and on, gesticulating and waving her hands around. I suspected bad toilet training as a tot, but who knows. But at least she was carrying on with the sound off.

"This event is coming to us in real time, live from the Women's Lawyers' Caucus Against Porno-Rapists-Pimps Convention."

"I'm sure it is," I noted. "Free speech and more free speech and crazy people too. But where's Jean-Jacques? Selling the lewd postcards in the lobby?"

Lenny made a pass of one hand over the image of the bloated anti-porner. Slowly, the face of J-J appeared from within the corpus of the loud-mouth. Rosseau looked terrified. He saw us watching him and he made a direct appeal.

"Sound up!" Sage ordered. Mede waved his hand.

"All very cute for you all to enjoy this," he sounded desperate. "But it's not a pleasure to be trapped inside of this woman. That noise just reverberates through this lard. *And she never shuts up!* It gives one a whole new appreciation for being in the realm of the dead. BUT I CAN'T GET OUT! HELP ME! DO SOMETHING!"

"I suspect you have just forgotten how." Sage was counselor. "And, anyway, you just crossed over to get some drugs."

I noted, with interest, Sage's middle-class moralism.

"Not drugs!" Rosseau quibbled. "Sex stimulants."

"I won't argue, as it's all the same," Sage was sanguine. "But now you are trapped inside all that blubber."

Lenny chuckled all too enthusiastically.

"Believe me, Sage, I've tried all the standard physical release mechanisms, the aural formula, even the Last Ditch emergency pulls, which *you* assured me were fool-proof, but nothing has worked. I'm still stuck here. I WANT OUT!"

"We'll do what we can, darling." Lenny was smug.

"Meanwhile, enjoy the anti-porn crusade. It may help you to clean up your act." Sage flicked his wrist and J-J and The Great Blubbery One on the window disappeared. "As to *you*, my friends"—Sage glared at Voltaire and me—"there is a cautionary tale in all this. Take care in your travels. First poor old Mary Renault gets trapped in some slave on a trireme as it spoons its way around the Mediterranean. And now poor Rousseau is forever implanted in the body of an anti-porn fanatic. Something is in the wind. *QED*."

Mede leaned over and brushed his cheek against mine. "And have a nice day," he whispered. His breath stank of whiskey. The three of them continued on their merry way, *their* day obviously made.

Voltaire took my arm as we strolled along. "It appears that, for whatever reasons, our ranks are being selectively thinned. The daring ones are being taken away and cast into hideous and, I presume but do not know, permanent fates." He clucked his tongue.

"I fear both our names are on that list." I was glum.

"Mmmmmmmm." Voltaire stared hard at me. "Now, as to this nice day, any suggestions?"

We stepped off the bridge, shrugged our shoulders, closed our eyes, only to open them to find that we were in a semi-lit casino in a Hi-Tackola hotel in Las Vegas. Was this our preferred destination? It must have been Voltaire's wish.

Scantily clad hostesses bustled about. We found ourselves surrounded by people who frequent such spaces, lots of polyester suits and odd-color hair rinses. I looked at Voltaire. He was wearing a white linen suit, pale blue shirt, a white tie and white patent leather pumps. I was garbed in a soft velour short coat, belled trousers, Qiana shirt and short boots that came to a point.

Voltaire's eyes lit up when he spotted the gaming tables. The tables were, of course, surrounded by gambling junkies. Was my dear friend one of that tribe?

"My one short-attention vice," Voltaire noted. I hate gambling and its hideous subculture. Voltaire pulled a small pile of chips from his coat pocket and placed them on a fashionable single number in red.

It hit.

The croupier gave Mr. V. a steely smile and raked over an even larger pile of chips. Voltaire scooped them up and we went to cash them in. As the bills were counted out, he gave me a patronizing smile. "I never linger after a big win. Once a philosopher, twice a pervert."

"Wrong, Frank, you've always had that backwards."

"Who cares? Everyone's a critic. You know, it suddenly makes sense. It was da Vinci."

"*Who* was da Vinci?"

"That Lenny we met on the *ponte decripito*. His former address was the Elysian Fields. Distant there and a bit on the arrogant side. But Sage and his crew have now crossed him over, and they've butched him up and he's doing a South Philly wop number. But I saw right through it. Such a weak sister, that one."

"Tell me. What is going on? I thought they were supposed to be pissed off because I got you over. Now, if Sage has brought over DaVinci, what can it mean?"

"My friend, nothing we can't handle." We walked into the lounge and ordered Bloody Marys. The place was filled with loud, vulgar and badly attired Canadians. Voltaire, in the dark lounge "atmosphere," seemed to be even more dominated by his huge set of peepers. He ogled every blond white thing that went by. There were many. I was not impressed. The Canadians were, for me, menacing. The whole country is a machine to cough out hockey players and hockey fans who are let loose onto the poor ravaged United States, celebrating their victory by whooping it up in Vegas.

"The nicest change in being here over chez Elysian Fields is the rediscovery of libido, a word not used in my time, but lust by any other name can be life stirring." Voltaire had his peacock feathers up and on display. "Life in the Elysian Fields revolves around parlor games and gluttony. That's why your friend Wilde enjoys it so much. At any rate, what I wanted to say, Bunny, is that while you slept, and I can't recall how many weeks it seemed, but Sage & Co. have not only decided that crossing over a select few from E. Fields is a good and trendy idea, they are lining up the slots and, as I glean from the grapevine, each shade requires different frequencies and other variables and, well, just too boring. And, *voila!*, the fabulous DaVinci shows up. I hear Capote has weaseled his way to the head of the line to be the next on the dumb waiter up to our heady land."

I burped. Loudly.

"We agree." Voltaire sipped his BM. "It was just awful when little Truman bounced down our way. We were so hoping he'd go *anywhere* else. Many of the formerly religious actually prayed. It didn't help. We got him. He has his fans. To me he is nothing but a nasty piece of business and I speak with some authority when it comes to that category." He sighed.

"The Fates are cruel."

"Worse, my dear. They are stupid, fickle and inattentive. Like audiences. Which reminds me, when I get some time I want to produce a rewritten Oedipus cycle with an audience-activated ending. Stop the action. 'He killed his father and now he wants to fuck his mother. *Should we let him do it?* Vote now!' Dump it all on the paying crowd. Why not?"

I laughed. "Sure to be an instant success."

"At least keep them awake! Slapping the murder genre onto the classics, as though poor dull Sophocles needed it."

"They're snakes," I said into my drink, "Sage and his crew. They want to bring over the beer bellies and the twisted sisters and have the resisters among us get trapped in anti-porn psychos. It's perverse and not even grand enough to warrant admiration. Can Sage be nailed to the drying board?"

"Who knows? I'd suggest that you woo him first. It might be more productive. Now, that's the bad news. I haven't told you the upbeat side yet. It seems that President Diderot has appointed Marie as his Minister of Culture. Isn't it a sensation? Robespierre is pounding out propaganda for the government. Danton has his drinking under control—Marie has introduced AA and a twelve-step program, and we'll see how far she gets with *that*—and Danton still has his head attached to his body, which is something. Dear Marie seems to be quite the mover-and-shaker. In fact, the Assembly voted Marie "Miss Liberty of 1794." She is quite pleased. Marie actually dropped by while you were sleeping—I have it all on tape—and she still wants to finely tune the whole number. Revolution as cooking class. Just follow the recipe and try and try again. Season to taste."

The public address system in the lounge crackled with a low-pitched voice. "Paging M. Voltaire and Mr. Bunny LaRue. A call for you at the front desk."

Voltaire and I stared at each other, shocked that we were still surprised that odd things happen. We finished our drinks, paid, rose and walked through the boisterous bevy of ill-mannered Canadians.

At the front desk, Voltaire took the phone. "Hello? Hello! Speak up! But there is no one there!" he said, holding the phone.

"There's enough of us here to take care of you boys." The two of us looked over our shoulders. Three greasy bruisers glared at us. Voltaire turned to address them.

"If you're lost, the men's room is over there. You look like you could use a good scrubbing."

"And *you* a good drubbing. We're here to be your chauffeurs. We're going to take you boys for a little ride."

"The ambience has changed," I sneered. "Have the prices?"

"That's enough out of you!" The goon, wearing a maple leaf baseball cap, clamped cuffs on me. Another put the bracelets on Voltaire. They dragged us out of the casino. Voltaire and I were screaming at the top of our lungs. No one bothered to notice. It must happen on a regular basis.

We were lugged out the front door of the building where a BMW, with driver, awaited. Voltaire and his jailer got in front. I was pushed into the back seat and wedged between fat-faced goons. The car sped off. I had no idea what might happen, but I had a hunch it wasn't going to be pleasant. Voltaire just stared at the driver.

"*I know you!*" Voltaire said excitedly. The thugs then all pulled on ski masks. "That won't help. I recognized you immediately from those posters in the Elysian Fields. And now you're on *their* payroll. The hired muscle."

"All I know," said the driver, "is that Canada wants you boys removed from the face of the planet. We're under instructions from the PM personally. You're going to your deaths!"

"Hardly likely," Voltaire laughed, "as I'm dead already. My death is in your hands. And furthermore, you and your silly Canadian government know that either Bunny or I can end this charade any time we want."

"Ha, ha, ha," cackled the driver. "The Canadian government is more powerful than your sick fantasies."

"Well, then slow down for chrissake or you'll smash this German junk into that billboard."

The driver slowed a bit. Suddenly, all four tires blew out. The BMW careened about the roadway, which was completely devoid of other cars, and finally came to an abrupt halt on the gravel shoulder.

"Now unlock this jewelry, big boys, let us out, and be on your way."

"Can't do it," said one of the thugs sitting next to me. "Canadian pride and perhaps even the future of Canadian sovereignty hinges on the success of our mission."

The driver's door fell off. Still, there was no move to free us. The hood flew up. Still not a move. Voltaire looked at me and gave me a wink. The car's engine fell from the chassis.

"You want more?" Voltaire teased. "How about I make all your hair fall out?"

We quickly got unlocked and were released from the heap. Voltaire and I calmly strolled away from the scene. Voltaire leisurely looked back and snapped his fingers. The BMW blew up; the four bodies were tossed into the nearby woods by the blast.

I was impressed. "Seems to be a high risk occupation."

"A crude kidnapping attempt," Voltaire said, "and not to be allowed."

We shut our eyes. Opening them, we found ourselves in Voltaire's conversation pit. Twain was there, bathed in light, scribbling on foolscap.

"A close call for you boys," he said, not even looking up at us. "If you keep up that level of excitement, you might start looking for a commercial sponsor."

"It was nothing," Voltaire said. "Just a night in Vegas. And well-scripted. The shorter the vignette, the bigger the punch required at the end. It's only the long, ruminative, blowsy stories that can afford to go nowhere."

"Meanwhile, back at the ranch"—Twain consulted his notes—"events unfold. I've made a list. An appeals judge, whom I assume was Sage in mufti, overturned the conviction of Mary Baker Eddy and set her loose in the land. The indictments against the Mormons and the various fundamentalists have been dropped."

I scowled. "I'm in the mood for serious revenge."

"An ugly impulse," Voltaire observed, "but understandable in these circumstances."

"Where shall we strike?" I was ready to move.

"Well," Twain took his time, "I never thought John Wilkes should have been convicted of blasphemy. It was a stupid law. Still is, as I think it's the law of the land in England. Want to go throw that trial?"

"I'm game!" Voltaire smiled.

"Me too!"

We mapped out a strategy and took our leap back to the scandals of the Enlightenment.

Arriving at our destination, and the fog was thick, we stumbled our way along a cobblestone street. There before us was a public house. We entered, took a table and ordered whiskey. The pub was filled with the chat of the English drinkers.

"Those crazy frogs. That Napoleon lunatic. Just an idiot, he is. Should have done away with him in Egypt. Bury him with all those other mummies." Laughter.

Voltaire was serene but said, "Something's wrong."

The barmaid walked passed us. Twain grabbed her arm.

"What's that talk about Napoleon?"

She looked at us as though we were from another planet. "Ain't you seen the papers? He calls himself the emperor now, crowned himself they say. Imagine that. Means more war. Ever since that French Revolution, ain't been nothing but trouble." She went on.

"Seriously wrong, I think," I said.

"Not only have we not made it back to the eighteenth century to undo Wilkes's conviction but I'm afraid Marie's work in the early nineties is now being undone." Twain lit a cigar.

We left the pub and went back into the fog.

"Let's at least try again," I suggested. I think I knew what they were thinking.

"Bunny's right. One more try." Voltaire seemed determined.

We held hands, closed our eyes and concentrated on the court-room where poor Wilkes was on trial for a crime against the Christian deity. When we opened our eyes, we were still in the fog, still outside the pub. We could hear a distant, if feeble, laughter. But from *whom*?

"Back to my digs for some regrouping," Voltaire proposed.

We did our exit and found ourselves in the conversation pit. Depressed. We sat, staring through the floor-to-ceiling windows at the valley below.

"That's it then," I sighed. "The leadership Mafia has blocked off the eighteenth century for folks like us. Too bad. It seemed like such fun."

"But *how*?" Twain was adamant.

"What of Marie?" Voltaire seemed concerned. "Will she be able to cross back over to give us updates? What if she gets into trouble again? What will we do?"

We kicked that around for a few minutes.

"I thought you boys would be thirsty after such an exercise." It was a very white whine. We looked over our shoulders. There stood Truman Capote, in a chef's hat and an apron over his jumpsuit. He wore sandals and a Playboy ankle bracelet. "So I whipped up a pitcher of piña coladas. It's one of my specialties." He twinkled at us.

He set elegant glasses in front of the three of us and filled them with his brilliant concoction. Both Voltaire and Twain stared at Capote—surely he was used to it at this point—and looked grim.

"I like the climate here," Capote babbled, pouring his own drink and sitting next to me. "So much more direct sunlight than in the Fields." He sipped his drink. "Purrrfect! I would have made a pitcher of martinis but, honestly, looking at the lot of you, you don't come off as the martini type!" He made a dramatic gesture. "You know, back in the fifties, I could make martinis dead. And now that I *am* dead, and have transcended death with my arrival here, martinis are the last thing on my mind. Isn't it screwy?" Capote licked his lips.

"Sage brought you over, I presume?" I had to ask.

Capote smirked. "*I'm* not telling. That bunch! They said the most perfectly awful things about you all. So I had to run right over. And, *you*, Voltaire! Always going out of your way to avoid me in the Fields when you know I'm just as good as you are—or *were*! Such bad manners. If that's what the *ancien regime* taught its troubadours in the courtesy department, it's no wonder it was overthrown by the ruffians. I was chatting with Marie Antoinette the other day, and she was just aghast, as you might imagine, and—"

"*Can it, Capote!*" Twain was sharp. "We know the rap."

Capote smiled his sickly sweet grin. "But now that I'm here, let's all be bosom buddies."

"You won't be staying with me, will you?" Voltaire asked, not in the friendliest tones.

"Not to worry, ducks. I'm lining up this fabulous sub-let across town. It's really fabulous. It overlooks the East River and the Seine at the same time! Imagine that! Primo real estate with an option to own. Having a very good location is so important to own's social life. So many possibilities here. Hope you don't mind, dear, but I borrowed the use of your phone to call Elsa Maxwell and we're putting together this elegant costume ball. You all must come. Voltaire, you can be Lear. Twain and Bunny can come dressed as Goneril and Regan. You'll be a hit. Be nice to me and I'll fix it up so you can win a prize!"

"Have another drink, Truman," I said, filling up the wispy one's glass.

"Now that you have joined the club," Twain was inquisitive, "what plans have you for meddling?"

"Weeeeeeellllll"—Capote radiated attitude—"there is one project I'm already kicking around."

"Do tell," I encouraged him.

"I have this absolutely terrific idea for a TV special. Needless to say, I have very important friends in the high echelons of both NBC *and* ABC. But I think I'll do it through Lorimar—more creative freedom and what not—and then sell it to one of the networks. The concept? It's me and Arthur Godfrey doing *A Salute to The Fifties*. I'll be in drag throughout, big poodle skirt, Peter Pan blouse, and Arthur will wear a tux, and we'll do great numbers, 'How Much Is That Doggie In The Window,' '*Que Sera, Sera*,' 'Old Cape Cod.' Soft lighting. Guest spots by Imogene Coca, Jackie Gleason, the McGuire Sisters, Dick Clark and Teresa Brewer. Admit it, it's total box-office!" Capote was all wide smiles and bright eyes.

"*I love it!*" I enthused. "You're just the right number to do the fifties up proud."

Capote pouted. "People underrate the fifties. They were grand."

Not for everyone, I thought to myself.

"We'll all be watching," Voltaire was polite. "But since we're all best buddies now, you must confess that it was Sage who brought you over."

"*Please! You are all obsessed with Sage.* I don't know why. He's so easy to twist around your little finger when you have my gifts." Capote looked at us severely. "Here I am in the den of three pretty big heavy hitters and you're telling me you haven't figured out Sage's number yet?"

"You're right. We haven't." I said.

"Well, I learned this in the Fields, and I hope the gossip is as good up here as it was down there. Despite what you may think, very little was censored *down there*. Word got around." Capote sniffed. "Turns out your great nemesis, Sage, was once positioned to be the soul of

The Dialectic. He had a great run of it. Made things move right along, if not always in harmony. He adores the early part of the nineteenth century, when his biographers revealed him to the masses. But then things changed. As we know they must do. Things started becoming a little too undialectical for his tastes. Events were not going as planned. Human invention went on its own course. In fact, Sage loathes, just loathes, the early twentieth century. He's madly anti-modernist, you know. Well, *everybody* knows! He wants a dull, mechanistic world. He's fascinated with progress but not gutsy enough to ride it out."

Capote sipped his cocktail, set it down and stared at me.

"Which is why *you*, my dear, or at least so I have heard from very reliable sources, were brought over. Sage thought you might be his cat's paw in the post-modernist struggle to battle this trend to nihilism and random experimentation for its own sake. It was a daring and risky move considering you weren't that famous yet, and fame is all that really matters in our realm. But he does love you, even though, at this moment, he sees you as a wandering child. He's waiting for your return to him for advice and direction. Twain and Voltaire he regards as pure poison."

This last observation, I noted to myself, was the only fact to fall from the little one's lips.

"What do you recommend?" I asked.

"I'm new here. But I've done my homework. Your crowd wants to go off and change all these crazy things. It smacks of idealism. It belongs in the eighteen-forties or nineteen-sixties. When all that shit was fashionable. I'm a hedonist and I plan to do well right where I am. I'll get the TV gigs. Then some marvy parties. Folks like my parties. Then some swank deals on the side. I'll be set up for all eternity, as long as eternity doesn't turn out to be *too* tacky!" He took a deep breath and then pulled a rumpled piece of paper from a pocket. He stared at it. "As for these few select enemies, I have all the time and, now, all the power of the universe to get back at them. Won't that be fun?"

"The very force of The Dialectic." Voltaire chuckled. "It sounds like hard work. And pretty gritty."

"A slave to conditions, enemy of spontaneity," Twain noted.

Capote stood, gingerly removed his chef's apron and tossed it on the vast sofa. "Sorry, but I really must fly, duckies. I'll be staying with Marie Laurencin for a few weeks until I get my new digs done up right. Something French Quarter with all the views. You *all* must come to what will be The Ultimate House Warming Party! *Everybody will be there!*" Capote waddled to the door, opened it, turned back to the three of us and whispered, "Bye, bye!" Then was gone.

"As they say, there goes the neighborhood," Twain was cutting.

"Swallows at Capistrano and hummingbirds in heaven," I said.

We were all depressed. *Was* Sage the grim deposed force of The Dialectic in the nineteenth century? Does history have a jockey? If yes, what *was* his problem? What was he up to?

"I need to cheer myself up," I said, rising. "And, Twain, I want you to come along with me on this one. A small but satisfying gesture."

Twain held onto my arm. I tossed back my head and set the program.

We opened our eyes. It was dark. The waves of the Atlantic Ocean gently rolled in over the sandy beach. The stars seemed somewhat too numerous throughout the sky, but I was pleased to see them all nonetheless. There was no moon. We heard the sputter of a two-engine prop plane passing overhead.

"I've never been to Fire Island before," Twain said softly.

"Somewhere out there," I pointed vaguely, "the remains of Margaret Fuller were carried out to the ages. Along with her book on the Italian Revolution. Maybe Marie will write her book on *her* French Revolution."

Twain clucked his tongue. "When it comes to the Fuller story, I always suspected there was some sort of cover-up. I think the body was found, but the family, scandalized by the husband and the baby, whisked her off to Concord and had her secretly buried with the other Great Ones."

"All I can say is good for Margaret! At least she got out of Massachusetts." But Fuller was sideshow. We had more urgent business. "One tragedy on this southern exposure is quite enough. Our mission is to spare another literary loss."

"You're my guide." Twain tagged behind. Sometimes he seemed such an old and tricky man. I was never certain what his act was, but it didn't matter; we were best friends.

We could hear the party house before it came clearly into view. But there it was, bright lights illuminating an all-wood and glass Pines manse. The latest pop music. Shrieks and laughter. Alcoholics. We spotted a figure ahead of us. Just his outline in the dark, sprawled on the sand. From behind us, we heard the rev of a dune buggy, another menace from the sixties.

"Hurry, Mark! Help me!" We jogged to the figure. "FRANK! GET UP!"

O'Hara turned to us, soggy-looking and not terribly interested and *not* about to move.

"Let's each take an arm," I snapped at Twain, "and just pull."

We could hear the dune buggy getting closer.

Twain took O'Hara's left arm, I the other. We lugged O'Hara across the sand and toward the wooden staircase that led from the beach to the noisy house.

O'Hara broke out laughing. "Off to jail, I suspect. What, constable, is my crime?"

We dropped him against the wood stairs just as the dune buggy whizzed by, spitting a spray of sand in our faces. O'Hara wiped the wet sand from his face and was suddenly alert, aware he had been saved.

"That lunatic!" He shouted. "Why are those god-damned things allowed on the beach?" He looked up at us. "You guys just saved my life!"

"Exactly our goal." I twinkled.

The shock was setting in. I feared O'Hara might hyperventilate but his breathing remained steady. He slowly assumed his famous self-confidence. He rose from his supine position.

"Once again, one relies on the kindness of strangers." He brushed the sand off his bare legs, his knee-length madras shorts and his knit shirt. "I am Frank O'Hara," he said, holding out his hand. "May I have the pleasure of knowing the names of my saviors?"

I shook his hand. "My name is Bunny LaRue. And *this* is Mark Twain."

O'Hara stared at Twain. He stepped back and stared harder.

"Well, I *do* believe you *are* Mark Twain." O'Hara chuckled. "You should have seen Jimmy Schuyler at Ned Rorem's party last year. He was *marvelous* as Nurse Edith Cavill!" He smoothed the lapels of Twain's white suit. "Now, let us do the right thing. Let's go inside and have a drink and I'll introduce you around. There's a lot of name-droppers here but none, to my knowledge, will have had the privilege of hosting *the* Mark Twain. If you can navigate the Mississippi, coasting through this crowd will be a breeze."

Twain was diplomatic. "Bunny and I would love to," he said sweetly. "But we're already running a bit late. We've go to get over to Cherry Grove to meet friends and watch the Truman Capote TV special."

"Little Truman is on the tube? I hadn't heard. Just like the witch. Well, in that case, what can I say but the obvious? Thanks, boys, for saving my life. I owe you one. And unlike poor Fitzgerald, I guess I now get a second act."

"Indeed you do," I said softly. "Just make sure it's spectacular."

"I think that's the easy part."

Twain and I were on our way and didn't look back. We continued on our leisurely walk, in the tire tracks of the dreaded dune buggy which was by now miles down the beach, looking for another victim in the dark.

The salt breeze, not to mention our daring adventure, had tired me. I felt groggy.

"Twain, I think I'll retire to the digs of my other quick self and get rejuiced from the living, among whom, I occasionally remind myself, I still belong."

Twain nodded, saying nothing. I walked away from him and strolled into the calm waves of the Atlantic with my arms held high above my head and my eyes closed.

Before I knew it, I was back in Boston, sitting in my big armchair, watching the TV. My real-time self was there as well. We stared at each other. He was entertaining and looked at me like unwanted baggage. I surveyed the party-goers. They were Stacey Brazzi, the Empress Carlotta de Cambridge, Kay Wieners, Boston City Councilor Derrick Tsongopoulos and the celebrity hair bender Kitty Katz. It appeared to be a *GAYOLA!* editorial meeting, the literary rag published when they felt like it. It was a ditzy effort, even though it had established itself as very important in the prose and poetry micro-circles of the unpublished, a vast throng. They seemed to be discussing one of the poetry submissions. I felt so removed from this world. I just wanted some sleep.

None of the others seemed to notice me, which had its advantages. I felt like one of the ghosts in *Topper*. The TV was on. It seemed to be one of the news shows. Carlotta turned it up. President Nixon was shown in front of a map, with a pointer, indicating where our nation's troops were having success in the military campaign against Canada. I did a double-take.

"Meet me in the kitchen, toots," my ordinary self said to me.

We both retired to the stove as the others argued over poetry.

"You're a great burden on me, I hope you realize," my quotidian self accused. "At first, it wasn't so bad. But, like tuning in a weak radio signal, the longer I'm stuck with it, the clearer it becomes. Now I get distracted by your doings. People at work think I'm bats. My friends don't care. They have me pegged as a loon anyway. It's just not fair."

"Sorry, my dear, but there are big things happening up above and I *must* be involved."

"I don't doubt that at all," my dull side said. "But can you imagine what those waves of change *feel* like when they wash in here? Every day it's something different. It's like getting up every morning and not knowing what play you're supposed to be in. One day Arthur Miller. Next day Odetts. Next Robert Patrick. No one seems to know why Nixon is President again! They just seem to accept it. Some of these quakes you generate from above are burps and some are big-time tidal waves. Each time you do something up there, or anyone else among your clique, to change things, it's like an energy field zapping me. Worse than a sonic boom. And after it's over, it's as though it has always been that way. No one can remember what the scenario was before, much less why it changed so suddenly. *Except me!* Since I'm the only one left with an historical memory or understanding of what's happening, they all think me on the road to madness."

I leaned over and kissed my other self on the cheek. "Treasure it. Something useful may come of it when events take a weird turn."

The Empress Carlotta waddled into the kitchen, looking for a dividend of Dr. Pepper. Carlotta wore his famous farmer's overalls, an army fatigue blouse and pink carpet slippers. "Talking to yourself again, Bunny?"

"As a matter of fact, I *am* talking to myself, Carlotta. But in a more profound way than is visible to you." The correct response, thus, easy.

"Well," Carlotta sniffed, filling his huge glass with soda pop, "it's like masturbation. People who enjoy that sort of thing enjoy that sort of thing." Carlotta, no dummy, looked around slyly, perhaps sensing both of my selves. "Anyway, you better wrap it up and come back into the living room. Nixon has declared total victory and is finally off the screen. The Truman Capote Special is just starting. It's sure to be a scream."

We all trooped back to sit in front of the old black and white monster-sized TV. Music up. A big proscenium stage. Plush curtains.

"Ladies and gentlemen," boomed the basso voice, "tonight, A Salute To The Fabulous Fifties. With Truman Capote and Arthur Godfrey. Brought to you by Hazel Bishop. *When Color Really Counts.*"

The curtain parted and Truman paraded onto the stage, dolled up in a tight woolen skirt, a flirty blouse, a pageboy wig, on spike heels, spinning a hula hoop about his middle, to thunderous applause.

"Tonight's special guests include Kay Thompson, Rosemary Clooney, The Jewel Box Revue and Dion and the Belmonts. But first, let Hazel Bishop dazzle you with color to conquer the world." The screen filled with huge close-ups of fingernails, black and white for our crowd, ravishing color for the rest of the audience, though, if memory serves, we didn't have color TV back in the fifties. A tiny anachronism shouldn't get in the way of a *fabulous* Truman Capote Special!

I knew exactly where this treacly display of vanity was going and I wanted to spare my poor tired eyeballs. I retired to the guest bedroom of my own apartment, sickened by the thought of the gushing triviality which was about to be screened. I undressed, curled up in the bed. Sleep came quickly.

When I awoke, I was in my own bed in my abode in Paradiso. The satin sheets were a mite chilly. The air was different. The sunlight constant. I rose, made my bed, showered, none of which I had to do as this was a place transcendent. But keeping to a familiar routine had its paybacks. Sometimes.

I made a cup of tea, adding a tiny mushroom into the brew, as I have been told it is good for the nerves. I took my mug into the living room. I found Sage sitting on my sofa.

He looked at me and smiled.

"I've been admiring your microcosm."

I sat next to him. "Yes. It amuses me." I had no idea how it had got here on my table, but I suspect I had willed it there while I was asleep, as I had willed, during REM, my return to Shangri-La.

"Cute, the way you've got them in there in miniature." Sage pointed.

I peered at the rectangular glass tank. Two-inch figures of Roy Cohn, Joe McCarthy and David Shine crawled up on the rocks and leafy plants, waving at us.

"This is something totally new. I fear the fad will sweep our little colony." Sage raised his eyebrows. "Homunculi as pets until they tire of them and then flush them down the toilets to clog drains and back up sewage."

"It wouldn't surprise me." I was suddenly clear as to what it was all about. "I was so disgusted with your bringing Capote over and his endless obsession for a TV jag pushing the fifties back in our faces, I made this small response as a gesture of my revulsion. Just cage these creatures."

"You shouldn't feel bitter." Sage leaned back. "There's a hydraulic principle at work here. If you and your friends continue to meddle in the eighteenth century, then there must be a counter movement to obliterate the nineteen-sixties. Tit for tat. Everything must be paid for."

It was time for me to turn coquette. I snuggled closer to Sage and began coyly touching him. My eyes radiated hunger—the mushroom helped. He received my attentions with welcome.

"You know, Capote said the strangest things about you," I purred. "That you were the embodiment of the deposed positivist thrust of the nineteenth century."

"I know. I watched him tell you." Sage chuckled. "Some folks say the wildest thing about me and they always get it wrong. Happily, none of it sticks."

I began nibbling at his neck.

"In fact, I *adore* the nineteenth century. All that progress." Sage sighed. "Looking back, it was a wild time of many forces loosed into the world but also a time when a sense of order imposed itself on these inchoate energies and shaped them into a working and pro- ductive world."

Where *had* he learned his history? "I've never heard it put better," I cooed, dropping my hand into Sage's lap. He wore bulky corduroy trousers. I massaged his crotch. Sage stretched out on the sofa. Cohn, McCarthy and Schine, in their miniature forms, came to the pane closest to us and pressed their hands and faces against the glass, eager to watch the show. *Aren't we all voyeurs?* How many were watching us on the screens?

"So many think so many funny things about me. I never bother correcting them. I enjoy the confusion." Sage seemed completely relaxed.

159

Little did he know *I* had his number and that he would be under my total control in a New York minute. I slowly unzipped his trousers and reached into his fly. He wore cotton boxer shorts and my hand dove into them. I reached for his cock and balls. They weren't there. I felt around on both sides, up and down. No cock. No balls. No nothing. Just smooth, seamless skin all over the groin. I reached in even further—in for a penny, in for a pound—back to the buttocks. Did he have an asshole?

I was a sight, at least for those viewing it all on the screens. Bent over with my arm deep in his pants. Had I lost my art of seduction? Or was there nothing here to seduce? I looked up at his face. Sage was amused.

"If you are searching for my bunghole, my friend, you are searching in vain."

I withdrew my arm. "You must be a god or a freak!"

"Perhaps both!" He zipped up his fly. "But thanks for trying. It makes me feel wanted." He sat up very properly on the sofa and asked me to get him a glass of water, which I did.

"And now comes my confession, if you can bear it. Even though I *appear* to be on opposing sides of the little battles we like to wage in Ethers-Ville, I am very much on your side. It's just that I have so much more power than you, Bunny. But, truth be told, I'm bored with it. No, not quite King Lear yet, but sort of on that trajectory. I actually enjoy your rambunctiousness and your scheming. I find it wholesome and refreshing. It clears the air a bit and adds some excitement to what is, let's face it, literally a dead world. This is what I was hoping when I brought you over."

"Just as you personally brought Capote over," I pouted. "Clearly either perverse or promiscuous."

Sage scowled. "At least give me the benefit of the doubt. I like to provide talent with opportunity."

"You sound like a Hollywood agent but at least without the obligatory sex to get the audition."

"Look, I've been around this crowd for a long time. Most are airheads, solipsists, little stuck-on-themselves figurines busy in their stuffy agendas. I was the originating and remain the continuing force in this space we thrive in. Yet I have no eternal commitment to it. When the critical mass arrived, I just went on automatic pilot. The bloom was off the rose, so to speak. The willfulness and the ambitions of the others sapped my energies and made a mess of my schedule. I have never had children, much less had to raise any, but let's just say it was a learning experience. *Don't the members of your race ever grow up?*"

Sage looked at me, expecting a response. I was silent.

"I started distancing myself from all the day-to-day lifting, pursuing my own amusements. You and Twain, and Voltaire, also our lovely Marie, like to meddle in the times and places you came from, though I still do not know whence Marie came. But she's part of the cast now, and that's that. But I never came from there. So I meddle here. This creation is my world. Which is why you are present here right now. A whim to my fancy."

"Well, thanks for picking me. You have good taste." I smiled. "Even though you haven't any genitals or an asshole, and since I'm not in the mood to get blown by you, and I won't ask, I'd still like to invite you to see my very own private black room."

Sage grinned. "I adore you modern degenerates. Keeping up the tradition of the dark caves, magic rooms and whatnot. That's the problem with poor de Sade. He trivialized the rituals of sexual groveling and brutality by moving his grubby floggings into the most bourgeois setting of all, bedrooms and drawing rooms. It's one thing to merely abandon the gods, something more severe to deflate the rituals of sex and humiliation in their proper contexts."

"Then, please come with me." I took Sage by the hand and we walked to the rear of my house and descended the back stairs to the basement. *This* was my black room.

We entered.

In the moody, hesitant lighting, the room seemed endless. Tiny flecks of light twinkled on the periphery, like a planetarium. Sage was impressed. I showed him around. Pointed out the mats, the cushions, the restraints, the racks of sex devices and small bottles of stimulants.

"A pleasure dome for the sensate." He was in awe.

"I try." I grinned.

"I realize that we're not going to have any sexual encounter," Sage said, "but surely there must be something here I could experience."

I crossed my arms and drummed my fingers against my cheek as I looked about. My plan was working like a charm.

"Well, yes, as a matter of fact, there *is* something. This brand-new sound wave I've just installed. It washes the body with low-frequency sound waves and tingles the flesh. Sort of a high-tech foreplay device."

"Let's do it!" Sage beamed, the fool.

"OK. Just stand over there." I positioned Sage in the center of the room. I walked back to the entranceway and waved a hand over a just audibly humming box. There was a huge surge of energy and Sage suddenly rose two feet into the air. His arm splayed out from his body and his legs formed a modest arc. He hung there, in mid-air, unable to move. I walked over to him.

"How's it feel, big boy?"

"It's an odd but not unpleasant sensation," he said. "But, even already, rather boring."

"You look nice. Sort of an electro-magnetic crucifixion."

"Perhaps. But thrills have such short half lives. Time to bring me down and we'll try something else."

"Wrong, my friend. You're going to stay there for awhile."

"I can end this any time I want. Be gracious enough to let me out of this force field."

"If you're so omnipotent, do it yourself. I'd love to watch." I put my hands on my hips and waited.

Though making no visible signs of resistance, I knew Sage was trying every trick in his bag to undo my spell. Nothing worked, as I was certain would be the case.

"Give it up, darling," I advised. "Take my good word on this. I've finally got you, like a poor bug in my invisible spider's web."

"But this is not possible!" Sage protested.

"Not only possible, *but a fact!*" I smirked, satisfied.

"But how did you figure it out?"

"Simple. I assumed that Capote was partly correct. You either are the force for linear positivism or you pretend to be. Your actions and your confessions only reinforced my analysis. This room, which I created exclusively to be your trap, is a concentration of critical theoretical forces, prismed through a deconstructivist focus. It is the warring tensions of everything operative in history, which I and my friends seek to exploit, the clash of tastes, fashions, egos, ambitions, interpretations, givens and excluded, among which your singular vision literally can't move. Which is why you are now trapped, suspended, in this jumble of conflicts and contradictions. One which, given your narrow perspicacity, you cheerfully walked right into. I'm only a smidgen sorry to have to do this to you, Sage, but let this be a cautionary tale. Not only of the limits of your power, which I don't necessarily abhor, but of the source of your construction, the fundament of your assembled choices. Yours seems to be the will and the ideology of the successful middle-level entrepreneur."

"That very well may be true," he sounded a bit panicky. "But do you intend to just leave me here...*dangling?*"

"You are in no pain."

"I am not, as it happens. But I find it a terrible inconvenience."

I laughed. "You are displaying the mentality of a TV sit-com producer."

"I don't know any from among them, thank you. Still," Sage pouted, "it's unfair."

"*That* I'll give you. Though I will note your sudden interest in equity as a heavenly desideratum. I will return to this black room after some necessary changes have been made. In the meantime I won't leave you here without any distraction. Boredom is not a torment I would wish on anyone."

I held my arm up about two feet from his face and drew down a screen in mid-air.

"This is so you can watch and keep up on the neat and rapid changes about to take place." I gave him a nice little pat on his asshole-free butt. "By dinnertime, it will be a changed skein of worlds."

Sage sighed. I walked to the door.

"Bunny," he called, "if you disappoint me, I will hate you forever and be cruel to you in ways you've never imagined could happen."

"You're on!" I gave the thumbs up sign. "And, meantime, Happy Trails!"

I ankled the black room, went up the stairs and found Twain in my living room, watching the scene just transpired on my TV screen as he pitched bits of burnt toast to the McCarthy trio.

"Such fancy talk from a country boy from Ohio." Twain winked at me.

"I'm a country boy from Ohio *only* when useful," I twinkled.

The TV went off at Twain's command. Voltaire joined us from my library carrying a bunch of old Sears catalogues.

"We're home free. I've just set it up perfectly."

"Oh, really?" He sat next to Twain.

"Yes. I've put Sage out of commission for a bit, and with him out of the way, let's wrap up our plans and settle history to our liking once and for all, set it in concrete and then move on to newer and more adventurous things, perhaps throwing in just a dollop of critical theory for the fun of it."

Voltaire looked at me. "Critical theory and concrete don't mix as metaphor *or* as a strategy."

"You know exactly what I mean!" I was sharp. What were these two lugs doing to reshape history anyway? I had no impulse to get angry with them. They *were* the best of the bunch. Still, I did expect a little more enthusiasm from these dead activists. I was reluctant to try to do it all on my own.

"I'm just fascinated looking at all these old catalogues," Voltaire said, leafing through the top one. "How quickly, in the so-called modern world, everything changes. And how ugly it all is. *Didn't anyone notice? Or care?*" He held open a two-page spread from a 1950s catalogue. It showed faux-families wearing the retailer's latest offerings. "Imagine going to a party where everyone is *dressed like that.*" He laughed. "It's shocking when you take the long view, to which I am inclined. I went to the Screening Room downtown and watched these old Pathé news reels. And then the various signal events of the age, called Feature Presentations. It makes me dizzy trying to figure out how the population puts up with all this stuff. You'd think it all would drive them even crazier."

"Don't be a fool, Voltaire." I cautioned. "It seems like forever when you have to live through things. *Even* when you're old. That's why documentaries are so appealing. They telescope just the highlights. The most enjoyable media can successfully skim anything. Have you ever seen that wonderful production of the twenty-five minute *Parsifal*? An exquisite diversion. As to the quotidian of existence, it's something else all together."

"Happily the quotidian of existence is something I never need bother myself with again." Voltaire was crisp.

So there we sat. Voltaire flipping through old Sears catalogues, making notes in the margins, Twain engrossed in a picture book on the film career of Miss G. Garbo. *I*, on the other hand, was full of energy. I rose and left the room without their noticing. I would do this patrol unescorted, my mission.

First stop: Boston, 1903. Mother Eddy, still loose in the land, was quickly arrested again, tried, convicted and sent up the river. The church's entire property was seized and put up for auction. I bought it and in 1917 gave the entire portfolio to Margaret Sanger. She immediately opened the first mammoth Complete Women's Health Care Facility in the United States. It was endowed in perpetuity with the assets from the sale of Mother Eddy's other vast holdings. The Sanger facility sent shock waves through Catholic Boston but I never doubted Sanger's capacity to hold on to it and make it grow. Margaret was always a safe bet. And Boston officialdom had always proved itself to be eminently agreeable to a piece of the action. I told Margaret, before departing, that even the Cardinal could be taken care for no more than twenty dollars a week. Sanger thought it vulgar but *practical*. In a few days, I planned to drop in on Dorothy Day; I think she'd get the picture in a glance.

Then *on to Chicago*. This time I visited the gum factory and poured bags of cyanide into the batter. Thousands might die, in their lust to smack gum, but chewing gum would be quickly flung onto the dust heap of consumer products.

It was a short hop to the western frontier. A caravan of Conestoga wagons struggled, bit by bit, towards the Utah Territory. A pick-up band of mercenaries, hired and trained by yours truly, appeared out of nowhere and suddenly attacked. They had been well paid—OK, I admit, I skimmed a few thou from Mother Eddy's pot to underwrite this gig—and the gang was ordered to carry out their instructions to the letter. They did. Their assault was a complete success. The massacre was brutal—is there any other kind?—complete and to this day remains a puzzle to historians. The legacy of Mr. Joe Smith had now been reduced to a mere clip in the time line of freakish superstitions.

After all this excitement, it was time for a break. I went to Paris. It was 1794. Apparently the prohibition on our visiting the century some wanted proscribed had passed its sell-through date. There I was, in a city that seemed pure serenity. Summer breezes teased the town and the citizens seemed to be in a buoyant mood.

I walked to the offices where I would find the various ministries. I walked up the stairs, looked at the directory and continued on until I found Marie behind her desk. She looked every bit the Cultural Minister of the Republic. She looked up at me and smiled. She was busy with a pile of paperwork; she looked tired. Revolutions are not good for the aging process, even for those who survive them.

We embraced. There were charts tacked to every wall, flow charts, that sort of thing. What were the pay scales in the First Republic? I did notice a typewriter sitting on a corner of her vast desk. This was good news. Marie had somehow, and I wasn't about to ask, broken the rule about transporting technology from one age to another.

"It's the little things I still find shocking," Marie told me, as we went to sit on a divan on the other side of her office. "No one in Republican Paris can figure out to file things properly. I'm determined to revolutionize printing. It will speed up the process of governing. Think what offset printing will do for the cause! And since we've now decimalized everything, it's now urgent we streamline the perception of time itself, decades before the population learns to gauge its activities by train schedules. *This* political revolution will succeed by *precision* as much as by battle."

"Speaking of which, *how goes the battle*?"

"The Turks keep the Austrians busy. The Prussians like our money enough to keep out of the wars. And those terrible fires that swept through the English Navy late last year"—Marie gave me a big wink— "have proved to be a crippling blow. All we get from that nasty island is the breeze from their fustian. I got a report that Edmund Burke choked to death in Parliament, presumably on his own vomit. Makes you wonder: should apoplectics serve in government?" Marie was aglow with her triumphs.

"And what of Dr. Guillotine's knife and string gizmo?" I was curious, as this was a major plot point in Marie's scenario.

"It's been touchy. The Committee on Public Safety has been packed through Diderot's doing. You know, Bunny, he has turned out to be just a masterful manipulator and administrator. He's wildly popular throughout the country. I'm introducing a select few from among the modern public relations techniques to enhance his effectiveness. Direct mail updates. Literature drops. Appeals to the populace. Without the threat of war, the Assembly has settled down to handling your basic legislation. The Jacobins are still full of bluster but they are, ultimately, politicians. They've gotten with the program, but it wasn't easy. Please notice my hair has turned grey in this effort. The Treasury is in fairly good shape, thanks to the sale of the royal properties and all the church holdings. They went rather quickly; odd, some of the English were the first and most ferocious bidders. I must admit I was a bit startled by how much property the church owned."

"The cult of superstition can be faulted for many things, Marie," I replied, "but failed greed is not one of them."

Marie continued right on, ignoring me. "The guillotine, used briefly in Lyons, was quickly removed by order of the Assembly after a stormy debate. And no whiff of its reappearance. Some émigrés, now certain they won't be decapitated, are trickling back, giving less base for foreign agitation. There are border raids and things like that but nothing to shock the nation or make people lose confidence. Furthermore, I'm pleased to report, I'm revamping and reenergizing the arts. So, if you are taking back a status report to Sage and the gang, everything's looking peachy keen."

I smiled and gave a slight nod. "But one question, my dear. Can you get through this revolution without any trace of the Terror?"

"It's just been a hellish struggle. Every time I propose something, some jerk tosses out a speed bump. Turns out I win most of the battles. People who have avoided me now fill my appointment book. Polite inquires from old adversaries. All quite delightful. Diderot told me they find me novel, something completely new. The French like that."

"Absolutely true, Marie, and my doing, completely, I'm pleased to inform you. But I will spare you the gory details."

"I've never been so satisfied with any undertaking in my entire life."

I stared at Marie. *Who was this woman?* What was her past? She reminded me of a regional shoe rep who had made his quarterly quota. I liked Marie but her vision, through her work, had become pedestrian. It was no longer a great bold, wonderful and tragic opera. She was Gower Champion making it into a box-office musical *with a message*. She was transforming the French Revolution into something you could take home to Mother, book onto a panel discussion where panelists agree to disagree. It was beginning to reek of "acceptable role model." She had spared history The Terror. What was left?

"What of Napoleon?" I asked. "Will he still barge into the spotlight?"

"I'm keeping my eye on him and that whole Corsican Mafia. Needless to say, I am not sympathetic. He's a vile opportunist. We've got him doing some boring garrison duty down in Burgundy and there he will stay, as long as *I* have any influence."

"But, Marie, you must advance him into the government. The general must lead the French forces to Moscow! I have it all planned. The best of the French Revolution must be used as a battering ram to smash decadent feudalism."

Marie suddenly stiffened and became tetchy. "Bunny, you are a dreamer." She smiled, but it was a cold and unfriendly smile. "The very success of the French Revolution will be its best advance. Change will seep into other cultures. It will not have to be forced."

Having just slaughtered the proto-Mormons, I was not persuaded by Marie's cheerful progressive inevitability. I could never forget that Marie was clearly the protégé of Sage, perhaps his distaff alter ego— *but was Sage even male?* Was I up for yet another confrontation? At least I had one thing working in my favor. I was a freelancer. Marie was wedded to her singular event.

"Marie, darling, I would hate to go head-to-head with you in this French matter, but it appears to me you have misplaced your urgencies."

She cackled. Her voice became that of a harpy, sound waves that scratched across the cortex. Perhaps she was just tired.

"Whatever you're thinking," she shrilled, "don't waste your time." She leaned towards me and became decidedly nasty. "This is my turf and I'm pretty well-protected. No one here in France *or* from our realm can touch me. I'm under sail all on my own."

*Was she right?* Would a constitutional Republic in France just lumber on? I had my doubts, the French being the French.

"It was I who personally recommended to Diderot that he remove the royals to New York City. They'll love it. The way I have it scheduled, they'll wind up buying an estate up in Connecticut, next to Paine. The stain of regicide is something no social movement can wash away." Marie winked at me.

"You'd be the perfect cleaning lady for Madame Macbeth."

Marie sniffed. "Fine. Make jokes. History is nothing but one-liners for you anyway. I should remind you: I am in the trenches, actually doing something positive. You can gallivant around blowing things up, poisoning people, killing the religious. I keep tabs on your exploits on my screen, which I should note, and somewhat resent, is smaller than the ones I was used to in our paradise. Why did you come to pester me? Why don't you run off to Dealy Plaza and settle that mess? That's more to your tastes." Marie was huffing and puffing by this point. Could she get her meds crossed over to the 1790s? Why not three weeks at a fashionable spa?

"Not to worry, Marie. Dallas is near the top of my list. But meanwhile I'm concerned that you just may fuck up here in Paris. For example, you fail historical progress and the requisites of theatrical necessity by denying history the execution of Louis and his bride."

"This is my gig, fool!" Marie banged a fist on her desk. "*And I don't need any buttinskis!* So get out of my face and beat it!"

I rose and left in silence, only partially pleased with the outcome of my visit. I thought I might just rush right out and partake of just a tiny dabble, my thank-you to Marie, but I decided against it. One thing I was learning: not to dabble in another's obsession. It was a no-win game. Poor Marie had forgotten the fun of it all. She was consumed by one single narrative, something I made sure was not my fate.

I returned to the domicile of the dead writers, our palmy Parnassus. I arrived in the midst of what appeared to be some sort of demonstration. I was in a public square, cute little brickwork in front of a vast beaux arts building, as my colleagues milled about carrying placards. I wandered through the crowd. It all had a familiar odor to it. The women in granny dresses and wire-frame glasses, the men in jeans and plaid work shirts with a variety of stickers on their attire.

I ran into Twain, standing grandly in his white suit and hat, puffing on a cigar, a cagy look in his eyes. Voltaire was a few feet away, had his peacock feathers up and was cruising outrageously.

"Voltaire tells me," Twain was blasé, "that any man can be made. I told him I didn't believe it."

"It's not something to doubt, really." I was a pedant, of the Kinsey School. "It's more the matter of opportunity than willingness. And public demonstrations, for reasons still not understood, work wonders on the libido."

We both looked at Voltaire who was engaged in bright talk with some young Trotsky look-a-like.

"So what gives?" I asked. "What's the demo?"

Twain sighed. "Well, dear friend, with you away on your peregrinations, much has transpired in this realm, as usually happens. This is surely not the quiet grave that was promised. Your chum, Frank O'Hara, back in your real time, was named Poet Laureate of these United States, a position they created just for him. Was that your doing, by the way? Anyway, he thanked both of us *by name* in a speech before a combined session of *both* houses of the Congress. But no one picked it up. Politicians think poets are crazy anyway, failing to appreciate what both professions have in common, the manipulation of words. And then, with your swift move on Sage, our fellow denizens are having a merry old time. William Dean Howells, another country boy from Ohio, formed this committee and called for a demonstration to protest the lack of commitment on our part for fighting historical injustice. I like Howells, who got me on the committee. The rest are big yawns. I'm always shocked with true old news: there's lots of bad writing out there."

"But Twain," I replied, feeling heady, "this is the event of the season!"

I scanned the crowd. It was Celebrity City. I saw Isadora Duncan, looking tall and willowy. Next to her was Anaïs Nin, moving in on the number Voltaire was ensnaring. I stared at this object of desire and suddenly recognized him as Richard Fariña. He was wearing gobs of makeup which, on inspection, altered the impact of the Trotsky drag. Oh well, each to his or her own.

"Who's speaking now?" I asked Twain.

"Robert Ingersoll. Milton came just before him. Just these gasbags. They seem to know nothing about the tricks of public speaking. They just spout."

Ingersoll roared over the sound system. "And many of us here have done nothing more than be hedonists. When you truly understand that our obligations and imaginations summon us to public action and that our combined power is mind-boggling—"

The applause rippled through the crowd. I saw Capote, chatting away, clapping politely. Capote wore a long angora scarf, trailing to his knees.

"Our ranks seem to be somewhat supplemented," I noted.

"Yes, all too true." Twain sighed and looked at me. "In your absence, the floodgates have opened. The Elysian Fields have been depopulated and they all washed up here. Puts a bit of a crunch on the housing situation. There was one proposal before the Howells Commission that we formally merge with the Elysian Fields and enfranchise them all. Perhaps you shouldn't have put Sage on that suspension rack. I think that was the triggering event."

"Wilde came over?" I asked, excitedly.

"One of the first through the gates. With slave girls throwing rose petals before him."

"*Where is he*?" I was giddy at the thought of a new co-conspirator.

"He's over there, somewhere," Twain waved vaguely. "Holding his own little court."

I rubbed my brow, trying to adjust to the changes that had been made. "So all the barriers are now down?"

"Are you kidding? It's open admissions. Die and come to the heaven of heavens. The good sign is that this demonstration is happening. Yet who knows what comes next?"

"And now," bellowed Ingersoll, "I think it's high time I brought to this podium the one person, and I say this in complete accuracy that he is *still* a person, the fellow many of us owe so much to for this exciting moment of our liberation. Friends, I present *Bunny LaRue!*"

Twain gave me a little punch on the arm. "Your turn."

I seized the moment. Through the applause I heard a fair number of catcalls and hisses. I ignored them, though secretly pleased by the antagonism.

I climbed the steps and strode to the speaker's stand. Ingersoll shook my hand, though it was a spectral feeling, and creepy. I took the microphone. The plaza splayed out before me, the crowd filling nearly every inch. Clearly, no personage was off meddling today; every and all wanted to be in the moment, to see and be seen.

"My dear friends," my voice was a rich baritone and cold. "I've just come from the French Revolution. Our beloved Marie, as many of you must know from watching your screens, has enacted an amazing change, and has just about everything under control. She has recreated the Revolution—so far!—*without The Terror*. And no guillotines!"

The cheers arose. It was an easy crowd.

"But Marie's example is not enough. Many of you are new arrivals and I salute you and welcome you to this land of ultimate opportunity, where only imagination and ambition are our guides. And I would particularly like to welcome the arrival of brother Oscar Wilde. He's right over there!" I pointed him out in the crowd. More enthusiastic applause. Wilde waved a pudgy hand and gave a slight bow. "Though I am a relative newcomer here myself, it is clear that the yoke of inaction has weighed heavy on our community. This situation is now abolished!" More applause. "And to good cause. Now I propose, *let us do something together!*"

With a wave of my hand, I transported the entire milling throng to Dealy Plaza that Friday morning in late November, 1963. We schmoozed in with the Dallas crowd—if they only knew!—and were all nicely dressed, except for Dicky Fariña whose face was still slathered with make-up. We waited to get a glimpse of the royal couple as they cruised past. Each of us held a mirror; each mirror was sized at two feet by two feet. I ran around the crowd, instructing how to catch the sun, which was just then breaking through the clouds, and blind potential assassins in their various lairs.

Voltaire, Twain and I had our mirrors trained on the grassy knoll. We were in luck. The angle of the light was perfect and the combined reflected sunlight could do nothing less than bleach the retinas of anyone lingering on the knoll.

The motorcade sped through, the occupants waving and smiling. Our ganglion of mirrors created a dazzling *sparkle* of dancing spots of light, not just on the knoll but on the adjacent buildings as well. Also the overpass. And the other spectators.

Nonetheless, we heard the pop of gunfire. A bullet nicked a bystander. The featured couple didn't even notice. They sped on to the Trade Mart to a cheery reception and a greasy Texas lunch.

I ran into a CBS newsman who looked an awful lot like a young Dan Rather. He cornered me for an interview. He asked about the mirrors. I turned to the camera and explained.

"We are the Texas Festival Of Light and we have practiced months and months to get our 'Salute to The President Mirror Drill Team' just so." I smiled a pretty little smile. He looked at me as though I were just another Texas nut. Then his expression changed and he pushed his earphone more deeply into his head.

"Just one minute," he sputtered. "We're getting reports from all around the country of a strange popping noise."

"Oh, it's nothing," I said, flicking my wrist. "Just the sound of highways, schools and public buildings being *unnamed* for John F. Kennedy." Again, I got the look of being a loony.

Mission accomplished, I transported the entire heavenly herd back to the rally site.

I was back at the microphone. "Now, *wasn't that wonderful?*" I asked of the vast throng.

There was cheering and applause. All seemed to be happy. Group participation builds community.

"And it was something we did together and something that made a difference. Let's keep it up! Two, three, many historical diversions. And make sure we wear it well."

I left the speaker's platform with great dignity. There were hands outstretched to me, slaps on the back—all that soft impact of the dead-alive—and as I walked past what looked like a languid clique centered around Proust, I heard this whisper: "The new Queen of Heaven!" It was a money notice. I stopped, turned sweetly to Proust and said, "Time is *found* once again."

I jogged home. I entered. I was alone and went to check up on Sage. He still floated above the floor, trapped in a web of contradictory impulses which kept him immobile.

I sat in a lounge chair in a corner of the black room and had a cigarette. Just one.

"Just as I feared," Sage said. "And I watched it all."

"*You like?*" I twinkled.

"Only those with a lust for chaos could enjoy this mess. It's just madness out there now."

"Let's not go negative at the top. To begin with, I am not responsible for the wave of immigrants that washed up from the Elysian

Fields. *That* tide just came in."

"Of course, it's *now* your responsibility!"

"What should I do? Just cart them back down into the Fields? Not an easy task. They've tasted the high life."

"You might consider it. I did it with Henry James and Chesterton some time back. Just took them by their coat collars and pitched them below. A quick show trial and then the Big Bounce. But terribly effective. You must understand, Bunny, the Elysian Fields exists for a reason."

"Well, they're all here now. The whole lot. And I think I'll let them stay, until I have my plans worked out. Though it won't be easy."

"Nothing is easy," Sage seemed weary. "I had thought you would have learned that by now."

"I don't fatigue."

"There are other measures of the rigors of things beside fatigue."

"I'm content to see which way things develop."

"Right. OK. So am I." Sage closed his eyes and then slowly reopened them. "It appears that the deed to this joint is in the process of changing. Something not to be ignored or denied. I'm willing right here and now to tell you everything—it's a deep backstory, I should warn you—and then turn over the whole kit-and-kaboodle to you. You can try your hand at running things."

"I'll sleep on it. Then ponder doing things my way."

"As you say." Sage hung in silence while staring at me. "While I was watching you on the screen," he continued, "I detected a severe contradiction in your own existence which you carry on your back, *unresolved.*"

"Who, pray, *likes* a resolved contradiction?" I snapped.

"You seem to resent that Marie is succeeding in remaking the French Revolution into a proto-liberal social-democratic model."

"I just don't think it will wash. It's likely to be washed away by some greater force."

"Ah, *force*! You have this proclivity for these dramatic meddlings, blowing things up, killing people—"

"You keep a short list. I saved Kennedy's life and Frank O'Hara's."

"Noble deeds, revealing a passion for the Irish. But must you opt for violence as the primary action? I know you dislike Marie's and my approach of gradualism, but the hard work over time—"

"You're wrong there. I don't dislike it. In fact, in some situations, it's just the ticket. But, looking out over the horizon, it's a fucking disaster out there and someone has to clean it up. Marie's hard work will prevent Napoleon. The Emperor will not try to take Moscow, and poor Russia will stay stuck in its morass for another century. Which is why, in a few minutes, I will have to make a visit to Lenin at the fabled Finland Station."

Sage smiled and then actually winked at me.

I climbed up the stairs to my living room, where I found a lively cocktail party in progress.

Voltaire, done up as a cheap-looking barmaid—something out of the catalogues, no doubt—rose, champagne flute in hand, offered me another and said, "A toast to our brave Bunny, impresario of our new ages."

We clinked glasses. I looked about the room. I saw Twain, Keynes, Wilde, McAlmon, Victor Chapin, Peter and Mede.

"This bubbly is delicious," I said. "Is it on you or me?"

They laughed. Currency, as in money, never noodged their noggins.

"Something you don't realize, Bunny," McAlmon said, as I sat next to him, "is that your have this aura. Literally. It comes, I suspect, from your being alive, actually generating heat. It's a novelty and gives you some added cachet. And we," he said, with a sweep of one hand, "are just moths to some flame."

In fact, I was feeling rather chilled at the moment and for no discernible reason.

"I *am* a bit concerned," McAlmon continued, sotto voce. "I admired your trashing of the Hemingway Collection at the Kennedy Library, though, amongst our colleagues, this is a minority opinion. But since we all just saved Kennedy's life, I fear things have a new events vector and that the Kennedy Library may sprout once again at another time, giving Hem's posthumous career yet another venue."

"These are the risks," Wilde snorted. "Let's take a look-see." Wilde flicked at the screen and programmed it for the ground-breaking at the Kennedy Presidential Library. The scanner raced through the data. A picture jumped into place. It showed an old John Kennedy, accompanied by his ancient mother and other assorted kin. The voice over noted that the former First Lady, having divorced the former President thirteen years ago, had been invited but declined, preferring to stay with her current spouse, a Sultan, in Brunei.

The Kennedys all stuck their shovels into the soil on the banks of the Charles River and scooped up dirt, to polite applause. The image cut to an artist's rendering of the monumental glass pyramid to be constructed on the site, a see-through edifice to rival some of the lesser pharaohs. The voice over announced that, following the former President's wishes, the Library and Museum would also house the complete Edna Ferber collection."

We all laughed.

"Good for Edna!" It was Keynes. "Denounced Bunny for burning down the Hemingway collection but didn't waste a minute lobbying to get her own papers to replace it. Writers and their artifacts seem to be very moveable feasts."

"You should do something about collecting *your* papers, Oscar," I suggested.

"I've thought of it," he sounded sad. "But after that vicious plundering of my house on Tite Street, I just can't imagine where all my personal effects wound up. So much loveliness grabbed and ripped apart by the vicious. The very thought of it drove me crazy when I was in the clink. I think I'll just let things stay as they are. Always subject to change at a later date, of course."

"By the way," Peter had to break the delicate mood, "this is for you, Bunny." He handed me a folded piece of paper. "I'll spoil the surprise for you," he grinned obscenely. "The indictments have been handed up. You have been indicted for mass murder in Chicago."

An excited "ooooo" went about the room.

"For the chewing gum caper." Peter raised just one eyebrow.

"Well," I sighed, "just one more reason to stay out of Cook County."

"My sentiments exactly," Twain said, exhaling a cloud of cigar smoke. "Drop in on Cook County and *be* cooked."

"Darlings, I hate to schmooze and run," Wilde said, rising, "but I've asked Roland Barthes out on a date. Isn't it mad? But he's so shy, elusive and oblique. So I tackled him straightaway. Look!" Oscar held out a pretty little plastic box. "I've even bought him a corsage." He opened the box and showed it to us. There was a flat, sickly looking orchid pinned to some Styrofoam. "Isn't it heavenly? We're going back to Berlin in nineteen-nineteen, when cocaine was ten cents a deck. We'll get wired out of our minds and pick up some sailors."

"Be careful, Oscar." It was Chapin. Oscar reboxed the orchid and fled.

Mede had on his best Junior League horse-drawn face as he said: "Oscar's gotten so *faggy* in his antiquity."

"Oh, *shut your hole,*" I snapped at him. "Who invited you anyway, you air-headed pretty boy? Be careful, little dove, lest I cover your beautiful skin with pink pustules."

Mede looked worried. He turned to Peter. "Can he really do that to me?"

Peter nodded. Mede sank into the sofa.

I swilled my champagne. "Don't anybody move—fat chance—for I have one more bit of dusting up to do before we can shift into forward gear."

"Where now, Bunny?" Keynes asked.

"A liquidation of no importance." I walked out onto the patio to find a pink brick road before me. I skipped along it for quarter mile or so, ran into a heavy fog and, then, suddenly garbed in a heavy fur coat, entered the Finland Station. It was cold. I pulled down the flaps of my beaver skin hat. I stood on the train station platform, blowing warm breath onto my icy hands. A darkened train slowly pulled up on my platform. There was the engine and three cars. All windows were covered with blacking. Soldiers were stationed up and down the platform but none challenged me. I walked up to a bulky looking type, obviously German intelligence. I flipped him my papers. He let me board the train.

Lenin sat with Krupskaya, both looking impossibly grumpy. I stared at Lenin and reminded myself how intensely I dislike the lean, wiry ambitious type who celebrate the personal affections of the *cheap* poor. I smiled at them and approached. I opened my briefcase and presented my papers.

"Disturbing news, Nickolai," I growled. Why must revolutionaries pose at being so butch? This malady of the all-too-predictable.

I showed the comrade reports of recent developments in Moscow, Berlin and Paris. I kneeled aside his seat. Krupskaya eyed me, then looked away. She needed a set of worry beads. As Lenin scanned the documents, I opened my coat and slid a small bomb beneath the bank of seats.

Lenin flipped through the papers.

"So, you can see, comrades, it is best for the two of you to remain on this train for another few hours, until we can be sure of your safe transit." I gave a comforting look. "I know it has been a long and cold and difficult journey. But it will come to an end. I will arrange that something warm be sent your way."

Lenin leaned over and hugged me. His lady gave me a look that could kill. The railroad car was damp and smelly. I rose to leave, gave Lenin one last look. If nothing else, my handiwork, if successful, would spare him that gelatinous stuffing in odd light in Red Square, such an odd tourist attraction that it ranks among the top indignities of "scientific" morbidity.

I stepped off the train. I walked through the station and waited. There came a sudden explosion. The ground seemed to rise. There was not a chance of surviving this devastation. The Russian Revolution, already in progress, would have to stumble along without the loud-mouth leader of the Bolshies. I hoped Marie, lolling in her decimalized office in Paris, would feel—even, perhaps, enjoy—the shock waves from the future.

I paused to savor my success. Whatever I tried to do always seemed to work. I had no problems with the ethics of the matter. I was on a roll. Let others quibble about my so-called "moral structure." *At least I got things done.* The monsters had to be stopped. And there were so many!

But was I really *that* interested? The way I had selected my targets seemed dull, repetitive and not box-office. How many times would I have to go out to Chicago to poison the gum? Did I really want to become the Cleaning Gal to the garbage heap of history? Perhaps there was another way.

I strolled from the carnage at the Finland Station. Was I sure I knew what I had actually done? I turned to look back. Standing there, I felt a gentle roll of atmosphere as I knew history texts and popular movements and general references were being rearranged. It seemed that the closer my actions got to my actual live time, the more visceral was the sensation of things being reformed. It was the shock that my real-time self complained about on my last visit. He—*I*—was the only creature subject to this awareness of things before, during and after these changes and all the attendant dislocations. Changing history, to my taste, was worth a moment of nausea. On the other hand, *why was Nixon still President?*

I continued on my stroll. I got something in my eye and blinked. When I got the fleck out of my eye, I looked about to find that I was at Muscle Beach in Santa Monica. I sat on a bench. It looked to be the late nineteen-fifties, Capote's favorite time. The boys lumbered about, in tight shorts and even tighter swim trunks, all their flesh oiled. It was the overt and crude kind of exhibitionism so perfect for American culture. The girls lingering about ogled the beefcake and played with their ponytails. *None*, I noticed with a sense of satisfaction, was chewing gum.

An old man sat beside me on the bench. He opened his afternoon paper and began reading it. I glanced at the headlines. President Harold Stassen was moving troops from Canada to support the Belgians in the Congo. Fifty thousand from the military services were being sent in as "advisers." Secretary of War Joseph McCarthy had announced two new detainment camps for violators of the Bomb Shelters In Home Program. The hepatitis epidemic had claimed another twenty thousand.

I couldn't read any more. Something was wrong and getting wronger. I left the bench, cruised the muscle boys for one last voyeuristic thrill and headed home.

The cocktail party was over. McAlmon and Chapin had left. So had Peter and Mede, no loss. Voltaire was peeling off his cheap waitress drag. Twain was scribbling on a legal pad. Keynes was staring out the window.

"Back to Pandora's famous box," Twain said, "whence everything jumps out."

Voltaire shook out his wig and placed it on a wig stand. "Just too dizzy here, Bunny. Perhaps I'll take a vacation. But where can I go for some rest? Is there yet some higher order?"

I didn't want to hear this chatter. I went right downstairs and entered my black room. Sage still hung there, suspended in space. I went over to my magic control box and waved my hands over it in six different directions. Sage slowly descended until his feet hit the floor. A soft lighting came up. He looked no worse for his ordeal.

"I thought," I said, affably, "you'd like a cocktail and some in-depth discussion."

"Delighted." Sage rubbed his arms and shoulders. He put one arm around my waist as we climbed the stairs. We joined Twain, Keynes and Voltaire as they watched a broadcast of some evening news from nowhere. I went to the kitchen, squeezed some fresh orange juice and made a pitcher of lovely screwdrivers. I carried the pitcher out on a tray with smoked glasses as the four of them were chortling away; I served the booze. I came in on a diaper ad.

"They always suggest the piss, never the shit. So much more unpleasant," I editorialized.

"Imagine paying all that money to show a baby pissing on TV," Twain smirked. "The fundaments rule the popular media." He snapped his fingers. The TV screen went dark. Soft rock filled the room.

Twain flipped through his notes. "I'm a keen note-taker and I've been keeping a little list. While you were busy blowing up Lenin, which, by the way, takes top honors in the drama department in the past hour, I thought you might like to know the doings of the others in our busy little colony."

Sage sighed and drank deeply.

"Read me the wire." I was brusque.

"Here we go. Lenin and wife get blown to pieces. Robert Fulton's steam ship falls apart and sinks. Steam-powered transport is abandoned."

"Wait a minute!" I protested. "I thought we couldn't meddle with the progress of technology."

Twain looked at me as though I were a booby. "All bets are off. Garibaldi was made king of Italy. Mad Ludwig has murdered Wagner in a fit of jealous rage. The Duchess of Windsor has demanded she be made Queen and all Britain is in a state. Franklin Roosevelt has been impeached and awaits his Senate trial. John Calvin has sent his agents south and they smashed the David to bits, claiming it was pornographic and a bad role model for the children. Part of his virtuous clean-up campaign."

"Oh, my god!" I snapped.

"Sit tight. There's more. *The Dinah Shore Show* will *not* be cancelled to make way for *Bonanza*. That was Capote's doing. Prohibitionism was reenacted in the United States in nineteen sixty-seven. The northeastern states are considering setting up their own republic. In California, possession of a controlled substance has just been made a capital offence. Seven mainline churches have gone out of business, unable to pay their taxes. Meanwhile, fourteen fundamentalist sects have gotten, through some sort of ruse, government funding for their so-called church schools."

"*What is going on?*" I bellowed.

"Everything, apparently," Keynes was the soul of calm. "All at once."

"I haven't finished my list," Twain protested. "Somebody's been tinkering with Hollywood grosses because after nineteen thirty-nine,

Louis B. Mayer puts the kibosh on his studio doing any more musicals. His catalogue goes for weepies and westerns."

We all sighed heavily.

"In nineteen fifty-three, the World Health Organization mandates circumcision for all member countries of the United Nations. It sets off the most unusual debate in the General Assembly. Marie has gotten the decimal system accepted as standard—"

"That doesn't surprise me at all," I said.

"—including the calendar!" Twain twisted up his mouth.

"The decimal calendar was one of the weirdest things to ever issue from the human brain." I hated to be trapped by tens.

"The twelve and sixty units of the ancient Sumerians is not only familiar but has a certain strength," Voltaire noted. He was still peeling off his outfit, down to garter belts and dress shields. He was skinny and rather sickly looking. Maybe I would start a healthy diet-and-exercise program for the dead writers.

"To continue," Twain said, taking a deep breath, "one of our little angels cooked up a family fight between little Wolfgang Amadeus Mozart and his old man. Wolfgang went to kill himself and jumped into the icy Danube. He was fished out, went into shock, came out of it but with considerable damage to the frontal lobes. He will now write nothing after his twenty-fifth year." Twain looked up at us from his clipboard. "Shall I go on?"

I was disgusted, disappointed and disillusioned. "Haven't these creatures done *anything* to the good?"

Voltaire, now naked, pulled a nylon caftan over his head. "Well, we *do* get to keep *The Dinah Shore Show* instead of those blunder butts of *Bonanza*. That's something."

"That was Ed Sullivan's slot anyway," Keynes reminded us. "But the intent shows promise and may indicate the limit of positivity of our crowd."

"None of you seems to care!" I snapped at them. I needed some Valium. I was being ungracious but felt I had every right to be snippy. This was serious business. Everybody in these heady glades was just running off every which way, changing things willy nilly, ripping and rending the fabric of history, ignoring my fine example, lacking vision. The result? Making human history look even more ridiculous and mean-spirited than when we began.

Sage, who had been listening without demonstrating any reaction, rose from the sofa, took his drink—and I did wonder, how did he pee without a pecker?—and went over to admire my shelves of plants. "Healthy looking avocado. Such vibrant basil. And the mint's divine." Then he turned to me with a scowl. "But, of course, it's all your fault, Bunny. All blame can be laid at your plaster feet. This anarchy bears your imprint and yours alone."

"Easy enough for you to say." I wasn't giving anybody an inch, times being what they were.

"All too easy for me to say, as a matter of fact, since I *was* often a god. And since I did create this special place, and it is really my only creation, and furthermore since it was I who personally selected you and brought you over with hopes and my own plans for the future, this is one time when I feel completely at ease in making a judgment. Clearly, I have made a mistake. I have your full measure now and a track record. Your education was startlingly deficient and your sense of things quite mad. Just look what you have done! My lovely special ambience, the graceful cadences of living we have all enjoyed are now being trampled by the rush of this mob, ground to bits by the clattering juggernaut of petty ambitions being enacted, all loose in the land, under no instructions and guided by no authority. *Is this your vision?* I didn't mind being strung up in your black room. It absolved me of any lingering guilt—something I first picked up being god to the Hebrews and later made double with the Irish—about what has happened to our delicate enclave. As a result, I abdicate everything to you. Bunny, you can now be god of this mess." Sage paused, gently squeezing a mint leaf, then smelling his fingertips. "I am not human and never was. I was invented as a god and I have a little retreat where I can retire, a place where the prayers of the people and the designs of the writers can no longer reach me. As a god, now a former god, I must live defensively. And it is to this little retreat that I will soon retire. For good."

"Can you sing?" Twain asked. "It's a great swan song. We could ring up Wagner, of course before Ludwig kills him, and have him stitch up something in the Faust mode, except from the other side of the deal."

"Arias are not my long suit, dear Twain. If you must use an opera analogy, I prefer the useful recitative, the exposition, the narrative, without the flamboyance of grand passion which always stuck me as phony and cheap. I have seen enough of grand passion and do not hold it in high regard."

"A god abdicates!" Voltaire chuckled, refilling his glass. "A new history lesson. This is where I get interested."

"This is where Sage comes clean," Sage said. "For those with vulture-like curiosities."

"I suspect Sage prefers the reptiles to the mammals," Twain suggested.

"All life forms are equally curious to me," Sage went on. "But the modern humans and their immediate predecessors have a certain distinctiveness. They create for themselves, and I repeat *for themselves*, deities. Whence I came. The god pool."

"So we were correct all along," Keynes said, unwrapping a butterscotch candy and popping it into his mouth.

"As you wish. Everyone's always right until they learn otherwise." Sage sat on the arm of the sofa. "Just settle in because I'm only going to run through this saga once. It's impossible for you to imagine how tiresome this is for me to gloss over. I say this not out of vanity but from sheer exhaustion."

At that moment, Wilde burst into the room, back from his date with Roland Barthes.

"Don't get up. I'm only passing through."

"It must be love," Voltaire teased. "You have that glow."

Wilde struck a pose. "Yes. Roland and I hit it off. I asked him to join us for a brandy. He declined. Thought I was terribly forward. I kissed him on the cheek. Seduction is such an oft-prescribed formula. Whoever holds that patent must be making a fortune."

"Well," I told Wilde, "plop your fanny down," patting a seat on the sofa next to me. "Sage is giving us the low-down about his life as a god." Wilde sank into the cushions and took my hand.

"How exciting! All those mad headdresses and gay sarongs!"

"As a matter of fact, I *do* have a scrapbook, but I only started it somewhat late in the game. It's been a *very* long journey." Sage folded his hands.

"You must start at the very beginning!" Wilde was enthusiastic.

"It was somewhat foggy back then. I just came into existence, with lots of others. Animal gods, planet gods, whatnot. It was like a deranged cattle call for some grand epic. Chaldea, Sumeria, Assyria, Canaan, so many tribes with so many gods. And then a rapid turn over. Just a jumble. Some overlapping. Multiple-use deities. All ensemble playing. Personally, I was happiest in Egypt. It was all so structured. Reasonable. Precise. Easy work. Until Iknaton. For some reason, it was I who got the slot. Suddenly so lonesome. I felt a modernization campaign underway. As you mortals, past and present, know, a certain personality known as Moses came along not too long, in my accounting, after Iknaton and enforced the idea of a single god—nothing is new, my children, *take my word on it*—and then within centuries there was this mania for monotheism. After Iknaton, given my job experience, I was assigned to be god of the Hebrews. It was certainly novel. In quick gestures, I was transformed into this hideous, old, nasty, anti-hedonist deity whom no mortal in his right mind would worship. Yet there I was stuck. There was no review board and each of us had to accept the working conditions. The powers of the believers kept me locked in place. It was not a happy time for me. I envied those gods of the Greeks. I watched in awe and admiration as Olympus came clearly into view. What a zany and fun-loving bunch, with no prejudice against mortals or their normal passions. Needless to say, Olympus gave me many ideas but what could I do? The Greeks, and I want to be delicate about this, were much better writers than the Hebrews. Their gods, and their numbers were in the plural range, frolicked, fought, made love, had boyfriends. *Where was my Ganymede?* Olympus was, for some time, considered *the* primary slot. I could only part my long grey beard, peer at the fun bunch on Olympus and sigh. Time passed. My constituency got dispersed and I felt less constrained by their power. One of their flock, however, had branched out on his own and did a slick update on the mean old god. Claiming to be his son. Sort of early modern public relations. In fact, I was so lonely I would have welcomed anyone. But this *soi-disant* son turned out to be just another bitter pill. Once again, I found myself being transformed. I now had two roles, stern old god of the Hebrews and the family man, single-parent variety, of this new sect. People complain that gods are merciless. How well I know this to be true. Look at my fate! I was glued to this peculiar firmament. The more *they* believed, the less freedom I had. I was their invention after all. The cult of monotheism got grafted. Other prophets sprang up and tacked on their avalanche of prayers. I came to share space with a Virgin and a Spirit, not my first choice of company. Clever writers! Then a gaggle of saints. It came to look like a very unnatural Olympus.

The weirdest of relationships. But since no questions were allowed, I continued to play my role well. Suddenly, there was a slackening off of belief among the devout. It was like a stone slowly lifted off my shoulders. People in the world became more self-involved. I had limited powers, but I encouraged the trend. By the time of the high renaissance in the West, I was feeling a little giddy and liked the way things were going. The sixteenth century in the West, from my point of view, was quite delightful. Is that when they had the Diet of Worms? I can't remember. But things always go in cycles and came the seventeenth century. The writers and fanatics once again got me in harness. There were schisms, new religions, and each new heresy was more devout than the congregation it had left. There hadn't been such a frenzy of religious writing since the fourth century. But back then the scribblers didn't have presses, and The Word or words had a limited market potential. In the seventeenth century, we're talking mass marketing of the superstitions. What could I do? I jumped through the hoops and some of the most horrible crimes were attributed to yours truly. My good name was bandied about by those legions of self-publicists, a species that always seems to be with us. It was a hard time. Subsequently, people of perfectly honest motivations blamed *me* for the nastiness of those who had invented me. When the eighteenth century rolled around—that century which seems to hold such a fascination for so many of you—it created another breathing spell for me. I was allowed to become more distant. The brighter of the mortals found new gods, the laws of physics and whatnot. And good wishes to them was my thought. I took up knitting, was called upon for an occasional miracle. After that nasty earthquake in Lisbon, I thought it was all over. I felt released. Of course, there are those who will always believe. I've decided *they* don't really require a god or a theology. Theirs is the cul-de-sac of faith, the madness of unreason. I had a bit of a fright at the invention of yet another new nation, the United States. I was pleased when its inventors opted for official disinterest in establishing a faith—*can you imagine being god of the Americans?*—though most throughout the new nation seemed obsessed with promoting religiosity in a weird, truncated way as the ideal way of life in the republic. The old religions were not, apparently, to their satisfaction so they invented new ones! I looked on with horror. The mad religious writers tried their darnedest to get me back in harness just as I was looking forward to a peaceful retirement. The mortals, over the millennia, having created me in their various twisted images and for their purposes, for a variety of perverse needs, might have allowed to me some of the grace they said I was famous for in permitting me a suitable disappearance. Happily, the nineteenth century's fetish for gadgets really did free me. That's where Capote had it wrong, Bunny. Poor Truman would hardly know a historical development if one ran him over, but that's why he saw me as the embodiment of historical development or whatever his idiotic idea was. People only needed belief in their own invincibility. I can do that on automatic pilot, a phrase which itself indicates that their deity is no longer self-referential but requires a world of material constructs. After nineteen-eighteen, I'm pretty much home free. There was so little impulse for me. The other gods and goddesses who had been created by the needs of the humans, well, it's sad to report but I have no idea what happened to them. I suspect they ended just as they began. There is no god graveyard; isn't that sad? They just evaporated when no longer needed. Yet, I remained about, some sort of evolutionary trick, to put it in modern terms. I was blessed or cursed by my fortune to just stick around."

Sage stopped for a moment and took a deep breath. He looked tired, an exhausted god who had given his final recap.

"You see, Bunny, everything does connect, a concept more dearly understood when your race was young than now, among you ancient of the species. The longer I was kept afloat as a god for the various tribes of the mortals, the more I became like them. Like an old married couple. Mortals, once I was liberated, became my hobby."

Wilde listened to Sage's rap with attention but looked skeptical. "Fine so far. But you haven't explained your shenanigans since nineteen-eighteen, when you took your open-ended sabbatical."

"I was getting to that," Sage continued, a flicker of interest lighting his face. "Since I hadn't evaporated, I realized I had some room to move around on my own. And with all those years of experience under my belt, I thought I might be of some use. Follow the age—become practical and in the arena I knew best."

"He's going to tell us," Oscar twinkled, "that he went into real estate."

"Very good, Oscar! We should have teamed up earlier. As a matter of fact, and this is a point you will understand, I was concerned about the writers among the mortals. I had been subject, dare I say victim, to their hideous god-invention impulses. Just a terrible curse among some of the quick. All this credo, all this faith, all this devotion. It's just prelude to betrayals, denunciations and slaughters. Take it from me; you can have no higher authority. I am the living proof of their evils."

"So you finally admit you are alive?" Keynes chuckled. "Just being a good lawyer, mind you."

Sage seemed amused. "I am alive, children, even if not mortal. I know, it's hard to understand. And my mission was to do something to control the scribblers. How I was to do this proved to be a difficult decision. The religious seemed to have played themselves out, and none too soon! Their ridiculous wars! And over the most trivial things! How many were murdered deciding the number of angels who could dance on the head of a pin? You could populate a small country. As a matter of fact, before I gave up that sort of thing,

I did a little research. Depending on the climate, and which angels you work with, and of course the pin—I use as my base model the standard Birmingham generic pin—you can get between forty and seventy-two angels on the head of a pin. Now, whether they will all dance or not is another matter. Those who have slaughtered so many over this issue were never in a position to get so many angels to dance. And angels being angels, they are tubby, indolent and are not prone to gyrate. On top of that, some of them had objections to the celestial music, preferring their own type of dance music. It was a thankless effort, just a nightmare. All in the name of some crazed writer's dictum. I hope you can understand why I'm glad to be out of that racket."

"Of course we do," Voltaire was gentle. "But finish your story. Bring us up-to-date."

"Well, it came down to this. I always have blamed the writers for my conditions. For this mess of the mortals. There were other factors, of course. But no one other than the writers could dream up these clarion calls, these righteous fantasies, these great impulses to move the masses based on the authority of their god. I didn't mind when they wanted to move mountains. It's when they wanted to move the heavens. As history demonstrates, a common ambition."

"And *this*," I sighed, waving one hand, designating the realm, "was your revenge on the writers? This holding action?"

"I wasn't sure when I set out," Sage continued. "I thought I'd just give it a try. I brought over a lot of dead writers and they turned out to be rather a lot of fun to play with. The meddling too was fun, up to a point. I encouraged them to cross over and defuse the religious maniacs. After a few spins in that cause, most developed their own narrower interests. If any got too testy or out of control, and some did, I would just ditch them down to the Fields. The Fields has an open admission policy. I became completely involved with this new community I had invented. And in the early days, it was such fun!"

Sage stared at me. His gaze was intent and something I had never seen from him before.

"Then I brought Bunny LaRue over. A live one. I had had some good reports, though a good report is never a complete indicator. Anyway, I thought it a good idea. Why I waited so long I'm not sure, not that time is much a matter to any of us here except, perhaps, to Bunny himself. Having served as gods to some many for so long, I thought I just might try my hand at playing one."

"A thespian at last!" Wilde quipped. "Give that greenhorn a union card!"

I rose from the sofa, closed my eyes and went on a daring journey for what I hoped would be my final effort at reformation.

I opened my eyes. The sun beat down on me. I was wrapped from my shoulders to my knees in a simple white cotton sheaf. I stood in the water, among tall reeds as they gently swayed in the constant current of the Nile River. I heard a cluster of women whispering just slightly downstream. I looked at my nails and passed the time. Soon a little basket drifted into view. I seized it as it floated in front of me. I opened the basket. The child bundled snugly inside gazed up at me with an inchoate curiosity. I paused for a minute. Hadn't I already blown up a library, bombed a train station, poisoned thousands with lethal gum? I pondered the squirming infant. It seemed such an easy thing to do, but … but … there was the future!

Slowly, I submerged the basket with its contents into the ancient Nile. The infant quickly drowned. I raised the basket from the river, let all the water run out of it, resealed it and let it float on its way.

I hastened back to my humble abode in Headys-ville. The bunch were still lingering about, awaiting my return.

I sat next to Sage.

"What have you done now, prodigal?" Twain aped The Fathers.

"I have nothing to say. Only to demonstrate." I made a gesture to Sage.

Sage's eyes suddenly flickered in a mad way, like a person having a seizure. He slid from the sofa as though he were turning into a liquid. Then he sprang forward, as though in a fit. He collapsed onto the floor, on his back. His body rippled with spasms. It was as though he were undergoing some ritualistic exorcism. He hiccoughed, gurgled and spat.

"Shouldn't we dim the lights?" Wilde asked, ever theatrical. He turned off the various wall and ceiling lights, ran to my kitchen and came back with a fistful of candles. Wilde lit them and placed them around Sage who continued his spasms in the flickering flames, his shadow dancing against our legs and feet.

Thirty minutes and it was over. Sage gave one last one death rattle moan and then fell into a repose. His eyes opened. He propped himself up on one elbow, looked about the room, at each one of us individually.

"I must apologize. I don't usually do this. I've made a horrible spectacle of myself in the company of friends." He got up quickly and brushed off his clothes.

"Quite all right, my friend," I said, helping him get back to the sofa. "It should happen all the time. And I think you might like a little brandy."

"We all would!" Keynes announced, getting up and heading for the sidebar. "I'll pour on the condition you give us the lowdown."

"Simple enough," I said, taking a pony of brandy from Keynes and handing it to Sage, then taking one for myself. "It was my last meddle. I drowned the baby Moses, sparing history so much. What we have just witnessed is Sage shedding so many of the incarnations he assumed over the centuries to fulfill the demands of the religious."

"I feel quite light-headed," Sage beamed, sipping his brandy. "Like millennia ago, before the layering got so thick."

"Total success." I gave him a flirty little smile. "Sage wanted to play at being a god, quite understandable, as that seems to be his only skill set. But it's an awful burden. We heard his story. Just heart-wrenching. And he is right. It *is* the fault of the writers, those busy scribblers who love nothing more than mischief. The tormentors of the gods *and* the mortals. I don't deny the gift of writers to make a world, just those who made *that* world, the world or worlds whose gods Sage has just purged."

"What does it mean, Bunny?" Voltaire stood and stretched, looking oddly chastened and a mite fearful, like a barnyard animal minutes before the earthquake.

"I've given it only as much thought as it deserves," I said. "And if I'm right in my instant analysis, we'll know soon enough."

I walked to the sliding glass doors that opened to the veranda and pulled them all the way open.

They all sat silently—Twain, Sage, Wilde, Voltaire and Keynes—while I leaned against one of the glass panels. We seemed half tableaux vivant, half séance awaiting the arrival of Madame Blavatsky. The candles' flames wiggled in the air.

We all knew when the moment had come. *It just happened.* Then we heard the after-effect; it was one simple thud, *but loud.* That was it. No winding down, no deceleration, no slow sinking. Just an unlovely dull clump.

Then all was quiet. *Very quiet.* The candles self-extinguished. The air didn't move. No one moved. No one spoke. It was such a novelty. It couldn't last.

Dorothy Parker was the first to wander in from the patio. Had she been lurking in the shrubs?

"I hope you boys are getting a kick out of this," she barked, helping herself to the brandy. "Because it ain't so funny to me. I was just on my way to have dinner with the Empress Eugénie and suddenly everything stopped."

"Cool your heels, Dottie," I said. "It's all over."

"I thought as much." It was Keynes. "Newton should be here. He'd adore it."

"What do you mean, *it's over*?" Parker was annoyed.

"Just what I said, ducks. Over. Caput. Finie. History as we have known it, and played with it, has completely stopped. You heard it yourself. The plug was pulled and it came to a clean and simple end. We've used it all up. Gobbled it all down. Munched up every moment. It's all still life now. *Nature morte.*"

Sinclair Lewis drifted in next. Followed by Natalie Barney and Jean Cocteau—the real Crisis Alert Crew. It made me wonder who was working the phone trees when it all ended. Others followed. My living room, and then entire house, was filled with a crowd of concerned and angry writers. Even Edna and Fanny drifted in, the Hedda and Louella of our set. The word spread, as did the hostility.

"It can't be over, Bunny," a plainly distraught Maupassant wailed, clutching my arm. Others were sniveling.

"Just when we were getting up to speed, it stops! *Just like that!*" It was either Amy Lowell or Evelyn Waugh; it didn't matter. None of their harping mattered. But I did let them ventilate. The din leaped in decibels, none annoyed by the screeching of the others, all on the theme lamenting that Their Great Plans Had Been Cut Off In Early Stages And What Would They Do Now.

Sage sat coolly as the yakking circled above and about him. A frantic Taylor Caldwell came up to him and made a demand. "Sage! *Do something!* This is *your* world!" Sage did not speak or move. "*Aren't you as upset as we are?"*

"Upset?" Sage's voice was like a fine-toothed saw. "You must be insane. I think it's wonderful. The absolutely best thing Bunny could have done. Why didn't *you* think of it?" Sage nodded at me and blew me a kiss.

"*YOU!!!*" The scream pierced the room. Everyone went silent, something I had not thought possible. It was Marie, hands on hips, full of rage. She was a mess and looked like a maniac; perhaps Marat was sharing his beauty tips. "What a rotten trick you've pulled this time. I demand you undo it immediately and make things just as they were before! *AND NOW!!!*" If looks could kill, I'd have been dead, but given the context, it wouldn't have mattered all that much.

"Marie, darling," I cooed, "you look like you've just snatched the grand prize in the Medusa Look-A-Like contest. As to your demand, there is no going back. It's all over. You look like you could use a drink."

"I'd just throw it in your face!" Marie was not amused. She raced across the room, pushing aside those in her way, and started pummeling my chest.

"Get him good, Marie!" went up the cheer. I expected her blows to be cotton taps but Marie's fists fell hard and I flinched. Such a small thing to transform her into a ruffian.

"You've ruined it! *Just ruined it for me!* Just when I had it near perfection."

I assumed she meant her make-over of the French Revolution. I wasn't unsympathetic but it did occur to me that she *might* have built up a diverse portfolio of interests, dog-breeding, indie filmmaking, *that sort of thing*. It makes a person more well-rounded.

"OK, you've had your outburst," I shouted, gently pushing her away. "So knock it off." She stumbled backwards, tripped on someone's foot and took a tumble. She fell to the floor and looked dazed.

The eyes of scores drilled me in the strange half-light.

"Some day, my son," I heard Sage mumble, "all this will be yours."

I signaled for Twain and Voltaire to join me. They did. Addressing the throng, I said, "We three will survey the ruins. The rest of you please stay here. Relax. Enjoy yourselves. The drinks are on the house. But before you spill too many tears in your beer, let me be the first to console you. Yes, I have ended history. I have taken the living history from you. For good. You can still fly through time and visit the still lifes. But there is now nothing for you to meddle with." There was a collective groan. "I did this for a reason. I wanted to reform as much of it as I thought I could, as did a few others, like lovely Marie here. But the rest of you got into the act and you tinkered in ways that were only playful, that had no vision or utility. And that frittered away the energy we needed to interact with the past. *You used it up.* Every silly dabbling that was not part of a plan depleted the pool of energy. The reservoir went dry. So, even though you blame me for ending history, I was merely the prophet who saw it coming and can now claim it as my own. In fact, it was the silly, stupid and sybaritic among you that pissed it all away, as though you never knew that everything must be paid for by someone. *Now we pay.*" I let that sink in for a minute. "But, in your lamentations for the past now gone, you have failed to see the other part of the story. *I can now promise you a future.* I can say no more."

In the confused silence, Twain, Voltaire and I quickly departed.

Our first stop was London. It looked mid-nineteenth century, dark, divided and full of dirt. Everything and everyone was immobile. It was like walking through a 3-D canvas. We strolled along the Thames. Though full of rubbish, the water didn't move. I peeked in some of the carriages carrying the rich. They smelled bad and their teeth weren't in very good shape. We continued on.

"*There!*" I said, pointing at Big Ben. "One reason the energy was used up. Someone went and put a Mickey Mouse digital clock on Big Ben. The technology tampering border clearly disappeared."

"I smell the work of Orton," Twain chuckled.

Next stop was Versailles. The Sun King was frozen in mid-stride in a garden, surrounded by a scrum of lords and ladies, equally immobile. The grand fountain was circled by pink plastic flamingos. It was like a twisted postcard from the 1960s.

Next we dropped in on the Bach freehold. It was filled with stop-action children and old JS scribbling away or, to be accurate, stopped at midpoint while scribbling in the family notebooks. I wandered around the house while Twain and Voltaire flipped through manuscripts. It dawned on me why Bach so liked *volume* in so many of his compositions; with a family that size, only big noise could be heard over the din.

I rejoined Voltaire and Twain who had sour looks.

"What is it?" I asked, gazing down at the work old man Bach was never to finish.

"A twelve-tone ode to Saint Joan," Voltaire sniffed. "*Not* in the catalogue and never intended to be."

"Severe tinkering," was Twain's judgment.

"Blitzstein?" I asked. "Or Adorno?"

"Probably Oscar Levant," Voltaire opined.

We whisked on to Athens. It was frozen during a theatre contest sometime in the fourth century before what used to be called the Common Era. *But aren't all eras rather common?* The amphitheatre was packed with emotive, unmoving bodies. The stilled actors were wearing large, bizarre masks and intricate headdresses. Few things seem to change in the world of footlights and greasepaint. We climbed into the guts of the Parthenon. It was painted in the oddest colors, lime green, yolk yellow and minty mist. The frieze was stained to look like carved woodwork. The monument had been made over by someone to look like an ancient version of some strip mall one-stop, an outlet for all things tacky. Our little band had certainly been busy.

One more stop was Paris, France, in the 1950s. We wanted to see the skeleton of Corb's mile-high building, never to be finished. Standing there like a sore finger, it had nothing to do with anything and would stay just that in perpetuity.

The three of us drifted into a bistro and liberated a bottle of wine, a corkscrew and three glasses. I pulled the cork, filled the glasses and we continued on our way. A Paris where nothing moved. Where each moment of its history was a page for us to flip, if we wanted.

Voltaire stole a city map from a kiosk as we passed. He unfolded it. He smiled. "The quai Voltaire is no longer there but the Centre de Voltaire seems to be the main exchange, even if largely a English concept. But I am an internationalist and never complain. Do I have Marie to thank for this?" He scanned the map. "But where is Lafayette? Poor creature seems to be gone from the geography. Military men are necessary, but so dull, no? And here's a monument I don't know. The Diderot Obelisk. We must go see it."

We walked for miles—this new world would be hoofing, no cabs or subways now—until we came across this strange construct. It wasn't so much an obelisk as it was a ziggurat. And an oddly asymmetrical one, staircasing unevenly on both sides. It had angled windows in random places. Could it have been done by Gaudí?

We entered the building through an aluminum and chrome archway. The interior of the building was completely empty, except for a huge silver pendulum that swung from a point at the acme of the interior over the floor that was done up as a map of France.

*The pendulum was still swinging!*

We watched it glide back and forth, in regular fashion, across the blue, pink and yellow tiles that depicted the regions of France.

"Well," I said, sternly, "this is a disturbing event. Something still moves."

"Don't be hasty," Twain seemed sly. "We just may need this. A little energy to respark when we choose."

"A kinetic Prometheus!" Voltaire announced.

"With the condition my liver's in, I'm loath to risk it," I twinkled. I was tempted to give the pendulum a little extra shove, but refrained. My meddling days were at an end.

Our tour was over. We had finished the bottle of wine.

"Come with me, fellahs," I said, with a toss of my head.

We were up and away, landing on a mountain in Bolinas. We three sat in the lotus position. The ocean filled the horizon. The sun dangled just above the ocean's edge like a glob of pop maquillage. We sat silently, in meditation, as the sun was absorbed by the Pacific Ocean. As the glimmering rays bounced off the pink clouds, a tear rolled from the corner of one of my eyes. Then another. And yet another. I made the appropriate noises. Twain and Voltaire looked at me with, I suspected, some admiration.

"Bunny," Voltaire whispered when the light was completely gone, "I do believe those are *real* tears."

I brushed the tears away on my sleeve. "You're right, Frank, real tears. At the moment I am a Niagara of sentiment. History, or at least *this* history, is like the film version of *A Streetcar Named Desire*, a one-hankie flick. And now it's truly over and the sun has set on it once and for all. We have taken this pause to share in our moment of achievement."

"Baby," Twain snorted then spat, "this thing is now completely your gig."

"I'm getting a chill." Voltaire got up. "And I would like to know where we go from here."

"Back to this," I said, pulling down a viewing screen in front of us. The scene was still full of the lot of dead writers, yakking away, making quick work of emptying my wine cellar. I kept the volume down. One group in the corner was doing The Twist. Others watched my screen at home, changing from image to image as all history was now nothing but pretty pictures. "I promised them a future, remember? Well, *now I have to deliver.*"

"This should be fun," Twain smirked. "Any ideas?"

"First of all, I think there must be a sense of the occasion. In the beginning, there was darkness."

"As there is every night," Voltaire was bland. "Let's not get too grand and make the same mistakes all over again."

I thought him sour and lacking my sense of fun, but I ignored it. "I think we should begin by setting up task forces and getting everything mapped out before we get the population involved."

"You're so modern." Twain didn't appear to be enthusiastic.

"Give me time. After I debut the future, you'll rave."

"Can I get a sweater?" Voltaire was shaking in the night breeze. He looked ill and terribly fragile. It might have been part of his act.

"We're going right back."

In a pop of my fingers, we found ourselves back in my living room. It was thick with cigarette smoke and sour attitudes. I saw someone in a tatty fox-fur stole, with the poor critter's mouth snapping its tail. I felt like a drop-in on some fifties Leslie Caron movie—the GP orgy scene. It didn't matter. I had to establish my presence very quickly.

"Where's Sage?" I asked Wilde as he glided past, carrying drinks.

"The bum slinked out without so much as a by-your-leave."

"But *to where?*"

Wilde shrugged and went on.

I stepped on the marble coffee table—it was liver shaped and black and white—and I clapped my hands. I let my famous piercing gaze machine-gun the room. Silence fell over the lot. Those who couldn't keep quiet coughed.

"OK, folks, now here's the deal. I hate being the master of the obvious, but we're all in this together." I paused. No dissent. "You've seen the video survey. Stillness reigns everywhere. Except here. Human civilizations are at an end. Even as I speak, the very traces of them recede to the origins of the beginning of light. A real chance to attempt, on a completely clean slate, what all those tired clichés, some written time and again by some of you in this room, promised. No, not just a new America, though that might be fun, but an entirely new human culture. Begun by us. As I am the only living person among this lot, I will be in charge."

I heard the catty remark behind me: "Hope it doesn't turn out like *Animal Farm.*"

"Our first task is to organize. I have designated Voltaire and Twain to be my VPs in charge of operations. Twain will be doing a comprehensive census to get an exact count of our numbers, our preferences, our directions and so forth. Voltaire heads the R&D wing. I've got my own outline of what should happen but I will wait for the committee reports. I have one warning and it is serious. It's about what *won't* be tolerated. No hack work. No clap-trap. No tired formulas from past successes. No meretricious pandering. No party-liners. No celebration of the dull and listless. You've got to be on your toes and in top form all the time. Our experiment will be nothing if not exquisite.

We're going to have a lot of fun and it's going to be better this time around, as much fun as you can get out of a bunch of dead writers."

A figure in a tight skirt and silk blouse came forward. Her hair was cut short and her bangs seemed stuck on her forehead. She was madly puffing on a cigarette. I was hoping it was Bette Davis. It was Ayn Rand.

"I for one don't think I'm going to enjoy this exercise of building a new society on your guidelines. It sounds far too cooperativist. I preferred meddling in the old one. I had lots of scores to settle. This new project offers me nothing but committee assignments and dull meetings." She took one long drag on her cigarette, swept the crowd with her hard gaze, did a little pirouette and then—POYT!—*she was gone.* Just a quick pop and then, *nothing.* Most odd.

Others stared in wonder at the spot Rand had just occupied. I was in no mood to be upstaged.

"If Ms. Rand had paused a moment longer"—I smiled—"then she would have heard my first directive of the new way." I raised my hand. "It is this. The end of male pattern baldness! *And it's retroactive!*"

An appreciative round of applause greeted this news.

"The women may not be too excited over this edict. But their good news will be forthcoming. For the men, I salute our forthcoming full heads of hair."

I heard another POYT!, and the dead writers looked around. Then, seconds later, came another POYT! Clearly, there was a dissident element. This was their protest, to absent themselves from The Creation. Too bad. And for reasons I couldn't fathom.

"Twain!" I barked. "Get on with the census before we lose any more of these creatures."

I stepped off the marble table and had my arm taken by Natalie Barney, who was grinning.

"Don't let these early returns depress you. You can't make an omelet without breaking a few eggs, to coin an old phrase newly for the first time." Barney was full of enthusiasm. "Those who are popping off are just leeches on the past. The thought of having to contribute to creating a new world, well, I'd say it scares them half to death—again! Let them stay gone for good, though I suspect, in their clever ways, they will slink back somehow. In fact, I spy two over there, behind the potted palm, I'd certainly like to help into eternal oblivion. It gives us breathing room."

A little old man bumped into us.

"Oh, Bunny, I don't think I've ever introduced you to Mr. Borges. You'll get on famously." Barney abandoned me with Borges as she glided across the room in a simple and elegant gesture, given that she had had so much practice.

The room itself then did a sudden transformation. It turned into a large high school gym, decorated with banners and crepe-paper. It appeared to be an Under-The-Sea theme. *I* hadn't willed this. Who had? High School. Prom Night. Just too depressing. Were we never to make any progress? I turned and saw Borges hanging onto my arm, smiling sweetly.

"I liked what you promised about our getting our hair back," he said running his other hand over his bald pate. His breath smelled just slightly stanky. "Now, my bold new god, what can you promise about vision?"

I patted his arm. "Only that all eyes and minds will be open."

"The dangerous road." He gave me a sly smile.

"We must prepare the way."

Borges sighed. "People said I was a dastardly old conservative, heartless and all that. It always hurt me. How can one be a conservative in a country that's still being invented, the invention of which I was trying my hardest? In fact, I, like all the others, was aspiring to be a successful opportunist."

"All?" I asked, as we strolled over to the refreshment stand. William Inge was done up in a mad swirl of chiffon and satin as he filled punch glasses in his prom queen regalia.

"*All*," Borges assured me, with a squeeze. "And, by the way, one of those POYTs you heard a minute ago was Nabokov, the lout. Someone told me. Very upset. He'll regret it. He'll miss us. Nothing is forever done in this new level of existence, is it, my Lord?"

His tone. His game. I sensed opposition; I certainly understood I was being patronized. Did Borges take me for a fool?

I turned and saw Wilde standing behind me, wearing a blue evening jacket, tight velvet trousers and smart leather pumps.

"May I have this dance?" he asked.

"Of course."

Suddenly, a big orchestra rose from a pit beneath the basketball court, which had opened and rolled back. A full-throttle waltz filled the gym. A mirrored ball slowly spun above us. I would have preferred a fox trot.

Oscar took me in his arms and, with me following, we twirled around the prom floor to the applause of others who, slowly, joined us. The orchestra finished with the waltz and segued into a tango. Wilde and I once again took center stage. Just as we went into a mad dip, Wilde asked: "*Must it be high school?*"

"I'm puzzled," I said, somewhat breathless. "I hate high schools."

"We all do. Particularly the American ones." The two of us cut a fiery blaze across the floor. We finished with a gay flourish. We went over to Inge, who was all aflutter with gossip of romances and handsome young men. We took cups of punch from him and found a corner of the gym.

"I see it this way," Wilde was all business. "Lacking a firm vision of what you want to project, this is the default mode, the automatic fallback. High school. So hopelessly ungrown-up and always to be that way. I think we can do better." Wilde gave me a quick buss—it was Prom Night!—and I smelled a perfume on him. This was new. The dead were not to be sensate, including the olfactory.

"We need the famous quantum leap," I suggested. "To get beyond this dull default."

"You have the power." Wilde winked.

And so I did. I casually flicked my hand in the air, and immediately heard POYT!, POYT! and POYT! again. Wilde and I were once again in my cozy abode, now cleared of the crowd but not of their detritus, ash trays filled with mountains of cigarette butts and glasses and Styrofoam cups littered about. It was the dark of night. We went into my work room. We stood before a large draftsman's board. A T-square, triangle, graph paper and sharpened pencils were all neatly laid out.

I loosened my tie. Wilde picked up a pencil and quickly made some random, though attractive, sketches on the paper.

"I have always seen myself as primarily a structuralist and not a basic designer."

Wilde sat in the comfy chair. He looked at me, sucking on the eraser, and cocked an eyebrow. "What does it matter? Designing a women's magazine. A poetry rag. A train. A career. A clever work of art. Or an entirely new society."

"We will design the famous new society, like those who did it at Philadelphia, minus, of course, the horse-shit on the street outside."

"If it adds to the authenticity, *bring in the manure!* At least this time, we're in control." Wilde continued with his sketching.

"I don't want anything that takes too much effort. Our idea is something that should happen casually and with comfort."

"I'll second that. It's the hard-driven conscientious who make it impossible. We shall have no gods, no obsessive demons, no souls to sell and no one to sell them to even if we wanted. Isn't it delicious? And all the time that we can make exist, thus getting rid of that horrible concept of urgency. The only thing to fear, as has just been demonstrated, is that if we don't get it just right, we all wind up back in high school. And baby," Wilde snorted, "being trapped in a high school is not my scene."

"A punishment fit only for the libidos of the young," I concurred. I leaned over the drafting table, picked up another pencil and started working on my own idea. I was so lost in my thoughts I didn't notice when Twain entered.

"A-hem!" Clemons cleared his throat.

I looked up. He stood there with a bound volume under his arm and a bottle of bourbon and three glasses in his hand. He set down the bottle and the glasses and then tossed the tome onto the drafting table.

"Here it is, toots, your census report." He opened the beverage bottle, poured drinks and handed them around. "The Domesday Book of our brave new world."

"Like a big cattle call for the final production." Wilde knocked back his bourbon.

"Spare me the big picture," I said, "give me the précis."

"Just the cold facts? Well, here we are, at the dawn of the new age, which, by the way, the population is clamoring for."

"A case of rising expectations." I was unconcerned. "It will pass."

"This new domain has a population of some three thousand four hundred fifty-two dead writers, as I counted. I may have missed a few, as some occasionally disappear. You, Bunny, are the only living one among us. They are dispersed all over the nation once known as the United States of America which, of course, no longer exists. Many have homes as well in what were other domains. It seems many have a fancy for what used to be Ireland."

"That's because they weren't raised there," Wilde was severe. "They only possess some atavistic attraction for it as a tax-haven for writers."

"But," continued Twain, "they are gadding about. Not tinkering any more. Instead the new fashion is taking a grand tour of the immobile moments. It's the new chic."

"Anything to avoid doing something constructive." I looked at my sketches "I think I've come up with something. Revoking our instant geographical mobility in favor of invention."

"I don't get it," Wilde stared at me blankly, having refilled his glass with the bourbon.

"Instead of all this mad larking about, I want to anchor these creatures and redirect their energies into creating madly interesting and diverse societies wherever they wind up."

"Ummm," Twain moaned. "It's still a big world. How would we get about?"

"*We* shall have no problem. *We*, meaning the three of us, will snap our fingers and be in Savannah in seconds, if we wanted. Though I think Charlestown would be more intriguing; we could stop in and visit Dawn Pepita Hall. So, yes, Twain, it will be just be us and Voltaire who can gallivant about. The others will have to stay put."

"They'll resent it." Wilde was politic.

"*So what?*" I was snide. "They're just a bunch of dead writers. They have always admired unobtainable privileges."

"And what of your own mortality?" Twain asked me, slyly.

"*Will* I die? *How can I*? History has stopped."

Voltaire walked into the workroom at that moment and stared at me. "Yes, history may have stopped. *But has time?*" He took a sip from my glass. "I've noticed that since history has ended, I once again feel corporeal and rather warm-blooded. Also a little on the horny side. It's been a heady and rather perplexing sensation as you might imagine, after all these years."

"Me too," Twain said. "I don't quite know what's happening."

"And if you take the gad-fly ability away from the dead writers, Bunny, they will become all the more flesh real. You and they, all of us, will be equal. Shall I stitch up a flag?" Voltaire looked wicked.

"Then one of these newly vibrant creatures," Twain mumbled, "will come kill *you*. For reasons none of our various commissions will ever be able to determine. Trust me. That's how it works."

"Insanity, other than the native writerly type, will be banished, like religions." I was uninterested in their talk of my demise.

We sat in silence, pondering the next move. Suddenly, out of nowhere, a folded piece of white paper drifted down from the ceiling and landed on my desk. We four just stared at it. At our age, most *new* news was *bad* news and we all knew it.

"I can't stand the suspense," Wilde preened.

Twain plucked up the note, unfolded it and read it to himself. "It's from Sage."

"And what does the defrocked deity have to say?" I wondered.

"Just this, and I think this is directed to you, Bunny. The text is, 'Like a child who has taken apart a toy, we'll see if you can put it back together again.'"

"The one thing I held against my elders," I was brisk, "is the horrible and vague threat '*We'll see*.'" I looked about the room and then gazed out the nearest window. "Sage," I said, hoping he might hear me, wherever he was, "I appreciate the joy you must be feeling in your concern. Just don't overindulge."

"There's a postscript," Twain said, holding up the note. "He says he's available for consultations for a certain fee."

I laughed. "A little late to be getting into *that* racket. But, then, he missed so much. The longing to get into the marketplace after it has been destroyed."

"The plight of the fallen aristocrats," Voltaire sighed. "Something to *write* about, perhaps, but *not* associate with."

I pulled open the desk drawer from the drafting table and found a safety pin. I snapped it open and took Voltaire's right hand and, while he watched, pricked his index finger. A little blob of blood formed. I took a tissue and wiped it clean.

"Needless to say," Voltaire told me, "that hurt."

I stared at Twain.

"No need to jab me, Bunny. If Frank is bleeding again, so will I."

This was a formidable twist to things. These dead confreres were now back among the warm-blooded. Should I take credit?

"It's something evolutionary. The next stage." I played it as though it didn't faze me. "With my having ended history, the dead writers have come back to life."

"*All of us*, I expect," Twain sniffed.

"Which presents you, Bunny, as de facto chief executive," Wilde told me, drubbing his fingers on the table, "with the frightening prospect of massive health care for old, once-again alive writers."

I pulled down my screen in mid-air and waved an image into focus. The image was my own, as I used to look in real time, before that concept lost its referent.

"Surprised to see me?" my face asked. "Thought you could leave me on the dust heap that is all history? No way, baby. I'm tagging along with you." I seemed supremely self-satisfied. "Mark, Oscar and Frank, welcome back to the active set."

"Let's play 'What's The Answer,'" I suggested to myself.

"Wouldn't it be easier to call up the Help Menu?"

I was firm. "It's 'What's The Answer.'"

"Very well. What's the question?"

"Why are the dead writers resurrected?"

"Through will and imagination, most things are possible. It's just a guess, but since there must be some energy left floating around out there, and since it can't be destroyed, it landed on the writers and reheated them."

"That seems far-fetched."

"You could always go back to that high school prom and find a drunken physics teacher for something more savvy."

"Next, what am I going to do with you?"

"That's an easy one. Since *you* stopped history, and since you and I are one and the same—"

"Only sort of."

"—I was not about to join the others and become some frozen monument out there, like Enver Hoxha or your friend Jefferson. I'm sticking to you like a barnacle. No freeze-framing me into oblivion. I shall become part of the decision-making process. Think of me as your media consultant."

"Tsk, tsk, tsk," clucked Twain. "Too many cooks."

"Oh, Sam," my screen face hissed, "just get over it. We're all in the game of the public double, and dualities in glass heavens shouldn't cast first stones. We might hit ourselves."

I looked at my face on screen and whisked it away. "I feel I'm in a cul-de-sac."

"You're not really," Voltaire was trying to be helpful. "You're just wanting what is the obvious way out."

"Which is?"

"Let's have a Constitutional Convention. People like that sort of thing."

"Why not?" Twain seemed to like the idea. "An exercise in our eighteenth century hobby."

Voltaire smiled. "I have files full of drafts for every situation. Constitutional monarchy. Federal republic. Universal suffrage. Unicameral. Bicameral. Tricameral. Try anything."

I saw no need to hesitate, so I willed it.

Suddenly, there we all were, in a large generic auditorium, seated in tiers, much rumbling, coughing, shuffling, like nervous investors on the opening night of what advance gossip rumored was sure to be a Broadway clunker. Voltaire had been designated to do the honors. He walked to the podium.

"Fellow patriots. *Welcome back to life!*" A limp round of applause was all this announcement gleaned. "So many of you were depressed with the end of history. Little could you imagine that this would mean our rebirth. In those times, they said the living feast off the dead. Under Bunny's new vision, we've turned it around. Our second coming. The democratization of the resurrection with no gods on hand to work *that* feat."

Twain and I sat on two rickety fold-down card-table chairs on one side of Voltaire and scanned the auditorium. Who could tell how this effort might come out?

"We have been summoned to write a new constitution for our society. A charter for our unique nirvana. We must bring all our gifts and experience to this noble effort. Your committee assignments are on the boards in the antechamber. Your reports are due in two weeks."

And what a time it was! A whirl! Smoke, noise, arm-twisting. Everyone mad at each other, position papers crumbled and hurled on the floor, boring lectures full of fustian about the importance of what we were doing, most of which were ruled out of order by Voltaire who pointed out that without history, our actions had neither referents nor traditions and only existed for themselves and were likely to be changed by whim. Perhaps.

William Blake made sketches throughout the excitement and had an exhibition on the day of the final drafting. I kept in the background as much as I could though it seemed everyone wanted my opinion about everything. *Why did Ambrose Bierce seek my opinion on what should be the national bird?* For my money, it could be the cuckoo!

My spies kept me up-to-date on everything.

The folks took to wearing funny clothes, period outfits, resort wear and weird rags. Some dropped out of the convention and opened little shops near the site with peculiar stocks of exotic items. Where the stuff came from and how it got here I didn't know and didn't really care. *And I have never seen so many drugs in my life!*

Sitting on the platform with the other dignitaries, I listened to the presentation of the final constitution as it was read, in full voice, by Mary Roberts Rinehart. Soon I would have to sign the thing. She droned on. I nodded off. Welcome sleep! At long last!

The flapping noise startled me awake. As did the shrill voice of my other self.

"Well, aren't *you* useless? Leave you alone for just a minute and it comes to this!"

I gazed at this figure on the screen before me, which was getting larger each time he appeared. He posed there, hands on hips, with a lethal smirk poisoning his face. I looked about. I was in the projection booth of a drive-in movie theatre. It was a twin theatre, two vast screens out there in the distance. Four enormous projectors were aside me. On the bottom of one projector, film was wrapped all the way to the rim of the reel. It was spinning around rapidly, and the loose end of the film was slapping against the floor on each rotation. A beam of very bright white light shot through the big lens. I heard a cacophony of car horns.

"You're off in slumber-land and you missed your change-over," Bunny 2 sneered. "You've just ruined the plot for all the loyal patrons of this dump."

I rose, turned on the second projector, threw the switch for the take-up film, centered the frame and focused it. The honking ceased. The couples could now resume their snuggling on their plastic seats. I took the full reel to the rewind table, laced it up and rewound it.

"It's *déjà vu* all over again," I sighed. "But what happened to the convention for the new constitution?"

My other self looked at me with impatience. "The best of all possible scenarios. It turned out to be a movie script. There was some bad blood when some of the hoity-toity types found out. But their moan-and-groan number dissipated when they saw the final product. Everybody just looks fabulous. They couldn't be more delighted. Some are demanding a sequel or a pre-quel or whatever you want to do."

Reel rewound, I carried it over to the first projector and laced it up. "Where are Frank and Sam?"

"Running the concession stand right underneath us."

I rechecked the picture, the sound level. All was fine. I had a half hour of film yet to go on the current reel. I trotted downstairs, the screen with the other me tagging right behind. I breezed into the concession stand which occupied the entire space underneath the projection booth. It was badly lit and stank of cheap refreshments.

Voltaire was done up in a chef's hat and apron and tended the grill. Twain had rolled sleeves, a green visor and worked the candy bar and cash register. I watched Voltaire as he filled a bin with frozen egg rolls and lowered them into a vat of boiling cooking oil, which looked murky.

"Can't we afford some new oil once in a while?" I asked.

"No one complains," Voltaire said without emotion, as he jiggled the egg rolls in the popping oil. "Well, that's not exactly true. Ronald Firbank complains, but I ignore him. He should be eating flowers anyway. Or weeds." Voltaire looked at me. "And it's about time you made an appearance around here." He feigned an attitude of being miffed. "We thought you were upset with us or perhaps boycotting the affairs of state for reasons we couldn't fathom."

"I've just been told," indicating my other self, "that I have been asleep."

"First he shuts down history," the screen Bunny was flippant, "and then he sleeps through the dawn of the new age. Fate must be a tired old sow."

Twain drifted over with a four-foot clear plastic bag of very limp looking popcorn. He untied it and emptied it into a Lucite popcorn display unit. The little sign that read "Hot Buttered Popcorn" flickered unevenly.

"Well," Twain said, wiping his hands, "to bring you up to date, something that seems to be my constant task, the film has legs. It's been running to a packed house night after night. They all come to see themselves. Alas, all writers being vain, we have discovered, Bunny, while you took your long siesta, how easily we can manipulate them. Sadly, some of them have become agents and are pitching deals. A harmless diversion, so far. And I suppose we can be grateful we don't reign over a society of actors." Twain spat in the sink and washed his sputum down the drain. "But we're all fully alive now and all in the bloom of good health. It's rather magical. Things just show up. Frank and I can't figure it out. The eggrolls, such as they are, arrive in vast deliveries, with no invoice. They get gobbled up every night. Same with the popcorn. We use gallons of the partially hydrogenised butter on the corn; the folks always want more. Every writer has a car and plenty of gas. Money is back in use and no one is wanting, except for the truly greedy. They want everything."

"A land of milk and honey," Voltaire smiled. "Or, to be precise, eggrolls and popcorn."

"Speaking of which," a voice growled, "could I get some service over here?"

We three—or four if you counted my screen self, picky,

picky—stared at the candy counter. It was Bernard Shaw, looking rather hopeless and forlorn.

"It's Old Whiskers," Twain whispered to me. "I'll take care of him."

"I'd like the deluxe box of Junior Mints, and I'll take some Dots," Shaw said, tapping on the glass counter. He looked my way. "Well, if it isn't the newly divine Bunny LaRue. The deity of the projection booth." Shaw ambled over. "Everyone's so jealous. You get to be the projectionist!" He gave me a little smirk. "Listen, I have this great idea for a new production. Something very sophisticated for our crowd, but gripping, with lots of suspense, real drama, and you can bring it in as a mini-major."

I smiled, not having a clue. "Sounds solid. Let's do lunch. Next week."

Shaw winked at me. He snatched up his boxes of candy, paid Twain in some oddly shaped coins and drifted back into the vast, dark expanse of the parking lot of the drive-in.

"Tell Bunny how the gate was tonight," Twain poked Voltaire.

"It was ninety-five percent of capacity. We let Wilde do the ticket booth. We figure he clips the other five percent because, in fact, the house is always full. But who cares? In our business, you can afford to overlook petty clipping as long as the money's flowing in. And, to be transcendent, when you have the power what does all this money collecting *really* mean?"

I sighed. "I would prefer something more intimate. A fine arts cinema screening French jobs with hard-to-read subtitles in English. This all seems suddenly so … odd."

Twain and Voltaire stared at me and then exchanged very knowing glances.

"Well," Twain said gently, "while you were napping, someone had to take the helm. We got a drift of things here as they developed. We all moved as though on some unconscious, though nonetheless planned, vector."

I heard bells ring in the projection booth, warning me of a changeover in three minutes. "In that case, I think I understand." I ran back up the stairs, the other Bunny still tagging right behind me in the screen.

I arrived just in time to start up the epic all over again. I shut off the second machine, lifted the heavy take-up reel, carried it to the rewind table and laced it up. The miracle of the movies seemed less miraculous from this end. My other self said, "Don't look now, but Oscar is busy previewing porno loops over in cinema three."

Oscar stood aside a 16-milimeter projector, screening old silent beefcake and soft porn gay films against a white wall inside the projection booth. He turned and waved at us. "It's such a pleasant release! But how the muscles have puffed up in so few years! It puts most of us out of the running. I will have to become even wittier to keep in the game."

He switched off the small projector. "Alas, even the flesh of others becomes tiresome after a few viewings. Why is that? The smell of control is so much more powerful than the spell of libido. I'm not complaining, mind you, as it's nice to have it back." Oscar took my arm. "I heard what those witches downstairs said about me, clipping from the box-office. If they only knew! I could clip the whole thing and those sillies wouldn't be able to fathom a thing. *But I've never nicked even a nickel!* Scout's honor! But let me tell you, it's no easy street working the box-office night after night. Cars stuffed with groups demanding discounts, giving me the most elaborate guilt raps. The other night Miss Hilda Doolittle pulls up with the Cord full of poets, all twisted on something. Now, usually I don't make a fuss because pearls before swine and all that. Most just pay their Jackie Kennedy coin and that covers the lot. But Miss Doolittle, backed up by Bryher, mind you, went into High Poetess drone, and that set off the lot of them, and I waved them all in just to be rid of them. Thus, Twain and Voltaire, the Goneril and Regan of the Twi-Lit Twin, have me pegged for clipping. You'll notice that neither one of those distinguished gentlemen has signed up for my job. They're happy to push the popcorn and those lethal eggrolls, which is where I suspect Doolittle and Bryher dropped their Jackie coins. But, still, it is such a woesome burden to bear. I had hoped for so much better."

I took the rewound reel of film and laced it up, once again, on the projector to show through the night and, apparently, all time.

"Well," Wilde cooed, "my gig is up and I'll go punch the clock. Let's blow this joint."

"I'd love to join you," I said, "but please remember that my latest job assignment finds me stuck here, running the film grind in perpetuity."

"Wrong, bubby." Wilde gave me a coy look. "Let me take care of that."

My other self, now posed in a grand manner on the screen, looked at the both of us with no interest whatsoever.

"YOU!" Wilde screamed, lunging his arm into the screen and grabbing Bunny 2. "It's time you started earning your keep!"

"What???" My left-over real-life persona screamed in protest. But to no avail. Wilde yanked him (me?) from the smug sanctity of the two-dimensional screen and pulled him out into the strange realm of our queer actuality.

"Back to the joys of three-dimensionality for you, my sweet!" Wilde was pleased with his work. "You are to run this projection booth while your divine spirit and I split."

"You can't do this to me! I haven't any idea how any of this works! I'll fuck everything up!" More complaining.

"Everything Bunny knows, *you know*," Wilde said smartly. "That's how it is and how it has always been. So don't play the dumb Dora card; it won't work. If, perchance, there is some emergency you can't handle—"

"The second amplifier can be tricky," I warned.

"—the home number's on the wall."

Wilde and I fled down the staircase and landed on the gravel surface. The huge drive-in movie screens hung there, out in the distance, with the Constitution pageant unspooling to the packed house, bovines at last.

We strolled across the lot to Wilde's pink Packard. People recognized me and whistled out of their cars.

"Yo! Bunny! Nice job!"

I waved, like the Roman pope used to do, before I destroyed him and his racket. Wilde held open the passenger door for me. I slid in. I was engulfed in garishness. Wilde sat in the driver's seat and slammed the door. He grinned at me, his three chins shimmering in the off-light of the night.

"Like it?"

We rolled out of the drive-in and glided along summery lanes until we came to Verdant Hills, where I lived, given its new name since I took up residence there. The neighborhood was definitely on the up-and-up.

"It's funny," Wilde noted, "I work the box-office every night. And I see the same faces time and time again. They pay their Jackie Kennedy coins, park, and watch the movie. But they never leave. Or at least, no one has ever seen a car exit the venue. I've seen the same John O'Hara pull into the drive-in every night for weeks on end but there's no indication that *any* John O'Hara has ever pulled out. Most bizarre. It's the same with the rest of them." He grimaced. "*How many John O'Haras can there be?*"

"As many as there are John Gunthers."

"*Inside The Twi-Lit Twin?*" Wilde quipped.

He pulled into my ivy-covered carport. We walked to the house. All the lights were on and we could hear the laughter. I opened the screen door. A fly buzzed out. Voltaire and Twain and two others were carrying on in my living room. Twain had on a funny-looking little party hat.

"Those silly swine," Wilde hissed at me. "Any excuse to swill someone else's good liquor."

I feigned cheer and buoyancy and approached my guests.

"Bunny," Voltaire took me by the elbow, "isn't it wonderful the Woolfs have dropped by? Virginia has been so deliciously wicked about so many whose names shall never pass my lips."

"Virginia. Leonard." I bowed slightly. "My digs are your digs."

Twain gave me a wink. "And, look," Twain pointed, "Virginia has brought over her lovely tomato aspic!"

I gazed at this quivering blood-like blob that sat in a plastic dish on the table.

"We'll have to have a slice. But first, Virginia, you must fink out and tell us your recipe."

Ms. Woolf leaned over and spoke in a hesitant voice. "There's lovely bits of mandarin orange in it," she said, indicating the ingredients, "and little sprigs of fresh garden parsley—"

I was wide-eyed. "A sensation!"

"Actually, Bunny, while we are here," Virginia went on, cool as a cucumber, "I thought I might bring up the *sewer* problem."

I raised an eyebrow, rose from my seat, walked to the glass sliding door and pulled it open. There, in the distance, I could see the two huge drive-in movie screens, just floating there, with the Constitutional assembly in mid-reel. Someone had told me that it could be seen all across the realm.

"We just can't seem to find anyone reliable to hook up our house's pipes to the grid."

I stared at her and Leonard and imagined all the shit that must flow from the two of them. I sympathized.

"My friends, I don't handle that." I turned to Voltaire. "Haven't we set up divisions and departments to handle the legitimate needs of the freeholders?"

"Of course, my liege." Voltaire gave a fancy little wiggle to his head. "It's just that work is behind schedule in their sector and there's much confusion."

"Which is their territory?"

"It's called Under-And-Over-The-Rhineland-At-The-Same-Time-Land."

"Oh." I looked sweetly at Virginia and Leonard. "I hear that's very up-and-coming."

"It is," Leonard answered, "except for the sewers."

"Here's where I need your advice, Virginia," I asked earnestly. "What should be the role of the poets in our new realm? Can they make a significant contribution? Or should they be slighted?"

Virginia, with perhaps memories of the plague of poets, took her own consul. "I think each one is actually different."

"It's a hard call," Wilde opined. "Frankly, there's practically no one who gives a wing-ding about the whole lot. But I do predict, that since we are all alive again, it will be a poet amongst our lot who will be the first do away with himself."

"*Herself*," Leonard said flatly, looking in his lap.

"Well, I can't wait." I, as host, always tried to be cheerful. "One place we have yet to invent is our own Père-Lachaise."

"But Bunny," Wilde sounded confused, "that's what I thought you achieved when you set up the twin drive-in. The place where writers can go to see themselves memorialized, over and over again, every one-hundred-twenty minutes, from now until eternity. They're stuck on themselves, like flies on flypaper."

I hadn't a clue what he was babbling about.

"Isn't that the point?" Twain looked at us like dullards. "That you just can't get rid of the writers. Here, back there, out there, up ahead. You can't dispose of them—*us*! We are temperamental, tricky and, ultimately, adhesive, even if most of the work winds up in the morgue."

"On the contrary," I smirked. "I got rid of Hemingway."

"*Who*?" they all chorused together.

I smiled, satisfied. "See? Dead. Gone. Forgotten. A clean excision." I walked over to Leonard and Virginia. They looked like used rag dolls at a yard sale. I glared down at them. "I don't want to seem ungracious but would you two mind leaving right now? You're not the kind I like to have loitering about."

They rose, giving no hint they had been insulted. I suspect it happened all the time. Virginia pulled on an old wrap. She had the smell of old clothes about her. Poor things. Oscar did honors and showed them out. I was livid.

"Do they think I'm some crappy ward-heeler?" I snorted, snatching off Twain's rainbow-colored party hat. "Some crooked city councilor they can come crying to when their shit backs up. Do I need to remind them that I have created this world and re-created them?" I made a silent style decision: less hippy, more *hauteur*.

I poured a drink and went back to the patio to watch the action on the drive-in screens that loomed so large on the horizon. That compelling constitution drama kept on flickering from scene to scene. To two full houses. In which even I looked fabulous, though I had no memory of even trying.

My reverie was interrupted by Twain's soothing voice, always a welcome diversion.

"Bunny, it's becoming like Voltaire's old place. No sooner do we dismiss one delegation but another arrives."

"Who is it now?" I sighed.

"A delegation of doctors. They're here to make a request of you. Shall I scare them away?"

"No. Leave that to me. We all need to practice to keep up our skills. Show the creatures in."

I assumed a slinky pose against the sliding glass doors. I would be a siren from a forties film noir man-eating flick. The doctors drooped in. The looked like the Three Stooges. With more degrees, honors and certificates of appreciation than I would ever have time to read.

"The doctors," Twain said, bowing.

"Doctors, my house is your house. A great temple for healing, I hope." I smiled, lighting galaxies with my *faux* gleam.

"We have come from another world but one close enough to allow us access," bleated doctor #1.

"This has been demonstrated," I was brisk.

"We come here purely out of clinical curiosity," doctor #2 informed me.

"Ah!" I sauntered before them, a Dietrich teasing the mere mice men.

"We have read all the publications of your new society and we want to do some cultural surveys. Our early preliminary research has led us to a puzzlement, which is why we are here." Doctor #3 was as opaque in presentation as he was ugly.

"Well, how can I be of assistance?" I purred, curling up in a lounge chair.

Doctor #1 leaned toward me, clasped his hands together and was intent. "We are interested in documenting patterns of deviancy in your new society."

"Is this, like, a review?" I trilled.

"In a way, it is." Doctor #3 was hot to trot. "We're just getting at the facts."

"I was thinking that perhaps our new little world was up for some kind of award." I winked at them. "That would be lovely."

They looked confused. I glided right on.

"Well, isn't this your lucky day!" I signaled for Twain to come close. He did. I whispered in his ear. "Run upstairs and tell Voltaire to get up in his duchess drag and come down here and do a number for these boys."

Twain quietly proceeded upstairs. I grinned at the doctors, who looked expectant.

"As it happens, noble doctors, I was on the eve of holding a meeting with every responsible authority in this new realm. We are pleased that the very Duchess of Deviancy herself, despite her old age and celebrated infirmities, could actually arrive and attend in person. She is staying with me. I have sent my agent to summon her. The Duchess has the latest up-to-the minute reports on deviancy patterns in our brave new world since its very foundation. All precisely recorded and some of it quite shocking. All worthy of your attention, I pray."

"We are most eager to meet the Duchess," the doctors said in unison.

"I have instructed the Duchess to preview her findings for our august visitors. All in the furtherance of science, I hope."

Out of the corner of my eye, I saw Twain flagging me from half-way up the stairwell. He looked panic-stricken.

I rose from my chair. "I am called for the moment. But I would like you to meditate on this question—why do hockey players at college always major in sociology?" With that, I raced to the stairs. "What is it?" I snapped at Twain.

"They're having a fight."

"*They*?"

"I'm sorry, Bunny, I won't get near it."

*Such fair-weather friends.* I went up to the master bedroom and threw open the door. There, on my queen-sized bed, on opposite sides, sat Voltaire and Wilde. Both held in their hands the fabulous chicken-wire, taffeta, corseted regalia of the primo duchess drag.

"Let go, you monster! I want to wear the duchess drag for the doctors!" Wilde pulled on the garment and tugged Voltaire half-way across the bed.

"Not on your life! I will be the Duchess of Deviancy for the doctors!" Voltaire yanked on the dress and Wilde fell on the bed.

"I want to be the duchess!"

"I'm the duchess!"

"Fuck you, idiot!"

"Drop dead, fool!"

"Give me the dress!"

I stood there, arms akimbo. "OK, boys, *STOP IT*! That's an order!"

They dropped the dress and looked at me with crestfallen faces.

I continued. "I've promised the doctors downstairs an appearance by the Duchess of Deviancy. This is my call, and I stand by it." I gave a severe look. "Voltaire will be the duchess. And I am counting on you, Frank, to give it your best. These boys deserve nothing less than a steamrolling."

Wilde looked pouty. "Just because I was married and had two sons, I feel discriminated against when it comes to playing bizarre roles."

"Spare me, Oscar," I sighed.

"I hate being obvious. Not to my taste at all. I did marry and raised a family, and after what seemed a millennium of editing women's magazines, this, mind you, when it *really* mattered, I am all too well acquainted with the obsession of transvestism in the normal heterosexual male. I am *still* better in drag than Voltaire, who treats it as just another put-on."

"What you say, Oscar, is no doubt true. We all carry scars. And festering grievances, which I hoped I had banished for good." I sniffed. A loss of my powers? Or homage to monumentalism? "Voltaire will be the Duchess and you will be the Lady In Waiting." You have to give a slot to all the whiners just to keep them on board. "You guys have two minutes. The doctors are waiting."

I went back downstairs and rejoined the three doctors.

"Gentlemen, I hope you will be more interested in our society than merely a brief analysis of our deviancy statistics." I smiled the smile of eternal grace. They stared at me as though they were a band of stigmatic brothers about to announce a crusade.

We came to a lull. I picked up a matchbook and pulled three matches from the pack. I coyly held them in front of the doctors.

"Short one wins a weekend with Lillian Hellman!"

Twain appeared at the foot of the stairs.

"Sire, the Duchess of Deviancy arrives!"

I dropped the matches—there were no takers anyway. I beckoned the doctors to follow me. We stood at the base of the stairwell, looking up the long, angled staircase. Voltaire appeared at the crest, shoulders, hips and mantilla out to here.

"Honored guests, may I present the Duchess of Deviancy herself!" I bowed and stepped back.

Voltaire perused the marks, stiffened his back and began his grand descent. Wilde, in a mini-version of the duchess drag, carried the train behind.

"Gentlemen, I leave you for your private conversation with the Duchess."

I slowly withdrew as I heard Voltaire, in his falsetto bray, no, *shriek*, "Science! At long last science! We must bring science to human relations! I have Newton under my skirt!"

"Ah, Duchess," droned a doctor, "we have determined an absolute correlation between imperfect vision and child molestation."

I was halfway out the door but paused to listen to the exchange.

Voltaire, stepping off the bottom riser, took the hand of the closest doctor and swept to the divan. Wilde stood behind him.

"How fascinating!" Voltaire snapped open a fan. "Does that mean you *arrest* the pedophiles?"

"Oh, no, Madame," cackled doctor #3. "We are strictly research scientists. What we try to do is sensitize the police before *they* arrest the pedophile."

Voltaire snapped his fan shut. "*Sensitize the police!*" He laughed loudly. "I see! Well, gentlemen, in that case, let's start with my *volume* of statistics. I propose we begin with incidences of oral-genitalism among the handicapped."

The doctors all moaned with pleasure. I was out the door by then.

Coming up the stone walk was Apollinaire, looking all the more ravishing with the sun at his back.

"Oh, Bunny, it's just terrible. I've come for your help." He took my hands in his, a lovely sensation.

"What now?" I was droll. "A plugged cistern? Green tomatoes?"

"It's Scott Fitzgerald. *Terrible car crash.*"

We hastened across a field and came to a narrow country by-way. An old Studebaker was slammed into a tree, which had fallen over on it. The driver's door was open and a limp Scott Fitzgerald hung out. We raced to help . He was semi-conscious, mouthing obscenities and bleeding from a severe wound to his forehead. I pulled Scott from the car and stretched him out on the nearest patch of greenery. He stank of liquor. Apollinaire gently held Scott's head in his lap and dabbed at his wound with a hankie, getting blood over his trousers.

"I suppose it had to happen sooner or later," Apollinaire said matter-of-factly.

"Why is it writers drink so much?" I snapped.

"I don't know. But it does seem to be only the writers. The composers and musicians barely touch the stuff. Maybe a few of the painters. It must be a different set of demons. Ours are thirstier."

Fitzgerald spoke. "Fuckin' no good lousy jew-faced, nigger-loving cocksucker..." Then he drifted off.

"Our little society is cluttered with bars and lounges. Our people spend half their time imbibing. Oh, and by the way, have you stopped in at The Blue Canary? Their happy hour is just delightful, or so I've heard," I said.

Apollinaire was thumbing through a small notebook he had pulled from Fitzgerald's shirt pocket. Scott drifted into consciousness briefly enough to start with the name-calling again.

"It says here that Scott can operate on two channels." He looked up at me. "Shall we give the other one a try?"

"Why not?" I shrugged.

No sooner said than done.

The courtroom was as neat and grim as a Protestant church in the suburbs. Scott sat in the docket, looking befuddled. Apollinaire and I sat among the rows of spectators.

"Isn't it true, Mr. Fitzgerald, that you repeatedly stole ideas from your wife, copied from her journal and plagiarized her without her consent?" The question was from a wiry woman with a stone face.

"It would be more accurate to say that we had an understanding." Fitzgerald's response seemed timid.

"Would you characterize this so-called understanding as preferential to you and exclusively for your own benefit?"

"Oh, dear," I whispered to Apollinaire. "this has a familiar ring to it."

"It's a suit brought by the Women Writers For Spousal Justice Committee."

I sighed.

"They're seeking to rewrite Fitzgerald's work and give some of it to Zelda. Plus correcting the contracts, disbursements of royalties, et cetera."

"I didn't think we were able to do this any more."

I snapped my fingers.

We were back at the roadside accident, poor Scott on his back, bleeding and spouting obscenities.

"Well," I mused, "given the choices, let's just leave him here. I've sent for an ambulance. This is what Scott would want."

Scott, hearing his name, aimed his torrent of abuse at me. "Good for nothing lousy maggots, fucking that royal pussy full of puss." He nodded off.

I stared at Fitzgerald. "You know, the Irish have done so well moving right up the social ladder. Look at famous Scott here. Surely a case of the two-toilet Irish."

"Yes," Apollinaire continued, "and at the moment, they both seem to be in his mouth." He put Scott's head back in his lap and stroked his forehead. I strolled away just as I heard the ambulance's siren on the horizon. Scott would be saved.

I took a leisurely stroll through a nice pasture. It wasn't long before I came across Twain and Wilde. They were sitting at a picnic table which was done up with a bright pink tablecloth, decorated with little embroidered white doves. A wooden basket was open and around it was set paper plates in floral patterns, yellow napkins in napkin rings, a bucket of fried chicken, slaw, a pot of potato salad, a plate of cornbread and a tub of butter in which a fly had committed suicide.

I joined them.

"Don't blame me for the appointments," Oscar was arch. "I swear, Twain is either colorblind or perverse in his tastes or both."

Twain nibbled on some cornbread, slathered with butter. I picked up a plastic fork and helped myself to some of the potato salad. It was delicious.

"By the way," Wilde said, wiping the corners of his mouth with a napkin, "Voltaire had a ball with those deranged doctors. By the time the Duchess was done with them they'll need three years of intense brain-doctoring just to bring them back to their previous state of dementia."

"Odd how they got in." I was not pleased.

"Our world," Twain noted, "seems to be more porous than we had planned. I wonder what that will mean down the pike."

"Alas," I said, "perhaps I've tried too hard with not enough effect." I looked above us. The tops of the trees swayed hard in a wind we didn't feel. The birdies tweeted in the branches. The sun felt warm. The moment hung there, as though forever. I felt resigned to having things merely continuing as they were. "I just don't get it, guys."

"Get what?" Voltaire appeared out of the foliage and went at the food. "Second helpings?"

"The whole thing. What I have created. With all the best intentions and the *correct* intentions."

"You're complaining?" Wilde said while picking clean a wishbone. "You do Olympus an injustice. It all looks pretty neat to me."

"And anyway," Twain was direct, "*your* type always complains. Just your way of saying hello."

"I destroyed history, brought that consecutive line of events to a halt, created a world just for writers, somehow brought them all back to life, and have now brought some organization to the colony. But what have I created? A society where the folks line up each night to watch themselves in a movie I made about their participation in the constitutional process."

We all gazed across the field and in the distance saw the drive-in twin screens, even in the bright sunlight, though the twin screens seemed to be enveloped in a bubble of nightlight, and the movie flickering on the two screens.

"It's the same old people. And the same old movie." I was deflated. "What have I done that's any different? Is it all just another mess for which I am to blame?"

"Not at all, *caro*," Wilde was full of himself, while polishing off a slice of rhubarb pie. "I think the whole job is near perfection."

"It was so much easier and so much more fun getting rid of the things, and the people, I wanted out of the picture."

"*That*," Twain sniffed, "you did awfully well."

"And, as should be noted, with a touch of humor, about which I am writing for the ages." Wilde let us know about his new assignment.

"*Will* there be 'Ages'?" I wondered. "I thought I had destroyed the whole march of history nonsense."

"Sorry to tell you this, but I think the French did it before you, Bunny," Voltaire was busy consuming a chicken wing. "But few pay attention to them. And, I think, it was only a passing fad."

"Anyway," Wilde went right on, "that was *that* history. Now it is *our* history, which I think we might refer to as a Drama." Wilde waved his hands in the air, all set to launch into a bit. Instead, he looked at me in a patronizing manner. "Now, now. No self-pity or we'll throw you right out of the club and you'll have to go out and start another world and the bad news there is that your new world won't be writers; *you'll get sports broadcasters*."

I cringed. "What I expected was exactly what you said, more Drama."

"We have all the Drama the folks need. For *them*, there is the Twi-Lit Twin Drive-In." Wilde waved a pudgy hand at the distant screen. "For us, there are universes of invention," he said, tapping his head. "After all, Sage didn't pick you at random. Have confidence and don't change a hair for me."

"Funny you mention Sage." I brightened up. "I was thinking of him as we left the drive-in." I pulled a screen in mid-air before us. "Let's call him up and see how he's doing."

The screen filled with fuzz that slowly came together to give us an image of Sage. He wore a loose caftan and a headband. It was a new look. He carried an atomizer and was spraying plants in a hothouse.

"Sage, my dear, I hope we're not crashing in at an inopportune moment." Could he hear me?

Sage sprayed some fine mist on a plant, the likes of which I had never seen. Sage looked at us and said, "Ghhyt julter, gossoggwat pfut. Onhhuxm, buttywuk woo...zerkawhiz toomgluzt."

"Sage, I can't understand you. Try again."

A mouse ran up Sage's arm, perched on his shoulder and also stared at us. "Koilyter couhfanso gylesanat logper."

"It's hopeless," Twain said. "May as well turn him off. We're on the channel of Babel. Our world has spun off on its own by now. We have our own language and civilization."

"Sorry, Sage. I'll write." I closed the screen and waved it away. It disappeared.

"We have become what we always wanted to be." Voltaire wiped his hands and set the crumbled napkin gently on the table. "We are a race without mortality, without predators, without religion, without hunger. It has been a remarkable enterprise, Bunny. And you pulled it off. And I didn't see you break a sweat."

"I needed dress shields for the Kennedy Library job. And some Depends." I lied, *but only slightly.*

"And let's not forget. You have put to death dullness," Wilde added. "A significant achievement.

"And complete?" I asked loudly.

"I challenge any to ask for more." Twain leaned back and stared at the three of us.

"Twain is right," Voltaire said. "We are freed from the apparent and transcendent shackles. And the process and the outcome were achieved in the best possible manner, *casually*."

"And what shall *I* do? I have no intention of suffering Sage's fate, reigning, against my will, as some jerry-rigged deity." I was confessional and didn't like it, but I was among friends.

Twain laughed. "Not to worry. This crowd isn't much on inventing deities. We have more satisfying diversions."

"When you get bored," Oscar advised, "we can work on the treatment for your next screen production."

"The society must be run!" I remonstrated.

"It runs itself," Oscar sniffed. "Those who complain, like the Woolfs, just don't have their asses in gear. Everything is available to them. When they stop bitching, they'll figure it out."

"We must accommodate ourselves to living in paradise," Twain reported. "And we will. By the way, your friend Fitzgerald is doing well in the clinic, to come out and slam into another tree once again."

"And look over there!" Voltaire pointed to a grassy meadow.

We all looked and saw a chubby old man chasing a little butterfly with a net in the bright afternoon sunlight.

"It's Nabokov, of course." Voltaire smiled. "He's back. He's nobody's fool. He came right back when he saw how good things are. He's probably jealous that, on account of his disappearing act, he didn't get a part in the movie."

"Maybe he can be in the sequel," Twain suggested.

I continued my confession. "It must be my Protestant upbringing. The actuality of salvation, no, *not* salvation, but eternal existence, I find ...formidable."

"You haven't been dead yet, thus a looming enterprise," Wilde was full of information. "For the rest of us, paradise is something we could only imagine. Yet, here we are. I live in a world where I will not face trials, imprisonment. I will not be spit on, not dragged hither and yon. At the most, I will face the writers' wars, which we all *adore*. We are insular, eternal and implacable." The width of Wilde's grin surely set a record.

"Happily," Voltaire said, "now we will only speak to each other. Quite enough, I'd say. That's why Sage was incomprehensible. *Shouldn't they all be*? Haven't most of them been that way for all time?"

Twain got up. "I think I'll go over to Nabokov and ask him to join us. There's still lots of food and maybe we can talk him into cleaning up."

"An excellent idea," Wilde said. "I have the perfect joke to play on him."

"I will stay for just another half hour. Then I really must make my excuses," Voltaire said. "That way I'll have a few hours before I have to report to the twin drive-in. You see, I've started this really magnificent garden, full of the oddest flowers, drooping plants and itty-bitty ferns. There's this mood I slip into while I tend my garden and it's so satisfying that it's really quite"—Voltaire paused, searching for the right word—"*indescribable*."